SANTIAGO WAS WAITING AT THE RESTAURANT WHEN SHE ARRIVED

A smile curved his lips when he saw her. Taking her hand, he kissed her palm, sending frissons of sensual delight coursing through her. "I did not think you would say yes."

"Neither did I."

Still holding her hand, he led her to a booth in a far corner and slid in beside her, his thigh brushing intimately against her own. "Yet here you are." He caressed her cheek with the back of his hand. "What made you say yes? Were you missing me as much as I was missing you?"

"Were you?" Regan asked. "Missing me?"

"Every night."

"Then why did you wait so long to call?"

"I was trying to be noble."

"Noble?" she asked, laughing.

He nodded, his expression somber. "Vampires and mortals do not mix well, as you know. And while I think you would be good for me, I know I would be bad for you."

"Would you?" she asked, her voice hardly more than a whisper. "Be bad for me?"

His gaze caressed her. "Very bad."

Also by Amanda Ashley

DESIRE AFTER DARK

NIGHT'S KISS

A WHISPER OF ETERNITY

AFTER SUNDOWN

Published by Zebra Books

AMANDA ASHLEY

DEAD SEXY

ZEBRA BOOKS
Kensington Publishing Corp.
www.kensingtonbooks.com

ZEBRA BOOKS are published by

Kensington Publishing Corp.
850 Third Avenue
New York, NY 10022

All Kensington titles, imprints, and distributed lines are available at special quantity discounts for bulk purchases for sales promotion, premiums, fund-raising, educational or institutional use.

Special book excerpts or customized printings can also be created to fit specific needs. For details, write or phone the office of the Kensington Special Sales Manager: Attn. Special Sales Department. Kensington Publishing Corp., 850 Third Avenue, New York, NY 10022. Phone: 1-800-221-2647.

Zebra and the Z logo Reg. U.S. Pat. & TM Off.

ISBN-13: 978-0-8217-7834-0
ISBN-10: 0-8217-7834-X

First Printing: February 2007
10 9 8 7 6 5 4 3 2 1

Printed in the United States of America

To the world's best dental hygienist,
Cynthia Hekimian,
because she always makes me laugh
before she tortures me.

Chapter 1

They called it You Bet Your Life Park, because that's what you were doing if you lingered inside the park after sundown, betting your life that you'd get out again. It had been a nice quiet neighborhood once upon a time, and it still was, during the day. Modern, high-rise condos enclosed the park on three sides. Visitors to the city often remarked on the fact that most of the buildings didn't have any windows. A large outdoor pool was located in the middle of the park. The local kids went swimming there in the summertime. There was also a pizza parlor, a video game arcade, and a couple of small stores that sold groceries, ice, and gas to those who had need of such things.

Large signs were posted at regular intervals throughout the park warning visitors to vacate the premises well before sunset. Smart people paid attention to the signs. Dumb ones were rarely heard from again, because the condos and apartments that encompassed You Bet Your Life Park were a sanctuary for the Undead. A supernaturally charged force field surrounded the outer perimeter of the apartment complex and the park, thereby preventing the vampires from leaving the area and wandering through the city.

Regan Delaney didn't have any idea how the force field worked or what it was made of. All she knew was that it kept the vamps inside but had no negative effect on humans. It was against the law to destroy vampires these days, unless you found one outside the park, but the force field made that impossible. Any vampire who wished to leave the park and move to a protected area in another part of the country had to apply for a permit and be transported, by day, by a company equipped to handle that kind of thing. What Regan found the hardest to accept was that vampires were now considered an endangered species, like tigers, elephants, and marine turtles, and as such, they had to be protected from human predators. The very thought was ludicrous!

It hadn't always been so, of course. In her grandfather's day, vampires had been looked upon as vermin, the scum of the earth. Bounties had been placed on them and they had been hunted ruthlessly. Many of the known vampires had been destroyed. Then, about five years ago, the bleeding hearts had started crying about how sad it was to kill all those poor misunderstood creatures of the night. After all, the bleeding hearts argued, even vampires had rights. Besides, they were also human beings and deserved to be treated with respect. To Regan's astonishment, sympathy for the vampires had grown and vampires had been given immunity, of a sort, and put into protective custody in places like You Bet Your Life Park. And since the Undead could no longer hunt in the city, the law had decided to put the vampires to good use. For a brief period of time, criminals sentenced to death had been given to the vampires.

The thought still made Regan cringe. Though she had no love for murderers, rapists, or child molesters, she couldn't, in good conscience, condone throwing them to the vamps. She didn't have to worry for long. In less than a year, the same bleeding-heart liberals who had felt sorry for the poor, misunderstood vampires began feeling sorry for the poor unfortunate criminals who had become their prey, and so a new law had been passed and criminals were again disposed of more humanely, by lethal injection.

Unfortunately, the new law had left the Undead with no ready food supply. In order to appease their hunger and keep them from killing each other, blood banks had agreed to donate whole blood to the vampire community until synthetic plasma could be developed. In a few months, Locke Pharmaceuticals invented something called Synthetic Type O that was reported to taste and smell the same as the real thing. A variety of blood types soon followed, though Type O remained the most popular.

Taking a deep breath, Regan shook off thoughts of the past and stared at the lifeless body sprawled at her feet. Apparently, one of the vampires had tired of surviving on Synthetic Type O. She felt a wave of pity for the dead man. In life, he had been a middle-aged man with sandy brown hair and a trim mustache. He might even have been handsome. Now his face was set in a rictus of horror. His heart, throat, and liver had been savagely ripped away, and there wasn't enough blood left in his body to fill an eyedropper. The corpse had been found under a bush by a couple who had been leaving the Park just before sunset. From the looks of it, the victim had been killed the night before.

"Hey, Reggie."

Regan looked away from the body and into the deep gray eyes of Sergeant Michael Flynn. Flynn was a good cop, honest, hardworking, and straightforward, a rarity in this day and age. He was a handsome man in his mid-thirties, with a shock of dark red hair and a dimple in his left cheek. She had gone out on a number of dates with Mike in the last few months. He was fun to be with and she enjoyed his company. She knew Mike was eager to take their relationship to the next level, but she wasn't ready for that, not yet. She cared for him. She admired him. She loved him, but she wasn't in love with him. It was because he was the best friend she had in the city that she didn't want to complicate their friendship, or worse, jeopardize it, by going to bed with him. She had seen it happen all too often, a perfectly good friendship ruined when two people decided to sleep together.

"So," Flynn said, "definitely a vampire kill, right?"

"Looks that way," Regan agreed, but she wasn't sure. She had seen vampire kills before. The complete lack of blood pointed to a vampire, but the fact that the victim's heart, throat, and liver had been ripped out disturbed her. She had never known a vampire to take anything but blood from its prey.

"So, you about through here?" Flynn asked.

"What? Oh, sure." She wasn't a cop and she had no real authority on the scene, but in the past, whenever the department received a call about a suspected vampire killing, they had asked her to come out and take a look. She had been a vampire hunter in those days, and a darn good one, but that had been back in the good old days, before vampires became "protected" and put her out of a job. Fortunately, she had a tidy little inheritance from her grandfather, though it wouldn't last much longer if she didn't find another job soon.

"I'll call you next week," Flynn said with a wink.

Regan nodded, then moved away from the scene so the forensic boys could get to work. It gave her an edgy feeling, being in the park after the sun went down, though she supposed there were enough cops in the area to keep her reasonably safe from the monsters. At any rate, it felt good to be part of a criminal investigation again, good to feel needed. Still, she couldn't help feeling guilty that she would be out of work in a heartbeat as soon as they caught the killer.

She remembered the first time the department had requested her expertise. Even now, years later, the thought made her wince with embarrassment. After all the classes she had taken at the Police Academy, she had been convinced she was prepared for anything, but no amount of training could have prepared her for the reality of seeing that first fresh vampire kill. At the Academy, the bodies had been dummies and, while they had been realistic, they hadn't come close to the real thing. Regan had turned away and covered her mouth, trying in vain to keep her dinner down. It had been Michael who had come to her aid, who had offered her a handkerchief and assured her that it happened to everyone sooner or later. They had been friends from that night forward.

Now, she stood in the shadows, watching two men

wearing masks and gloves slip the body into a black plastic bag for the trip to the morgue while the forensic team tagged and bagged possible evidence from the scene. Maybe they would get lucky downtown, but she didn't think so. She had a hunch that whoever had perpetrated the crime knew exactly what he was doing and that whatever evidence he had left behind, if any, would be useless.

Regan watched the ambulance pull away from the curb. Once the body had been thoroughly examined, the medical examiner would take the necessary steps to ensure that the corpse didn't rise as a new vampire tomorrow night. She didn't envy him the job, but if there was one thing the city didn't need, it was another vampire.

Regan was jotting down a few notes when she felt a shiver run down her spine. Not the "gee, it's cold outside" kind of shiver but the "you'd better be careful, there's a monster close by" kind.

Making a slow turn, she peered into the darkness as every instinct for self-preservation that she possessed screamed a warning.

If he hadn't moved, she never would have seen him.

He emerged from the shadowy darkness on cat-silent feet. "Do not be afraid," he said. "I mean you no harm."

His voice was like thick molasses covered in dark chocolate, so deep and sinfully rich, she could feel herself gaining weight just listening to him speak.

"Right." She slipped her hand into the pocket of her jacket, her fingers curling around the trigger of a snub-nosed pistol. She never left home without it. The gun was loaded with five silver bullets that had been dipped in holy water. The hammer rested on an empty chamber. "That's why you're sneaking up on me."

The corner of his sensual mouth lifted in a lazy half-smile. "If I wanted you dead, my lovely one, you would be dead."

Regan believed him. He spoke with the kind of calm assurance that left no room for doubt.

Joaquin Santiago moved toward her like a sleek black panther on the trail of fresh game. Supernatural power radiated from him like heat from a blast furnace. He was tall and well-muscled, with broad shoulders, strong arms, and long, long legs. In movies, vampires were usually depicted as pale and gaunt, with stringy hair and long fingernails, but there was nothing pale or gaunt about Santiago. His dusky skin and the contours of his face proudly proclaimed his Spanish and Native America heritage. He wore snug black trousers, a black silk shirt, a long black coat reminiscent of the kind cowboys had worn in the Old West, and a pair of supple black leather boots.

He looked like the angel of death come to call.

Regan took a deep breath. "Do you know who killed that man?" she asked, pleased when her voice didn't tremble. Even though she had never met Joaquin Santiago before tonight, she knew who he was. He wasn't your garden-variety vampire. Before the local Undead had been confined to You Bet Your Life Park, Santiago had been the undisputed master of the city, feared by vampires and humans alike. In person, he more than lived up to the hype that surrounded him.

"No." His answer was clipped and final.

"Well, somebody killed him, and all the outward signs point to one of your kind."

"My kind?" He lifted one black brow in an elegant gesture of disdain. "What kind would that be?"

Regan laughed. "A vampire, of course."

He shook his head. "Our kills are not so . . ." His gaze lingered briefly on her throat. "Messy."

She looked up at him, careful not to meet his eyes—dark blue eyes that were vibrant and direct and glowed faintly, even in the dark. Eyes that could hypnotize with a glance.

She lifted her chin a notch. "I don't know anyone else around here who would kill a man and drink him dry, do you?"

A muscle throbbed in Joaquin Santiago's jaw.

Score one for me, Regan thought with an inner smile of satisfaction.

She tried not to stare at him, but it was difficult. He was easily the most handsome individual, man or vampire, she had ever seen. Of course, all vampires, male and female, seemed to be beautiful. It was part of their preternatural allure, but she was willing to bet that this man had been drop-dead gorgeous even before the Dark Trick had been worked upon him. Though he looked to be in his early thirties, she knew he was an old vampire, perhaps ancient. Only the old ones possessed that eerie stillness.

"This is the fourth death in the last three weeks," he remarked.

"The fourth?" She hadn't been aware there had been others.

He nodded, once, curtly.

"Were the police notified?"

"No."

"No?" she exclaimed, her voice rising with her temper. "Why not?"

"We do not need any more bad publicity."

"Publicity? Three people were killed that no one knows about, and you were worried about a little bad publicity?" She shook her head, then took a deep, calming breath. "What happened to the other bodies?"

"They were disposed of."

"Did their remains look like the one found tonight?"

Again, that precise nod.

"The murders should have been reported."

He shrugged, a graceful movement of one muscular shoulder. "The victims would be just as dead."

She couldn't argue with that. Still. "Their families need to know what happened to them."

"I fear I cannot help you. We did not check their identification."

He talked of their deaths so calmly, as if those who had been killed were of no consequence. Feeling suddenly chilled, Regan wrapped her arms around her body. Three people had died violently and their loved ones would never know what happened to them. They would be listed as missing persons, their families left to forever wonder what had become of them. It wasn't right, and there was nothing she could do about it.

"Would you like to go to Sardino's for a drink?" he asked. "You look like you could use something to warm you."

Sardino's was a restaurant located on the southeast corner of the Park. It catered to humans during the day and the Undead after dark. The restaurant had long been considered neutral territory, a place where daring humans and curious vampires could mingle without fear, if they so desired. The restaurant had two doors—one you could enter from the park and one exclusively for humans that could be accessed directly from the safety of the street beyond the park's barrier. Out of curiosity, Regan had visited Sardino's once, soon after she graduated from the Academy, but it had been too weird, seeing vampires and humans sitting together like old friends, and she had never gone back.

"I don't think so," she said. The thought of sharing a booth with him while he drank a glass of warm Synthetic Type O wasn't the least bit appealing. Besides, she was supposed to hunt and destroy vampires, not have cocktails with them.

He laughed softly. "Afraid to be seen with me, Miss . . ." His gaze moved to the badge pinned to the lapel of her jacket. "Miss Delaney." There was an unspoken challenge in the depths of his midnight blue eyes.

She was afraid; afraid of the effect he had on her senses, afraid of that air of male supremacy that rolled off him in waves, but she would have chewed her tongue off and swallowed it whole before she would have admitted it. She had encountered vampires before, but never one this old, or this powerful.

She was still trying to think of a suitable reply when, without a word, he was gone.

Regan glanced around, surprised to find that everyone else was gone, as well, and that she was alone in the park. Though every instinct she possessed urged her to run from the place just as fast as she could, she turned and walked sedately toward the street where she had left her car. One of the first things she had learned was that showing fear in front of a vampire, or any predator for that matter, was never a good idea.

Regan slipped her hand into her jacket pocket. She was a hunter. She was supposed to be brave. Her finger curled around the trigger. Why had she parked so far away?

She was still a good distance from the curb when she realized someone was watching her from the darkness. She glanced casually over her shoulder, expecting to see hell-red eyes staring back at her. There was no one there, but she knew she wasn't alone. Someone was following her. She heard faint, mocking laughter off to her left and she veered to the right. Fingers of cold sweat trickled down her spine.

The sense of being followed grew stronger, the eerie laughter grew louder, and suddenly she was running. If anyone saw her and thought she was afraid, well, she would just have to live with it, because they were right.

Dead right.

She had almost reached the edge of the park when, without warning, she slammed into someone. She would have screamed, only terror froze the sound in her throat. At any rate, there was no one left in the park to come to her aid.

The vampire stared down at her, close-set eyes blazing red, thin lips peeled back to reveal sharp white fangs. He looked young and strong and hungry—and she was going to be dinner. It was her own fault. Anyone who lingered in the park after sundown was fair game. But she wasn't going down without a fight. She reached for her crucifix and her gun at the same time, but before she could use

either one, the master of the city materialized
between her and the other vampire.

"Karl," Santiago said, "go home."

The two vampires stared at each other for a long
moment. Regan could feel the animosity that
hummed between them, feel their power rise in a
silent battle of wills. For a moment, she was afraid
there would be a fight. She glanced at her car, wondering how long it would take her to get to the curb
and climb inside, because if there was one thing
she didn't want to do, it was get between two angry
vampires.

Several taut moments ticked into eternity and
then, with a hiss, Karl vanished from sight. She
knew he hadn't really vanished, only that he had
moved faster than mortal eyes could follow.

"Come," Santiago said, extending his hand to
her. "I will walk you to your car."

Regan stared up at him. Walk her to her car?
"How can you do that? You can't leave the park."

"Can't I?"

A sudden chill tiptoed down her spine. "Can
you?"

"No one tells me where to go or what to do," he
said with bold arrogance. "Least of all a human
girl."

"I'm not a girl," she said with asperity. "I'm a
woman."

A faint smile tugged at his lips. "Go home, little
girl, before the big bad wolf gobbles you up."

He didn't have to tell her twice. She was all too
aware of his heated gaze on her back as he followed
her to the edge of the park. He stopped where the
sidewalk began.

After punching in the code to unlock the car,

Regan slid behind the wheel and quickly closed the door. Resisting the urge to look back and see if the master of the city was still watching her, she punched in the ignition code and headed for home as if Satan himself was after her.

And perhaps he was.

Regan thought about the vampire Santiago all the way home and again later, while she soaked in a hot bubble bath. He had offered to walk her to her car. She had a terrible feeling that he would have been able to do it, too, if she had agreed. But how could that be? Vampires weren't supposed to be able to pass through the invisible force field. But what if he could? And if he could, did that mean others of the Undead were also able to leave the park? Had mankind been living under a false sense of security for the last five years?

The thought made her go cold all over.

Stepping out of the tub, she wrapped up in a large fluffy towel and went into the bedroom. After drying off, she slipped into her nightgown and a warm fleece robe, then went into the kitchen. She punched hot chocolate with a splash of extra chocolate into the computer, hoping it would help her to relax. Meeting Joaquin Santiago had unsettled her far more than she cared to admit.

Though Santiago didn't look a day over thirty, it was said that he was the oldest vampire in the city, perhaps the oldest vampire in the country. He was undoubtedly the most dangerous—and certainly the most handsome, with his long black hair, dark, penetrating eyes, and muscular physique.

With a shake of her head, Regan thrust him from her mind. Curling up on the sofa, she switched on the Satellite Screen, flipping through the online guide in search of a late movie she hadn't already seen a hundred times.

For the next two hours, she managed to avoid thinking about Joaquin Santiago. But later, while she was lying in bed, he invaded her thoughts yet again, walking through the corridors of her mind, an ache that wouldn't go away.

Chapter 2

Joaquin Santiago prowled the dark, deserted streets of the city. He was supposed to be concentrating on finding the creature that had killed yet another mortal in his territory, but his thoughts kept straying toward the woman. Miss Regan Delaney. Even now, her scent lingered in his nostrils, the warm sweet scent of woman, the flowery fragrance of her cologne, the deeper, more compelling scent of her life's blood. Rarely had he met a woman who stirred more than his hunger, but Miss Delaney, with her sea-green eyes and honeygold hair, ah, she aroused both his hunger and his desire. It was a dangerous and potent combination. The fact that she had worked with the police department added a hint of danger to the mix.

But he had no time for a woman, not even the very delectable Miss Delaney, not when there was a killer on the prowl, a killer who had dared violate the city that Santiago called home. The humans suspected a vampire of the murder in the park, but Santiago knew better. There were perhaps a handful of the Undead who had the power to mask their scent and their presence from him, but only one, other than himself, could breech the barrier that surrounded the Park. It was that fact that troubled him most of all, that aberration that convinced him he wasn't looking for a vampire at all, but for a creature he had hunted for hundreds of years. Was it mere coincidence that had brought Vasile here, to this place, at this time?

Santiago was about to turn back toward the Park when Miss Delaney's delightful scent surrounded him, a fragrance that was more than the mere blending of soap and toothpaste and cologne. It was the unique scent of her skin and hair, the female essence of the woman herself.

Pausing in the shadows, he glanced up at the apartment building to his left. He opened his senses, sifting through the myriad smells, old and new, that assailed his nostrils, until he found the one he wanted. Yes, she was there, on the fourth floor. The soft, steady sound of her breathing told him she was asleep.

A thought took him to her bedside. She had worn her hair pulled back in a tail earlier that night. Now it was spread across her pillow like a splash of pale gold paint. Her eyelashes made dark crescents on her suntanned cheeks. A faint sigh whispered past her lips, and then she smiled. Curious to know what she was dreaming about, he crept into her mind—and felt a smile of pure masculine pleasure spread over his own face. She was dreaming of him . . .

Hand in hand, they walked barefoot along a stretch of shimmering, sun-warmed sand, talking and laughing like ordinary mortals, pausing a moment to watch a couple of kids building a castle in the sand. It

amused him that she imagined the two of them together in the daytime. In reality, the sun would have
destroyed him in an instant, but this was only a
dream, and he watched through her eyes as they ran
into the frothy surf. When the water was knee-deep,
she stopped to splash him and he splashed her back,
reveling in the near-forgotten touch of the sun on his
face, the sound of her laughter.

And then he took control of the dream. The
other people disappeared, leaving only the two of
them on the beach. Her hand was soft and warm in
his as they walked along. He inhaled the scent of
sand and seaweed, heard the breakers wash upon
the shore, the screech of gulls overhead. He gazed
out at the ocean. A pair of dolphins rose out of the
water, somersaulting before they disappeared beneath the sunlit waves. He felt the heat of the
summer sun on his face, a warmth he had not felt
in centuries. He drew the woman into his arms and
she murmured his name, her voice laced with uncertainty and desire. He rained kisses along the
length of her neck. Her scent enveloped him, her
nearness aroused him. He held her tighter as the
predator sleeping within him stirred to life. She
shivered as his fangs brushed the tender skin of her
throat . . .

Regan woke with a cry, ending the dream and
driving him from her mind.

Santiago vanished from sight as Regan jackknifed
into a sitting position. She reached for the light on
the bedside table, her wide-eyed gaze darting around
the room while her fingers made a thorough investigation of the skin along both sides of her neck. He
sensed her relief when she detected no bites, no telltale marks.

Blowing out a sigh of relief, she fell back on the pillows.

His mind brushed against hers as she convinced herself it had only been a dream.

And then she sat up again, her eyes narrowing as she looked around the room a second time.

Veiled from her sight, Santiago stood at the foot of her bed. Though she couldn't see him, he knew she was aware of his presence. Never before had any human, man or woman, detected his presence against his will. Who was this woman, he wondered, that she had the power to do what others did not?

Lost in thought, he drifted out of her room to the sidewalk below. It had proved to be a most interesting night. A killer he had stalked for centuries was here, in the city, and he had met a beautiful and most unusual woman. Yes, he mused, a most interesting night, indeed.

Leaving the more affluent part of the city behind, he strolled through an area known as the Byways. It was here, in the dark underbelly of the city, where he felt the most at home; indeed, it was here that he hunted, here that he maintained his primary lair. It was true that he kept an apartment in the park complex, but he hadn't survived as long as he had by letting others know where he slept. Only fools permitted others, especially humans, to know their resting place, and Santiago had never been a fool.

He ghosted along the dark streets, his senses alert, the hunger that burned within him rousing at the tantalizing scent of prey. Anticipation hummed through him as his fangs lengthened.

He took the woman unawares. She was young to be working the streets. Her body was thin beneath the short skirt and low-cut spandex top. Her breath smelled of drugs and alcohol.

Lowering his head to her neck, he wondered briefly what had compelled her to embrace such a wretched existence, but all thought of her past was washed away as the warm red tide of her blood flowed over his tongue.

For a moment, he considered taking it all. Seeing the dead man in the Park had aroused old instincts, but he thrust the urge aside. Mortals lived such a short life span, it didn't seem right to rob them of the few years they had, though he thought this woman might welcome death. She had no family, no one who cared for her and no one for whom she cared. She hated her existence. She hated her life, but she lacked the energy and courage needed to break away from her old life and build a new one.

It was sad, he thought, but it was not his problem.

He closed the wounds in her throat, erased his memory from her mind, and sent her on her way.

The little streetwalker had been sweet, he mused, continuing on toward his resting place, sweet and satisfying, yet he couldn't help but wonder what it would be like to taste Miss Regan Delaney and he knew, in that moment, that the hunger she had stirred within him would never be satisfied until he had tasted her.

It was near dawn when he reached his destination. His dwelling place was in the basement of an old, abandoned chemical plant. He had bought the building for a pittance years ago. The first three floors remained as they had been when the previous occupant moved out. Dirt, debris, empty boxes, and crates littered the floors and shelves, along with a number of old beer cans, newspapers, and desiccated insects.

Derelicts and drunks occasionally crawled inside the building to spend the night or sleep off a hangover, thereby relieving Santiago of the need to hunt.

A wave of his hand opened a heavy iron door in the lower basement. Closing it behind him, he flicked a switch on the wall, filling the room with soft light.

Soon after he bought the property, he had hired a contractor to transform the basement into a comfortable home. Once the remodeling had been completed, he had destroyed all the paperwork and then erased all memory of himself and the job from the minds of anyone who had been involved, from the boss of the company to the woman who answered the phone.

He glanced around the living area, pleased as always by his surroundings. A large painting above the mantel depicted the sun rising behind a snow-covered mountain. A pair of smaller paintings, one of a sunrise, the other of a sunset, adorned another wall. Beyond that, his tastes were expensive but simple. The rugs and walls were a pale gray, the fireplace was of faded red brick, the tables were carved of ebony, the sofa and chair were of butter-soft black leather. A small glass-topped coffee table contained the few things he cared enough about to keep— a fine gold chain that had belonged to Marishka, a small silver-backed mirror that had belonged to his mother, a black leather riding crop that had belonged to his father, a gold pocket watch to remind him that he now had all the time in the world. A Satellite Screen took up one entire wall.

The bedroom where he kept his clothing was a light blue-gray and contained a king-sized bed with a wrought-iron headboard, a black leather chair, an ebony dresser, and a pair of matching nightstands. A small bathroom was adjacent to the bedroom. Santiago had never courted the Dark Sleep in the bed, though he rested there on occasion.

His lair, located behind a hidden panel in the bedroom closet, was done in the same shade of gray as the living room and contained little aside from a sleek black casket lined in black silk and a tall, free-standing, wrought-iron candelabra.

A prickling across his skin told him the sun was rising. Once, the sun had ruled his life. At its rising, he had been trapped in the death-like sleep of his kind, weak and helpless until the setting of the sun. But no more.

Bemused by the quirk of fate that had altered his destiny, he readied himself to take his rest, his mind turning once again to the Delaney woman. She had looked as innocent as a child, lying in her bed with her hair spread around her shoulders. Even now, his hand twitched with the urge to run his fingers through the thick golden strands.

Regan. He was still thinking of her when he sank into oblivion.

Chapter 3

The ringing of the phone beside her bed roused Regan from a deep, dreamless sleep. Picking it up, she muttered a groggy, "Hello?"

It was Michael Flynn. "Reggie," he said tersely, "we've got another one."

Instantly wide awake, Regan sat up and glanced at the clock. It was a quarter after nine in the morning. "Where?"

"About three meters from where we found the last one. How soon can you get here?"

"Give me twenty minutes."

Rising, she went into the bathroom, splashed cold water on her face, and brushed her teeth. After pulling her nightshirt over her head, she dressed quickly in a pair of old blue jeans that she had washed so often they were almost white, a long-sleeved sweatshirt with the words *Who Wants to Live Forever?* emblazoned across the front in bright pink letters, and a pair of old sneakers. She grabbed her gun from under her pillow and dropped it into her handbag, then went into the kitchen. She quickly downed a small glass of grapefruit juice, grabbed her handbag from the counter, and left her apartment.

Looking at dead bodies was a heck of a way to start the day.

Outside, the sky was thick with lowering gray clouds and the promise of rain before the day was out.

Flynn was waiting for her at the scene, his handsome face solemn. No one else was there, so she figured he must have called her before he notified anyone else.

The body lay on the dew-damp grass in a loose-limbed sprawl that couldn't be imitated by the living.

Regan's stomach clenched. This one was a woman in her mid-twenties. Regan surveyed the body without touching it, noting the opening in the chest where the heart had been extracted, the gaping hole where the liver had been, and the fact that there was virtually no blood to be seen. And no telltale puncture wounds on her neck. Of course, whatever marks had been there had been destroyed when her throat was ripped out.

"Same M.O. as the other one, right?" Flynn asked.

Regan nodded. "Identical, as near as I can tell."

"Two bodies in two days," Flynn remarked with a shake of his head. "I'm afraid we've got a serial killer on our hands."

Regan blew out a sigh. She was sorely afraid he was right. Though Flynn didn't know it, the death toll was five and not two. And while she hadn't seen the three bodies that Santiago had told her about, he had told her they looked the same as the one from last night. Even though she had no way of knowing if the killings were related, she had a feeling in her gut that they were. She should have questioned Santiago further about the other killings, she thought, and made a mental note to call his place and ask him to meet her in the park later.

Flynn swore softly. "Sure doesn't look like any vampire kills I've ever seen," he remarked. "I mean, look at . . ."

His voice trailed off at the sound of approaching sirens. Moments later, the forensics team and the M.E. arrived on the scene, along with a few cops who had nothing better to do so early in the morning.

Regan stayed out of the way as the medical examiner and his team got down to work. With that morbid sense of humor common to those who dealt with death on a daily basis, it occurred to Regan that if they didn't catch the murderer soon, she wouldn't have to go looking for a new job. She could go back to doing what she did best—hunting vampires. The thought brought a smile to her face, which she quickly banished.

She conferred briefly with the M.E., then waved to Flynn and left the park. There was nothing more for her to do there.

Going to her car, she pulled out her cell phone, called the Vampire Arms, and left a message for Joaquin Santiago to call her as soon as possible.

The rain started just before she got home.

Regan's phone rang almost the very instant the sun went down. A tingle of anticipation ran through her body when she picked it up and heard his voice.

"Miss Delaney, what can I do for you?"

He cut right to the chase. She liked that. "You said there had been three other murders."

"Yes."

"Were they in the park?"

"No."

Regan frowned. "But they were similar to the recent ones?"

"Yes, almost identical."

"Were they all males?"

"Two men and a young woman."

"I'd like you to tell me everything you remember."

"Of course, but this is hardly the kind of thing one discusses over the phone. Why don't you meet me at Sardino's for dinner?"

"I'm sorry, Mr. Santiago, but synthetic blood isn't on my diet."

His laughter sent frissons of heat dancing up and down her spine. "I am sure I can persuade Sardino to prepare something a little more to your liking."

"I don't think so, Mr. Santiago."

"Then I have nothing more to say."

She felt her temper rise. "That's blackmail."

"Indeed it is."

It was also flattering. "What time?"

"As soon as you can be there."

"All right," she said after a moment's hesitation. "I'll meet you there in forty minutes." It would give her time to wash up, fix her hair, and change her clothes. She shook her head. What was she thinking? The man was a vampire and this was a business meeting, not a date!

"Forty minutes," he agreed, and hung up the phone.

In spite of herself, Regan took pains with her appearance, choosing a long white skirt, white heels, and a dark green sweater that made her eyes appear several shades darker. She brushed her hair until it crackled, put it up in a fancy twist, and then let it down again. She rarely wore much makeup. Tonight, she indulged in a touch of powder and a bit of eye shadow and lipstick. Picking up her handbag, she checked to make sure her pistol was inside and loaded, and she was ready to go.

Stepping outside, she was glad to see that the storm had passed. She hated driving in the rain, but she loved storms, loved the thunder and the lightning and the way the rain washed away the dirt and grime of the city, leaving everything looking and smelling clean and fresh.

Sardino's wasn't yet crowded when she arrived. At this time of night, most of the humans had already left the park, while most of the vamps preferred to arrive later. She parked at the curb and took a deep, calming breath before getting out of the car.

Santiago was waiting for her. Dressed in ubiquitous black, he looked dashing and handsome and deadly. She could tell, by the heightened color of his skin, that he had fed not long ago.

He smiled when he saw her, displaying even white teeth. "Good evening." His smile was devastating, without a hint of fang.

"Hello."

He held out his hand. "Our table is ready."

Regan looked at him, hesitant to let him touch her.

Santiago raised one brow in a silent challenge.

Pursing her lips, Regan placed her hand in his and let him lead her to a table in a secluded corner of the room.

A waitress clad in a long black dress and a crisp white apron came to take their order.

Santiago asked the waitress to have Sardino fix Regan something to eat, then ordered a glass of A negative for himself.

Regan's heart skipped a beat. Was it merely coincidence that Santiago had ordered A negative, which happened to be her blood type, as well? But of course it was, she thought. How could he possibly know?

With a nod and a smile that showed only a hint of fang, the waitress moved away from the table. The fact that she couldn't completely hide her true nature proved that she was still a young vampire.

"Does all blood taste the same?" Regan asked what was uppermost in her mind without thinking.

"No." His gaze moved briefly to her throat. "Each type has its own . . . shall we say, bouquet."

Regan grimaced. It was more information than she needed. "So," she said, changing the subject, "tell me about the other killings."

"There is little to tell. They were almost identical to the one you saw last night. And the one today."

Regan wasn't surprised that he knew about the latest victim. She had a feeling that he knew everything that went on, not only inside the park but outside, as well.

"You told me that on the phone," Regan said. Leaning back in her chair, she crossed her arms under her breasts. "I thought you had some new information."

"There have been other killings."

"What do you mean?"

"Someone is also killing vampires."

That piqued her interest. "I hadn't heard about that," she said, leaning forward.

"Of course not. But I have."

"How many?"

"Four, so far."

"Do you think the same person is killing both vampires and humans?"

Santiago shrugged. "Perhaps."

"Perhaps?"

"The one responsible for the deaths inside the park is not a vampire. And not a mortal."

"Not a vamp and not a human? What else could it be?"

"It is a werewolf. A very old werewolf."

Regan stared at him. A werewolf? She sat back, stunned. That possibility had never occurred to her, but then, why would it? Werewolves were supposed to be extinct. She had never seen a werewolf, had been skeptical that they had ever existed except in fairy tales. The idea of a human turning into an animal just seemed so bizarre. And yet, it shouldn't be so hard to believe in werewolves, she mused, not when there was another, equally fantastic creature sitting across from her. Still, vampires remained humanoid if not entirely human. But werewolves . . . she shrugged inwardly. She supposed the two species really weren't so very different. Both werewolves and vampires were brutal killers that stalked the night in search of human prey. And if there could be werewolves and vampires, then why not fairies and goblins and trolls and elves?

She shook her head. She was being ridiculous now. Vampires and werewolves had once been human. Elves and goblins and trolls were just . . . make-believe. Weren't they?

"What makes you think it's a werewolf?" she asked, although the longer she thought about it, the more sense it made. She had never known any vampire to do more than take the blood of its victims. Sure, they usually took the life, too, but they left the victim's body intact; they didn't rip out the internal organs.

"I recognized his scent."

"You know him then?" she asked, startled.

Santiago nodded. "Our paths have crossed before."

From the tone of his voice, she didn't think they were friends. "The other night, you told me you didn't know who had killed the victim."

"I lied," he said with a shrug.

"So how do I know you're not lying to me tonight?"

"Because I know you better now."

Disconcerted by his words, Regan lifted her water glass and took a drink. What was she doing, sitting here with this . . . this creature? He was one of them, a killer of innocents, a drinker of blood. Looking at him, it was hard to believe he was one of the monsters. He looked like any other man, save that his teeth seemed a little whiter, his eyes a little brighter . . . who was she kidding? No ordinary man had ever looked this roguishly handsome, or made her heart do handsprings in her chest. No ordinary man had ever made her skin tingle just by looking at her.

She shook her head to clear it. It was hard to think straight when he was looking at her. "Are you the only vampire that can cross through the barrier?"

He hesitated a moment before replying, "As far as I know."

"Why don't I believe you?"

He shrugged.

She frowned thoughtfully. "What about the were-wolf?"

The vampire's gaze moved over her, probing, curious, and yet she had the feeling that he knew her better than she knew herself. "It would have no effect on him."

If only Joaquin Santiago had no effect on her! It was hard to think coherently when he was looking at her as if nothing else in all the world mattered. His dark eyes smoldered with unspoken desire. Her body warmed under his regard, aching for his touch. She told herself it was nothing. Vampires were notoriously charming and seductive. It was part of their appeal, part of their preternatural glamour, the very thing that made it so hard for humans to resist them.

Regan was glad when her meal arrived as it gave her something else to focus on. She had never eaten with a vampire before and she soon discovered that doing so made her extremely nervous.

"Is the food not to your liking?" he asked.

"No, it's really very good, but . . ."

He lifted one brow. "But?"

"I . . . it's . . ." She cleared her throat. "It makes me uncomfortable, eating in front of you, and . . ."

He glanced at the ruby red liquid shimmering in the crystal goblet in his hand. "And my drinking this doesn't help your appetite?" he guessed.

She nodded.

He signaled for the waitress and had her take his glass away. "Is that better?"

"Yes. No. I don't know. It doesn't seem right to eat in front of you when you can't . . . ." She paused a moment, then gestured at the basket of garlic bread the waitress had brought with her spaghetti. "Does this bother you?"

"No," he said, grinning. "The whole garlic thing is just a myth."

"Oh. How long has it been since you consumed real food?"

"A very long time."

"I guess you don't remember what it was like?"

"Ah, but I do. I even remember my last meal, though it was remarkably unremarkable. Ash cakes and a bowl of venison stew. A cup of tiswin."

"Ash cakes?" Regan shook her head. "They aren't really made of ashes. Are they?"

He laughed softly. The sound danced across her skin, sensuous and seductive, like the man himself.

"Not at all," he said. "They are made from ground mesquite beans or pine nuts mixed with tallow or bear grease, and honey. The women form the mixture into small cakes and bake them on heated stones."

"Do you miss it? Eating, I mean."

"Not any more, though sometimes . . ."

"Go on."

He shook his head, thinking it would be better not to go down that path. She had no need to know that when he drank from his prey, he could, if he wished, vicariously experience what they had recently experienced.

"Please," he said, "enjoy your meal."

She tried, but every time she took a bite, she was aware of his gaze. He was not a mortal man. He didn't eat food. He drank blood. She had been a fool to meet him here, alone, after dark. No one knew she had agreed to meet him here. If he should decide he wanted a snack, she was readily available.

The thought made her shudder. How could anyone drink blood? It was beyond her comprehension. Contemplating it ruined what was left of her appetite and she pushed her plate away.

"You have hardly eaten a thing," Santiago remarked.

"I'm not hungry anymore."

He regarded her through narrowed eyes. "I see."

Drat the man. She was afraid he saw way too much.

He signaled for the waitress and signed the check, leaving a generous tip.

After rising, he drew back Regan's chair, then followed her out of the restaurant.

Silently, he walked her to her car. Was it her imagination, or did she feel a slight tremor in the force field when he passed through?

Regan unlocked the door. "Thank you for dinner."

He flashed a smile. "I am sorry that the food, and the company, were not more to your liking."

"I . . ."

He held up one hand, silencing her. "You needn't explain." Indeed, her thoughts were clearly visible in her eyes.

Regan slid behind the wheel. If she needed physical proof that he could leave the park, she had it now. She punched in the ignition code, then looked up at Santiago through the open door. "If you uncover any more information on the werewolf, I hope you'll let me know."

Santiago nodded. "If you wish."

He closed her door, then watched her drive away. He would see her again, he thought, and soon.

Even if he had to make something up.

The vampire murders made headlines in all the newspapers the following day, and became the top story on the nightly news.

By the end of the week, the chief of police had declared that there was a serial killer on the loose and advised people to remain in their homes after dark. To date, eight bodies had been found inside the park, all of them brutally mutilated. For the public's safety, the mayor closed the park to all human traffic until further notice.

Various anti-vampire groups that had been silent up until now began demanding that the vampires be destroyed once and for all, while the bleeding hearts argued that anyone foolish enough to stroll in the park after sundown knew the risks involved and deserved whatever they got. The public demanded that something be done before it was too late.

At the beginning of the second week, Joaquin Santiago appeared on the eleven o'clock news. He expressed his sympathy to the bereaved and assured the city's nervous populace that none of the vampires that resided inside You Bet Your Life Park were responsible for the murders.

Sitting on the sofa at home, Regan listened to the telecast with interest, thinking that the master of the city was not only extremely handsome but was as tactful as any D.C. politician, as well. Obviously wary of adding fuel to the fire of panic growing in the streets, he hadn't mentioned his belief that a werewolf was responsible for the murders. No one would have believed him anyway, Regan thought, since everyone knew that werewolves were extinct. But then, people also believed that vampires couldn't leave You Bet Your Life Park, or the other complexes like it around the country, when she knew from first-hand experience that at least one of them was completely unaffected by the force field.

Leaning back against the sofa, she switched off the Satellite Screen. Vampires, werewolves, and murder, oh my. She had visited all the recent crime scenes and although she had not seen Santiago at any of them, she had been aware of his presence nearby. She was vaguely disappointed that he hadn't called her and annoyed with herself for feeling that way. Life was complicated enough without adding a vampire to the mix, especially a vampire like Joaquin Santiago.

Going into the kitchen, she pulled a can of soda from the fridge. The only good thing about the recent murders was that she was again on the police payroll, although it seemed wrong somehow to profit by the suffering of others. Still, the Department had asked for her expertise, such as it was.

Carrying the soda, Regan went back into the living room, switched on her computer, and did a Google search for werewolves. If it turned out that Santiago was right and the killer was a werewolf, then she wanted to know what she was up against. As far as she knew, there weren't any werewolf hunters in the city, which meant the job was wide open, and she was as qualified as anyone else, maybe more so.

She was about to shut down her computer and get ready for bed when the phone rang. She stared at it a moment and then, grimacing, she picked it up. Lately, whenever the phone rang, it was bad news. Tonight was no different.

"Our killer's struck again," Flynn said.

"Same M.O.?" she asked, reaching for her shoes.

"Looks like it."

"Okay, I'll be right there."

"It isn't at the park."

"Where is it?"

"Uptown, behind the high school."

Regan's hand tightened on the phone. "I'll be there in ten minutes," she said, and disconnected the call.

Behind the high school. Nausea roiled in her stomach as she slid behind the wheel of her car and drove uptown. *Not kids,* she thought. *Please, not kids.*

Fifteen minutes later, she pulled up behind Flynn's patrol car, which was parked at the curb next to the football field. While alighting from her car, she noted that the M.E.'s van was also there. Taking a deep breath, she cut across a corner of the football field, her shoes squishing in the damp grass. She passed a couple of police officers as she made her way to the storm drain located in a ravine behind the field.

The crime scene had been cordoned off with yellow tape. A number of uniformed police stood at the top of the ravine, looking down. She could see the M.E. kneeling on the ground beside the storm drain. The forensic team was bagging evidence, their voices low.

Moving carefully, Regan made her way down the slippery slope toward the M.E. She felt a wave of sympathy for a young cop who looked like he was about to lose his dinner. With a reassuring smile, she hurried forward so she wouldn't be a witness if he suddenly lost it.

Regan nodded to a few of the officers she knew, her steps slowing as she reached the crime scene. The bodies were sprawled in the dirt. The girl, clad in the bloody remains of a green polka-dot sundress and white sandals, looked like she was sixteen or seventeen. Her long, dark hair was tied back in a ponytail. The body of a young man wearing a mud-and-blood splattered white shirt and a pair of dark trousers lay facedown beside her. Both bodies had been mutilated. Both had been drained of blood.

"According to the M.E., they've been dead about four hours," Flynn said, coming up behind her. "The girl's mother said her daughter went to a movie with her boyfriend. She was supposed to be home by ten. When she wasn't home by midnight, the mother got worried. She called the boyfriend's house but his folks hadn't heard from him. What with the recent killings making headlines, the girl's mother called the police."

"What made them look here?"

Flynn jerked his head toward where a tall, skinny young man stood, a dog the size of a pony at his side.

"The dog found the bodies. The kid called nine-one-one."

Regan nodded.

Flynn swore, something he rarely did in Regan's presence. "We've got big trouble."

"More than this?" Regan stared at the girl's body, her stomach roiling. It was bad enough when this kind of thing happened to adults, but children . . . Regan crossed her arms over her stomach. The girl should be home with her parents, arguing about doing her homework or gossiping on the phone with her best friend. She shouldn't be a crime statistic.

"Think about it," Flynn said. "These killings didn't take place inside the park like the others . . ."

"Which means we've got a vampire that can cross the force field," Regan said, finishing his thought for him.

"Right."

Regan nodded. If this was, indeed, a vampire killing, then there were at least two vampires who could cross the force field: the killer and Joaquin Santiago. Unless they were one and the same . . . She thrust the thought from her mind.

"Maybe it isn't a vampire," Regan said, thinking aloud.

Flynn looked at her, his brow furrowed. "What else could it be?"

"I don't know. Maybe a copycat killer," she suggested, while a little voice inside her mind whispered *werewolf*. Legend said werewolves ate flesh. They didn't drink blood. Santiago had to be wrong. This had to be the work of a rogue vampire, one who drained his victims and then mutilated the bodies, perhaps to make the police think they had a serial killer on their hands instead of a vampire who was able to cross the force field. Either that, or the killer really was a madman, one who liked to collect blood and body parts. Or maybe the killer was some kind of Satanist who used the blood and internal organs in rituals of dark magic.

"Listen, I'll talk to you later," Flynn said. "I told the captain I'd call him and bring him up to speed."

"All right."

Regan was still contemplating who or what besides a vampire might have killed the teenagers when a warm tingle suffused her. She didn't have to turn around to know that Santiago was standing behind her.

"They're so young," she murmured. "So young to die such a terrible death."

She glanced up at Santiago, surprised by the sorrow she saw in the depths of his eyes. She had always believed vampires were past feeling human emotions, that the capacity for love and compassion and grief died along with their mortality.

"Is this the work of the werewolf?" she asked as he came to stand beside her.

"Is this between you and me?" he asked quietly.

"What do you mean?"

"I do not wish you to repeat what I tell you to anyone else."

"If you have information on who the murderer is, it needs to be reported," she said adamantly. "We've got to stop this maniac before he kills again."

"Then I cannot help you."

"It was a vampire, wasn't it? And you don't want anyone to know."

"I know who did this and I will deal with him in my own way."

"So, it is a vampire." It wasn't a question this time. She studied the two bodies, focusing on the wounds and not the horror reflected on the faces of the victims. "How can you tell? They look the same as the others."

"If you tell the police I told you a vampire did this, I will deny it," he said curtly.

"So now we have two killers running around," Regan muttered. "That's great, just great." She turned away as the M.E. shook out a body bag.

"This one will not be running around for long."

Regan stared at Santiago. He was the only vampire she knew of who could cross the force field. For the second time that night, she wondered if he was the one responsible for the horrendous killings.

He met her gaze, his eyes narrowing ominously. "You think I did this?"

"Did you?"

"Would I be here if I had?"

"But it was a vampire, wasn't it? What about the other murders?" she asked, frowning. "Were they the work of the werewolf or the vampire?"

"The three I told you about were killed by a vampire. I knew he was powerful. I did not realize he was powerful enough to ignore the force field."

"Why didn't you tell me this before."

"He was not killing children before."

Regan massaged her temple with her fingertips. She could feel a headache coming on. "How do you know it was a vampire who did this and not the werewolf? Did you smell the vampire's scent, too?"

"I cannot tell you all my secrets, Regan Delaney," he replied with a wry grin, "but after tonight, the one who did this will no longer be a threat to your kind, or mine."

Chapter 4

The vampire paused at the edge of the lake, his preternatural senses testing the night air. He had fed earlier, and fed well, but lately the hunger would not be appeased.

He glanced at the burlap bag in his hand, then flung the bag and its contents into the center of the lake, watching impassively as the blood-crusted organs floated on the water before slowly sinking out of sight.

He didn't know who was killing the people inside You Bet Your Life Park, and he didn't care. It provided the perfect cover for his own crimes, although he found ripping out hearts and livers a rather nasty business.

He grunted softly. He didn't know why he found it so odious. He had done far worse things without a qualm.

Turning away from the lake, he walked down the narrow, twisting path that led to the street and the park beyond. It amused him to know that the foolish mortals believed the vampires were confined to the park. Of course, it was true that most of the

Undead couldn't cross the force field—but he wasn't one of them.

He was almost to the park when he paused. It was hours until dawn, plenty of time to make another kill.

He was stalking a voluptuous young woman wearing a silver spandex tank top and a black leather miniskirt when he sensed the presence of another of his kind.

The vampire stopped, all thoughts of the woman forgotten. He had not felt fear in over two hundred years, but he felt it now. It was a sudden chill snaking down his spine, a clammy hand clawing at his vitals.

"Karl."

The voice came out of the shadows, as cold and unforgiving as death itself.

The vampire peered into the darkness. "Leave me alone, Santiago. You hear? Go away and leave me alone!"

"You have broken my law. You have killed on my turf."

"You're not the master of the city anymore," Karl said, his voice rising. "You're no better than the rest of us!"

"Am I not?"

Karl muttered a vile oath as Santiago materialized in front of him, his appearance so fast and unexpected that it came as a complete, and unwelcome, surprise.

Karl gasped as Santiago's hand curled around his throat.

"You have violated my law," Santiago repeated. "The tenuous peace we have achieved is at risk because you cannot control your thirst."

Karl stared into merciless blue eyes, his fear increasing as Santiago's voice grew softer and more deadly.

"I might have forgiven you for the others," the master of the city said. "But tonight you killed children. It is the one sin I will not forgive."

"I . . . I didn't . . . mean . . . to kill them," Karl said.

The other vampire snorted derisively. "One kill might be an accident. But two?" He shook his head.

Karl watched in horror as the master of the city lifted his free hand, the long fingers flexing, then curving into claws. He tried to scream as that hand moved slowly, resolutely, toward his chest, but terror trapped the sound in his throat. He thrashed wildly, his fear rising as he stared certain death in the face.

There was a blinding hot pain in his chest as his heart was torn from his body.

And then nothing at all.

Chapter 5

Regan stared at the clock on her bedside table. It was after two in the morning, and she couldn't sleep. Santiago's last words repeated in her mind, over and over again.

After tonight, the one who did this will no longer be a threat to your kind, or mine.

The words had been quietly spoken, but she had heard the ominous undertone. There was no doubt in her mind that Santiago would exact the ultimate price from the vampire that had killed the two teenagers. The very thought sent a chill down her spine. There were only a few ways to destroy a vampire. None of them were easy, or pleasant.

With a sigh of exasperation, Regan threw the covers aside and got out of bed. Going into the living room, she turned on the Satellite Screen, then went into the kitchen for a cup of hot chocolate. She punched in the code and then hit the marshmallow key three times. A moment later, the computer served up a cup of hot chocolate at exactly the temperature she preferred. Cup in hand, she returned to the living room and curled up on the sofa.

She had no doubt that Santiago had destroyed the killer. She should be glad, but she was so tired of all the killing, all the death. The image of the slain teenagers rose in her mind again. She was glad she wasn't the one who had to notify the parents, that she didn't have to see the looks of horror and disbelief on their faces, and that she didn't have to accompany them to the morgue to identify the bodies. Regan shook her head sadly. No parent should have to bury a child.

It was obvious that Santiago had a soft spot for children. Did he ever lament the fact that he would never be a father, never hold a child of his own in his arms? Never see that child grow and have children of its own?

She pounded her fist on the table. She had to stop thinking about him! He consumed far too many of her thoughts, walked in far too many of her dreams.

Where was he now?

Did he feel remorse for the vampire he had killed? Were vampires even capable of feeling human emotions like remorse or grief?

He felt passion, there was no doubt of that, or of the fact that his very nearness aroused her more than it should have.

She shook her head. She wouldn't go there. No matter how appealing he might be, he was still a vampire. There could be no future for the two of them. No sane woman would even consider such a thing.

"So maybe I'm crazy," she muttered, because in spite of everything she knew about Joaquin Santiago, in spite of what she knew he had done tonight, heaven help her, she wanted to see him again.

Feeling restless, Regan threw on her robe and stepped out onto the balcony of her condo. A bright yellow moon played hide-and-seek with a scattering of wispy gray clouds. She heard the faint wail of a siren, the barking of a dog, a baby's cry. Just the ordinary, everyday sounds of the city.

There was nothing ordinary or mundane about Santiago. What was he doing now? Was he standing on the balcony of his condo, looking at the same moon, hearing the same sounds? Or was he prowling the dark streets in search of sustenance? She lifted a hand to her throat. Did he prefer to prey on women, or was anyone who crossed his path fair game?

Folding her arms on the wooden railing, she stared out at the lights of the city. "Where are you, Joaquin Santiago?"

"Behind you."

Merciful heavens! Regan's heart plummeted to her toes as she whirled around, one hand pressed over her thundering heart. As usual, he was a study in black from head to foot.

"What are you doing here?" she demanded furiously. "You scared the crap out of me!" She jabbed her finger into his chest. In spite of her anger, she noticed his body was rock solid. "Don't you ever sneak up on me like that again!"

He grinned down at her as he captured her hand in his. "I thought you wanted me here."

Regan stared up at him. How was it possible for the slightest touch of his hand to make her insides turn to mush?

"How do you do that?" she demanded, unable to keep the tremor out of her voice.

His thumb made slow, lazy circles on the back of her hand. "Do what?" he asked in that sinfully rich, melodious voice that made her toes curl.

"You know what." She bit down on her lower lip, hating the breathy sound of her own voice. It was aggravating to think that he could probably hear the frantic beat of her heart, sense that his very nearness aroused her.

"I am not doing anything," he said, though the heat in his eyes belied his words. He gazed down at her, slowly drawing her closer, closer, until her body was a breath away from his. He looked down at her, waiting for her to make the decision.

Heart pounding, she pressed herself against him, her head falling back, her eyelids fluttering down in anticipation of his kiss.

It was earth-shattering, even more erotic than the phantom kiss they had shared in her dream. His mouth was warm and firm, his tongue like fire as it stroked her own, arousing her, making her think of hot bodies writhing on cool satin sheets. Black sheets. She knew somehow that his sheets would be black . . .

She opened her eyes and stared up at him. Did he sleep in a bed, or a . . . ?

He looked down at her, his eyes heavy-lidded with desire, his arms still holding her close. "Something troubles you?"

"Where do you sleep?"

"Would you like me to show you?" he asked, his tone suddenly soft and seductive.

"No. I mean . . . do you sleep, that is . . ."

"Ah. You are not wondering where I sleep but what I sleep on, or in."

She nodded, her gaze trapped by his.

"What do you think?" he queried. "And why do you ask?"

"I . . . I . . . never mind, it doesn't matter."

"No?"

"I . . ." She blew out a breath of exasperation. "I just had this mental image of black sheets . . ."

"Not blood red?" he asked with a wry grin, and

then he laughed softly. "You were right. The sheets on my bed are black."

"Satin?" The word was out of her mouth before she could stop it.

"Yes. Perhaps I will show them to you one evening."

"So, you don't sleep in a coffin?"

"I did not say that."

The image of Santiago stretched out inside a satin-lined casket cooled her ardor and she backed away from him. Vampire. He was a vampire. She had to remember that. "Did you find the one who killed those kids?"

He nodded.

"How did he get out of the park?"

"The barrier has no power over the ancient ones."

Regan filed that knowledge away. As soon as she got a chance, she would call the Department of Vampire Control and let them know that not all the vamps in the park were repelled by the barrier.

"Did you destroy him?" she asked.

He didn't answer. He didn't have to. The look in his eyes said it all.

Feeling suddenly cold, Regan wrapped her arms around her body.

"I think I should go now and let you get some sleep," Santiago said. He bowed from the waist in a courtly old-world gesture. "Good night, Regan Delaney."

"Good night," she murmured, but he was already gone.

Chapter 6

In spite of her resolve to put Joaquin Santiago out of her mind once and for all, Regan couldn't stop thinking about him in the days that followed.

When she shopped for food, she found herself remembering that his last meal had been ash cakes and venison stew.

When she changed the blue cotton sheets on her bed, she recalled that his were black satin.

When she drank a cup of hot chocolate, she pictured him sipping a glass of Synthetic A Negative.

When she watched *Dracula 2000*, she imagined Santiago in the Gerard Butler role. It wasn't hard. He already had thick black hair and a long black coat.

When he called and asked her to meet him at Sardino's for a drink, she agreed before her better judgment got the upper hand.

Santiago was waiting at the restaurant when she arrived. Tonight, dressed in a white T-shirt and black jeans, he looked like a teenage rebel from the fifties. All he needed was a pack of cigarettes tucked into his shirt pocket and a pompadour.

A smile curved his lips when he saw her. Taking her hand, he kissed her palm, sending frissons of sensual delight coursing through her. "I did not think you would say yes."

"Neither did I."

Still holding her hand, he led her to a booth in a far corner and slid in beside her, his thigh brushing intimately against her own. "Yet here you are." He caressed her cheek with the back of his hand. "What made you say yes? Were you missing me as much as I was missing you?"

"Were you?" she asked. "Missing me?"

"Every night."

"Then why did you wait so long to call?"

"I was trying to be noble."

"Noble?" she asked, laughing.

He nodded, his expression somber. "Vampires and mortals do not mix well, as you know. And while I think you would be good for me, I know I would be bad for you."

"Would you?" she asked, her voice hardly more than a whisper. "Be bad for me?"

His gaze caressed her. "Very bad."

Regan licked her lips, her whole body tingling with need, burning with desire and the kind of curiosity that the Pandora of legend had been unable to resist. According to myth, Pandora had unleashed all the ills of the world on mankind by opening the forbidden box that had piqued her curiosity.

Santiago slid his arm around Regan's shoulders, drawing her close to his side. Excitement and a thrill of danger unfurled deep in Regan's belly. What perils awaited her if she gave in to her curiosity? Would she live to regret it? Would she live at all if she surrendered to the unholy craving she saw in the smoldering depths of his eyes? *Play with fire and you'll get burned.* It was a cliché, but ever so true. How much more dangerous would it be to play with a vampire?

He pressed a kiss to her cheek, his lips cool and firm. "Come home with me tonight."

Regan swallowed hard. Like Pandora, she could feel herself reaching for that blasted box . . .

"Reggie, what the hell are you doing here?" Michael Flynn's voice hit her like a blast of cold air.

Regan looked up, startled to see Mike staring down at her, his expression grim.

"Mike," she said, her voice little more than a squeak. "What are you doing here?"

"There's been another murder. I was about to call you when I noticed your car parked out front." He glared at Santiago through eyes narrowed with distrust. "I hate to repeat myself," he said, looking at Regan once more, "but what the hell are you doing here? With him?"

Santiago gained his feet. He was taller than Flynn by a good four inches. "She is having a drink with me," Santiago said, his voice as smooth and cold as winter ice. "Is that a problem?"

"Damn right."

"Michael, knock it off. I'm a big girl. I can take care of myself."

"Yeah? I'll bet that's what the woman lying out in the park thought, too, before someone ripped her to pieces."

"Oh, no, not another one," Regan murmured. "How long ago did it happen?"

"The M.E. puts the time of death within the last fifteen minutes," Flynn replied.

Regan nodded, amazed, as always, at the wonders

of modern technology that allowed the medical examiner to determine the time of death to within just a few minutes.

Flynn's gaze moved from Regan to Santiago and back again. "How long have you two been here?"

"I don't know," Regan said. "Half an hour or so, I guess. Why?"

Michael looked pointedly at Santiago. "You're lucky you've got a good alibi, bloodsucker."

Keeping his gaze on Flynn, Santiago gave Regan's shoulders a squeeze, then smiled smugly. "Yes," he said. "Lucky."

"All right, boys, break it up," Regan said irritably. Grabbing her handbag, she slid out of the booth. "I'm sorry, Joaquin, but I need to go and have a look at the body and the crime scene while it's still fresh."

"I will go with you."

Flynn rested his hand on the butt of his revolver. "That won't be necessary," he said brusquely.

Santiago snorted disdainfully. "I live in the park," he remarked. "I am free to go wherever I please."

"Fine," Flynn said brusquely, "just stay the hell away from me. Come on, Reggie, let's get out of here."

Regan hurried out of the restaurant, aware of Santiago's gaze on her back as she followed Flynn out the door.

"Dammit, Regan," Flynn blurted as they walked toward the crime scene, "what the devil are you thinking, hanging around with that bloodsucker?"

Because she couldn't tell him the truth, she told him part of a lie. "I've been talking to him about the murders. After all, who better to catch a vamp than a vamp?"

"Yeah, right. He'd as soon kill you as look at you."

Regan felt a little thrill of excitement as she recalled the way Santiago had looked at her earlier. It wasn't death he had on his mind, unless it was what the French called *la petite mort*, the little death, in reference to making love.

The sight of the body sprawled beneath a flowering bush drove every other thought from Regan's mind. Though she had seen many similar deaths lately, it didn't make this one any easier to bear. Once again, she was glad she didn't have to notify the family, didn't have to see the faces of the victim's husband and children when they learned that their wife and mother wouldn't be coming home that night, or any night.

Frowning, Regan wondered what the woman had been doing in the park after sunset. She would never know now.

Regan looked up at Michael. "Did the M.E. say she'd been killed here?"

"As a matter of fact, he suggested she might have been killed somewhere else and her body dumped here."

Regan moved closer. Spotlights lit the area, making it almost as bright as day. The woman's body had been shoved under the bushes, apparently in an effort to hide it. As far as Regan could see, there was no blood on the ground, and none left in the body. There were gaping holes where her heart, liver, and throat had been torn out, but no blood.

"I think someone else is killing these people and trying to make it look like the work of vampires," Regan said.

Flynn snorted. "Why would anyone do that?"

Regan gestured at the woman's body. "Why would anyone do this?"

They stood back as the body was bagged and carted away.

"I need to go and check out the rest of the park," Flynn said. "Come on, I'll walk you to your car."

"Thanks."

"Be careful, Regan," he said as she slid behind the wheel. "Keep your doors and windows locked."

"Don't worry about me, Mike, I can take care of myself."

He closed her car door, then leaned down to look in the window. "I can't help worrying."

"I know. Good night, Mike. Be careful."

He waved as she pulled away from the curb.

Regan's mind wasn't on Mike or on the road as she drove home. Instead of traffic noise, she kept hearing Joaquin Santiago's voice, whiskey smooth and maddeningly sexy. Instead of streetlights, she saw his eyes, deep and dark and mysterious as they gazed into her own. How many centuries had he lived? How many secrets lay hidden beneath the midnight blue depths of his eyes? How many innocent lives had he snuffed out so that he could prolong his own unnatural one?

What if he was the killer?

That chilling thought brought reality rushing back to the fore. No matter how handsome he was, no matter how charming he appeared to be, no matter how blatantly sexy he was with his bedroom eyes and his roguish smile, he was a vampire and strictly off-limits.

Clearheaded now, Regan made a left onto her street, and noticed that the car behind her also made a left. Now that she thought about it, she realized that the same sleek silver-gray Mercedes had been following her ever since she left the park.

Overcome by a sudden sense of foreboding, she drove past her apartment and made a right at the next stop sign. The car behind her did likewise.

With growing apprehension, Regan continued on down the street and when the car continued to follow her, she drove to the police station and pulled into the parking lot. The Mercedes drove on past without slowing down.

Regan blew out a sigh of relief. She was getting paranoid, she thought with a shaky laugh. There was no reason for anyone to be following her. None at all.

Chiding herself for acting so foolishly, she drove home, checking the rearview mirror all the way. There was no sign of the silver-gray Mercedes. Pulling up in front of her apartment building, she switched off the ignition, then sat in the car, the hair along her nape quivering. Ordinarily, she parked in the underground garage, but not tonight. She told herself she was behaving irrationally but she couldn't help it. No way in hell was she parking in that garage tonight.

She was about to open the car door when she saw the silver-gray Mercedes turn the corner.

With a wordless cry, Regan started the engine. Tires screeching, she pulled away from the curb, her heart pounding a rapid tattoo in her chest, her palms damp on the steering wheel as panic gripped her. She couldn't see who was driving the silver Mercedes, didn't want to see who it was because she was afraid, so afraid she could taste it in the back of her throat. She told herself there was nothing to be afraid of. She had destroyed vampires before, she could do so again. She had a pistol loaded with six silver bullets that would stop a vampire cold. That knowledge did nothing to allay her fears.

She drove straight to You Bet Your Life Park, certain that the only one who could help her, the only one who could save her from the unknown terror that stalked her, was the vampire Santiago.

Chapter 7

Santiago stood on the balcony of his apartment, enjoying the moonlight while savoring the sounds and smells of the night—the faint hum of a small white moth doing a dance of death with a streetlight, the rich earthy scent of dew-damp grass and flowering trees. Being a vampire had given him a keen appreciation for the beauty and mystery of the night. It was a different world after dark, one feared by mortals because their vision was limited, or perhaps because they were the predators by day, but at the setting of the sun, they were prey, like everything else.

So many things had changed since he was made, and yet much remained the same, like the age-old struggle between life and death, good and evil. Mankind had made great strides in some areas—the oceans and the air were clean again, cures had been found for most of the diseases that had plagued the world of men, cloning had never become as popular as scientists had predicted it would, nuclear weapons were no longer a threat. There were settlements on other planets now. Solar power had, for the most part, replaced electricity. And yet, in spite of all that, there were still wars and rumors of wars. Doing away with poverty had not done away with the urge to steal. Prejudice still reared its ugly head from time to time.

Santiago lifted his face to the sky. How many nights had he stood thus? After the first few hundred years, he had stopped counting. Mortal time no longer held any meaning for him. Indeed, there was little in his existence, other than the need for blood and a lingering need for vengeance, that held any appeal for him at all.

But now Vasile was here and all that had changed.

Santiago felt his fangs brush his tongue as an old and familiar hatred rose within him. But for Vasile, Marishka would be at his side, as she was meant to be. The Gypsy girl had been his first love, his only love, in all his long years of existence.

He closed his eyes and let her image rise to the surface—tall and slender, with deep brown eyes and ebony hair that fell in thick waves past her hips. Marishka had been his first and only fledgling. She had been but seventeen when, on a foolish whim, he had brought her across. He had immediately had second thoughts about what he had done. He had, however briefly, considered destroying her before she rose the next night, but there had been something about her, some intangible quality, that had stayed his hand, and then it was too late. The bond between them had grown stronger with each night they had spent together. He had loved her as he had loved no other, had planned to show her the world and all the wonders it contained. It had been a wonderful dream, one that had lasted less than a year. A dream that had died a violent and bloody death one bleak wintry afternoon . . .

The sound of screeching tires and the smell of fear on the wind chased the distant past from Santiago's mind and brought him back to the present.

He recognized the car and the woman's scent immediately. A heartbeat later, Vasile's stink was borne to him on the wings of an errant breeze.

A thought took Santiago to the edge of the park and the curb beyond.

He was waiting for her when the driver's side door flew open and Regan spilled out in a rush.

"Slow down, girl," Santiago admonished, capturing her in his embrace. "I have you."

She glanced over her shoulder. "Someone's following me! I'm sure of it."

"You are safe now." He tried to ignore the rapid beat of her heart, the scent of her blood, but it was impossible. Still, this was not the time to ponder what it would be like to drink of her sweetness, to carry her to his lair and possess her, fully and completely.

Using one hand, Santiago thrust Regan behind him, his gaze focused on the silver-gray Mercedes that was cruising slowly past the park. Due to the dark tint on the windows, Santiago knew Regan couldn't see the man behind the wheel, but Santiago saw the driver clearly enough. It was Vasile, just as he had known it would be.

Santiago's grip tightened on Regan's forearm, but his gaze never left Vasile's.

You will not have this one, Santiago vowed, and knew in that moment that Regan Delaney had come to mean far more to him than he had ever intended. But then, so had Marishka. Knowing her, loving her, he had planned to spend the rest of his existence with her. Until Vasile found their lair . . .

"Santiago, you're hurting me."

Regan's voice chased all thought of Marishka from his mind. He murmured an apology as he released her.

"Was that him?" Regan glanced at her arm. His grip had left a red imprint on her skin. There would be a bruise there tomorrow. "Was that the werewolf?"

He nodded curtly. "Vasile, yes."

"Why is he following me?"

Santiago's gaze rested on her face. "Believe me, you do not want to know."

She started to argue with him until she saw the taut line of his jaw, the feral expression in his eyes. Maybe he was right. Maybe she didn't want to know.

"I think you would be wise to spend the night here, with me," Santiago remarked.

Before she could protest, he was taking hold of her arm again, leading her across the sidewalk and into the park's silent shadows.

The hair prickled along Regan's nape as they entered the grounds. A number of men and women, most of them dressed in black from head to foot, strolled through the park or sat on the benches scattered along the walkways. It was like a scene from some bizarre dream, seeing the vampires moving through the park in the middle of the night. She reminded herself that no matter how odd it seemed to her, the night was their day. Sometimes, on summer evenings, mortals paused on the sidewalk, their eyes wide with curiosity or narrowed in morbid fascination as they watched the vampires.

Santiago's apartment was on the top floor of a

five-story building. He opened the door with a wave of his hand and then stood aside so she could precede him.

She jumped when she heard the door close behind her. She was alone in a vampire's apartment, and no one knew she was there.

She turned to face Santiago, her heart pounding so hard and so fast she was surprised it didn't burst out of her chest.

"Afraid of me?" His voice was deep and rich and faintly mocking.

Hands clenched at her sides, she lifted her chin. "Yes."

His easy laughter filled the room. "Please." He gestured at a high-backed brown sofa. "Consider my home yours."

She sat down because she wasn't sure her legs would support her much longer. What was she doing here? What made her think being in here, with a vampire, particularly this vampire, was any safer than being outside, with a werewolf? They were both predators. And in the dark of the night, she was prey—for both of them.

Santiago loomed over her, tall, dark, and deadly. The words moved through the back of Regan's mind like a death knell. His mere presence made her feel small, insignificant, and defenseless. She knew all about vampires. She had studied them for years. She knew they grew stronger with age and that most of the things people believed about them were based on myth, legend, and the Transylvanian count made famous by Bram Stoker, and had little basis in fact.

Some things were true. They could change shape. They could travel faster than the human eye could follow. They drank blood to survive. Fire, sunlight, and beheading could destroy them. Silver and holy water burned their skin like acid.

She had yet to meet a vampire who was repelled by a cross, or one who cast no reflection. To the contrary, they seemed to love mirrors and never missed an opportunity to stop and admire themselves.

Of course, she hadn't met all that many of the Undead on a social basis, and certainly none quite like the one who was towering over her.

"It is late," he said. "You should get some sleep."

"Not here." She glanced around the room, wondering where his coffin was. She couldn't stay here, couldn't *sleep* here. No way!

"You will be perfectly safe, Regan Delaney," he said quietly. "Much safer than you would be at home."

"Now why don't I believe that?"

"You have nothing to fear from me. I have already dined. The bedroom is in there."

"Isn't that where you sleep?"

"No." Removing his coat, he tossed it over the back of a chair. "I would not leave here in the morning if I were you."

She frowned. "Why not?"

"He is a werewolf."

She stared at him a moment, then murmured, "Oh, right," as comprehension dawned. Vasile was a werewolf. Unlike vampires, he had nothing to fear from the sun's light. "What's to keep him from coming here?"

"My apartment has infinitely better protection than the flimsy barrier that surrounds the park," he replied smoothly. "And I am here."

Some help he would be, she thought, while trapped in the deathlike sleep of his kind. "Why is Vasile after you?"

"Because I have sworn to kill him."

"You have? Why?"

"Maybe one day I will tell you."

"But not now?"

"No."

She was too tired and too upset by the evening's events to argue. In any case, she didn't think arguing with Santiago would do her a bit of good. With a nod, she murmured, "Good night, then."

Going into the bedroom, she switched on the light, then closed the door. The first thing she noticed was the bed. It was an old-fashioned four-poster covered with a thick black quilt. Several plump red velvet pillows were scattered near the mahogany headboard. Since she was reasonably sure he didn't sleep in the bed, she wondered what he used it for . . . then quickly put an end to that train of thought before it reached its logical conclusion. The man was a vampire, but still a man, and the bed and its trappings clearly had seduction written all over them.

She didn't like the idea of sleeping in her clothes, but she liked the idea of undressing in a vampire's residence even less. Sitting on the edge of the bed, she kicked off her shoes, tossed the fancy red pillows on the floor, and crawled between the sheets. Cool, black satin sheets, she noted with a faint grin. Just as he had said.

Reaching into her handbag, she withdrew her gun and slipped it under her pillow. Always better to be safe than sorry.

With a sigh, she turned onto her side and closed her eyes, only to bolt upright a moment later. If he didn't sleep here, where did he sleep?

She glanced around the room, but there was no

sign of a coffin, no pile of dirt from the place of his birth. Maybe he had lied to her. Maybe this really *was* his bed! Maybe he was only waiting for her to fall asleep before he crawled in beside her.

That troublesome thought kept her awake for hours.

Santiago paced the floor in front of the hearth, keenly aware of the woman in his bedroom. In his bed.

Damn. After Marishka, he had sworn he would never again let a woman get close to him, never allow one to become important to him. He had seduced them and bedded them, but never, ever, let himself care for them. But this one, this Regan Delaney, had somehow managed to find her way past his defenses. And while his fondness for her might cause him a few restless nights, it could very well cost her a great deal more.

He swore softly. Loving him had cost Marishka her life, and while he had vowed that he would protect Regan Delaney from Vasile, he wasn't all that sure that he would prevail. Vasile was not trapped inside when the sun rode the sky. It was Vasile's very freedom of movement during the daylight hours that had given the werewolf the power to destroy Marishka while she took her rest. Had Santiago been new in the life, he had no doubt that he, too, would have died that day so long ago. But he had been an old vampire, even then. His age and his instinct for self-preservation had served him well that day.

He paused in midstride, listening as Regan kicked off her shoes, drew back the covers on his bed, and slid beneath the sheets. With his preternatural senses, he could hear each breath she took, each beat of her heart, hear the whisper of blood flowing through her veins . . .

His fangs teased his tongue. She was here, in his house, in his bed. His for the taking.

He resumed pacing, his hands clenched at his sides as he fought the urge to sweep her into his arms and succumb to the hunger burning through him. Every breath he took carried the scent of her hair, her skin, her life's blood. She would be sweet, so sweet. He could almost feel her in his arms, taste her on his tongue.

One taste. She need never know. She would never miss it.

A thought carried him to the bedroom door. He looked down to find his hand on the knob, unable to remember how he had gotten there.

Swearing a vile oath, he stormed out of his apartment, down the stairs, and across the park. He came to an abrupt halt when his foot touched the sidewalk. What was he doing? He couldn't go haring off into the night, couldn't leave Regan alone, unprotected, while Vasile was in the city.

Santiago's gaze swept right and left. The werewolf could be here now, waiting, watching.

Blowing out a deep breath, Santiago returned to his apartment. Entering his bedroom, he made sure the woman was sleeping peacefully. With a sigh, he settled down in the chair beside the closet, his every sense attuned to the mortal female in his bed. He was aware of every breath she took, every beat of her heart, the faint, flowery scent of her hair, her skin.

His hunger rose, and with it a growing desire to crawl into bed beside her, to take what he wanted, by force if necessary.

When his fangs pricked his tongue, he fled the room, afraid he would succumb to the sweet temptation she presented.

In the living room, he flung himself onto the sofa and closed his eyes.

It was going to be a long night.

Regan woke slowly, surprised to find that it was still dark outside. She stretched her arms over her head and out to the side, then paused with the sudden certainty that she wasn't alone in the room.

Heart pounding, she glanced slowly to the left. There was nothing there. Hardly daring to breathe, she slid a glance to the right, felt her blood freeze in her veins when she saw a pair of hell-red eyes staring at her from out of the darkness.

It was him. She knew it. The creature who had killed the people in the park.

The werewolf. And he had come for her.

She opened her mouth to scream but no sound emerged from her throat.

The eyes grew larger—and closer.

She had often watched movies where women in peril seemed unable to move. She had always thought of them as being weak-willed and too stupid to live as she mentally screamed at them to get up and run, for goodness' sake! She knew now why they didn't. She couldn't move, could scarcely breathe past the tight knot of fear growing ever larger and colder within her.

She was going to die. Quick visions of the mutilated bodies she had seen in the park rose in her mind, filling her with renewed horror. Where was Santiago when she needed him?

No sooner had the thought crossed her mind than the bedroom door flew open and the vampire was there, fangs gleaming in the moonlight, his eyes glowing as hellishly red as the werewolf's.

They came together in a rush, two preternatural creatures viciously lashing out at each other with gleaming fangs and razor-sharp claws.

She screamed as the werewolf's claws gouged a great hole in Santiago's chest and then, with a mighty roar, the werewolf ripped the vampire's heart from his chest . . .

She screamed and screamed again as strong hands folded over her shoulders, shaking her lightly.

"Regan! Regan, wake up!"

Her eyelids flew open and she saw Santiago bending over her.

A dream. Relief whooshed out of her in a sigh. It had only been a dream.

But then she looked into Santiago's eyes, eyes that glowed with an inhuman light, and wished that she was back in her nightmare. As frightening as it had been, she had been safe in her dream.

No such safety existed here.

Santiago took one look at her face and slowly backed away from Regan. Her fear was a palpable thing.

Crossing his arms over his chest, he said, "That must have been some nightmare."

"You have no idea," she replied, her voice shaky.

"Why are you sleeping on the floor?"

"I . . . because I . . ."

"Go on," he coaxed, his tone one of barely suppressed amusement.

She felt her cheeks grow warm under his knowing grin.

"Were you, by chance, afraid to sleep in my bed?"

"Of course not," she lied. "I . . . I must have fallen out during the night." That was a lie, too. Knowing she was in his bed had kept her tossing and turning until, at last, she had dragged the covers and one of the pillows onto the floor.

Clutching the sheet in one hand, she glanced around the room, still shaken by the last vestiges of her dream. It had seemed so real.

"Your nightmare," he said quietly. "Do you wish to talk about it?"

She shook her head vigorously. That was the last thing she wanted.

"You are safe here." One look at her expression told him she knew it for the lie it was. He was a vampire. She was prey. She would never truly be safe in his presence. "Go back to sleep, girl," he said, his voice gruff. "I will keep you safe until tomorrow."

"And then?"

Before she could protest, he picked her up, blankets and all, settled her on the bed, and tucked her in. "I give you my word that you will be safe so long as you stay here."

She nodded, the covers pulled up to her chin. "Would you . . . would you leave the light on, please?"

She didn't know what was wrong with her. She had never been afraid of the dark, never behaved like one of those gutless females she despised. She was a vampire hunter, for crying out loud, not some nervous Nellie. She had hunted vampires and even killed a few. But she had never been in a situation like this before, never had a vampire look at her the way the master of the city looked at her. Never felt such a primal attraction to any male before, man or vampire.

At her request, he switched on the light. It had been so long since he had needed any kind of illumination to see by, he sometimes forgot that mortals took comfort in it.

Leaving the room, he closed the door behind him. If only it was as easy to shut out his awareness of her. As prey. As a woman . . .

Going to the condo's only window, Santiago drew back the heavy blackout drapes and gazed out into the night. Only a few stars remained visible in the sky. It would be dawn soon. He could protect her as long as she stayed here, but if she left his apartment . . . a muscle worked in his jaw. He could keep her here by force, if need be, though he hoped it wouldn't come to that.

He thought back to the last time he and Vasile had met. Both had come away badly hurt. Both had drawn blood. Both had tasted the blood of the other, and in some way that Santiago didn't understand, it had changed them. Werewolves were influenced by the full moon. It was then that they changed shape, never during the day. But Santiago's blood had, in some freakish way, made it possible for Vasile to shift in the daytime, while Vasile's blood had given Santiago a certain immunity from the deadly effects of the sun, giving him the power to be active during the day if he desired, though he could not walk outside in the sun's light.

And now Vasile knew where he made his home, and that Regan was here.

Chapter 8

Regan woke to darkness. Frowning, she glanced around the room, wondering what time it was. She didn't usually wake up in the middle of the night, but the room was dark beyond the faint glow of the lamp on the bedside table. Closing her eyes, she tried to go back to sleep, but it was no use. She was wide awake. Maybe a glass of warm milk would help her relax.

Slipping out of bed, she went into the kitchen. She ran her hands along the wall, searching for the light switch. It wasn't until she opened the refrigerator and saw several plump plastic bags filled with red liquid that she remembered where she was.

Grimacing, she quickly closed the refrigerator door, thinking how bizarre it was that the condos at the Vampire Arms had functional kitchens, complete with ovens and dishwashers. But then, some of the vampires had human lovers, so maybe it wasn't so odd after all.

After turning off the light, she made her way into the dark living room.

A muffled "oomph!" escaped her lips when she

bumped into something. She let out a shriek when a hand reached out to steady her.

"Do not be afraid." Santiago's voice poured over her like hot chocolate.

Murmuring a quick, "I'm sorry," she backed away from him and cried out as she hit the back of her leg on a corner of the coffee table.

Once again, his hand was there to steady her. "Stay here."

A moment later, the lights came on and she found herself looking up at Santiago. "I couldn't sleep," she explained, unsettled by his steady gaze. "I was going to get some hot milk, you know, to help me sleep even though I'm not really tired, but . . ." A rush of heat burned her cheeks. She was babbling like a fool.

"It is late morning, Regan."

"How can that be?" She stared at him, her eyes wide. "You're . . . you're awake."

He shrugged. "So are you."

"You know what I mean. Why aren't you asleep in your . . . why aren't you asleep?"

He grinned, obviously amused by her reluctance to mention the traditional place where vampires took their rest. "I am not yet tired."

She glared at him. Stubborn man. He knew very well what she was asking. And she didn't believe for a minute that it was morning. Everyone knew that vampires were, you should pardon the expression, dead to the world until the sun went down.

Moving past him, she went to the heavy black drapes that covered the room's only window and pulled one back, just a little, in case he was telling the truth. After all, she didn't want him to burst into flame right in front of her eyes.

She squinted against the bright light of the sun, then glanced at Santiago over her shoulder. "How can you be awake?"

He backed further into the room's shadows. "Maybe someday I will tell you."

"Another secret?" she asked dryly.

He nodded.

"I guess you have a lot of them."

"More than you can imagine." He jerked his chin toward the window. "Do you mind?"

"What? Oh, sorry." She dropped the heavy drapery back into place, shutting out the morning light, her curiosity growing by leaps and bounds. She had thought she knew all there was to know about vampires. Apparently, she had been wrong.

"I regret I cannot offer you breakfast," he said with a wry grin. "Would you like me to order you something from Sardino's?"

"Spaghetti and meatballs for breakfast?" she muttered dubiously. "I don't think so." Although it was far more preferable than what he dined on.

His laugh was warm and rich as he picked up the phone, punched in the number for the restaurant, and handed her the phone. "Order whatever you wish. Tell Sardino to charge it to my account."

She didn't like the idea of eating in front of Santiago again and was thinking about telling him that she really wasn't hungry when her stomach growled, embarrassingly long and loud. With a sigh, she turned her back to him and ordered a waffle, bacon, coffee, and orange juice.

"Would you care to shower while you wait?" he asked. "There are clean towels in the bathroom."

A shower sounded heavenly. In Flynn's apartment, she wouldn't have hesitated, but Flynn didn't

affect her the way Santiago did. And Flynn wasn't
a vampire.

Santiago was watching her. Though his expression was impassive, she had a feeling he knew exactly what she was thinking.

Lifting her chin a notch, she said, "Thank you, a shower sounds wonderful."

Before she could change her mind, she pivoted on her heel and headed for the bathroom. She closed and locked the door, knowing, as she did so, that nothing as flimsy as a wooden door or a lock would keep him out. She told herself she was just being paranoid. Santiago had no designs on her; he had been nothing but kind to her.

But he was still a vampire.

And she was still afraid of him.

She turned on the shower, undressed quickly, and stepped under the spray. As wonderful as the water felt, being undressed in Joaquin Santiago's shower made her decidedly ill at ease. It was, she thought as she dried off, probably the fastest shower on record.

She pulled on her clothes and towel-dried her hair. She wished fleetingly that she had her hair dryer and her makeup, then chided herself for worrying about how she looked. He was a vampire, for goodness' sake, not a prospective boyfriend!

Taking a deep breath, she unlocked the bathroom door and went into the living room. She hadn't paid much attention to her surroundings earlier. Looking around now, she understood why. There was little to see. The walls were white and bare, the carpet a nondescript shade of beige. A brown sofa and matching chair were grouped in front of the fireplace. Somehow, none of the furnishings in this room, as sparse as they were, seemed to suit its occupant.

"You are just in time," Santiago said. "The delivery boy left your breakfast outside."

With a nod, Regan retrieved the tray and carried it into the kitchen. The walls were white and devoid of any decoration. The appliances were white and, as far as she could tell, had never been used. The space was so sterile, it reminded her of a hospital operating room.

Santiago followed her to the kitchen, then stopped in the doorway, one shoulder negligently propped against the jamb.

Sitting at the small, round, glass-and-metal table, Regan lifted the cover from the tray, pleased to see that Sardino had included utensils and a napkin. The waffle looked light enough to float away; the three strips of bacon were cooked just the way she liked them.

She looked up at Santiago. "Why do I have the feeling I'm the first person that's ever eaten in here?"

"Perhaps because you are," he replied with a faint grin. "Maybe I should stock the shelves."

Regan looked at him sharply. "I don't think that will be necessary."

He shrugged. "You know what they say, it pays to be prepared."

"Well, don't bother. I doubt if I'll be spending much time here."

"Maybe I could change your mind."

"Why would you want to?"

"I find myself enjoying your company."

She was flattered in spite of herself. Truth be told, she enjoyed his company, too, but there was no future in it. Even if she could get past the fact that he was a vampire, she wasn't sure if they were even the same species anymore.

With a shake of her head, Regan concentrated on the food on her plate, acutely aware of Joaquin Santiago's watchful gaze. She searched her mind for something to break the silence and said the first thing that popped into her head.

"Do you ever miss real food?"

His gaze slid over her throat. "Not for years."

"What do you miss?"

"What makes you think I miss anything?"

"Don't you?"

He thought about it a moment, then shrugged. "The advantages of being a vampire far outweigh what I lost."

"Advantages?" she scoffed. "Like not being able to go outside during the day? Like drinking blood? Like being unable to have children and being forced to live in this . . ." She made a gesture that encompassed his apartment. "This prison?"

"I call being alive a distinct advantage," he retorted. "If not for the Dark Trick, I would have been dead centuries ago."

"But you aren't alive. Not really."

"No?"

He moved toward her, his eyes so dark they looked almost black as his hands folded over her shoulders and lifted her to her feet. The fork in her hand fell to the table and skittered onto the floor.

"Not alive?" he asked, his voice soft and silky as he drew her into his arms. "Could a dead man kiss you like this?"

Kiss? The word jump-started her heart. He was going to kiss her. Before the thought had time to register in her mind, his mouth was swooping down on hers, capturing her lips in a searing kiss that sent frissons of heat exploding through every inch of her body before settling in the pit of her stomach. His lips were surprisingly warm, his tongue like a flame sliding over her lips, imprinting his taste on her skin like a brand.

It was the most incredible, unforgettable, mind-blowing kiss she had ever known. It heated her blood, made her skin tingle and her toes curl, until she was aware of nothing but the man holding her in his embrace, his mouth moving over hers, by turns teasing and seductive. But for his arms holding her upright, she was certain she would have melted into a pool of liquid desire at his feet.

She stared up at him, bereft and confused, when he broke the kiss.

His gaze bored into hers, hot and heavy. "Has any mortal man ever kissed you like that, Regan Delaney?"

Dazed, she shook her head.

He smiled at her, a look of pure masculine satisfaction. "I did not think so," he said arrogantly.

She couldn't think of anything to say, couldn't think at all. Her lips felt swollen and on fire, her legs felt like Jell-O, her mind like Swiss cheese. She would have done anything he asked, she thought, if only he would kiss her like that again. It was disconcerting to discover that one kiss could leave her feeling so muddled. No doubt making love to him would leave her in a disoriented state for days, maybe weeks.

Lifting one hand, he cupped her cheek. His touch sent shivers of awareness and anticipation skittering down her spine. Right or wrong, she wanted his kisses more than her next breath.

His widening smile told her he knew exactly what effect his nearness and his caresses had on her senses.

It was annoying that he read her so easily, she thought irritably, and then grinned. He was holding her close, close enough that she could feel the effect she had on him, as well. It was nice to know it wasn't all one-sided!

"I need to go home." She had to get out of here. She couldn't think clearly in his presence, couldn't think of anything but black satin sheets and his mouth on hers, hot and wet. She stepped out of his embrace. She needed a change of clothes, needed to check her messages, sleep in her own bed, and breathe air that didn't carry his hot, masculine scent to her with every breath.

"I do not think that is wise."

"I don't care what you think. I can't stay here indefinitely."

"Wait until dusk, and I will take you."

"I don't think there's any danger during the day. The killings have all been at night." She frowned. "I thought werewolves only shifted at night when the moon was full."

"Most do."

"But not Vasile?"

"No."

"Do you mean that he can shift anytime he wants?" Santiago nodded.

"And you don't have to sleep during the day." She frowned. "Why do I feel there's a connection there?"

"Perhaps because there is."

Regan sat down, all thought of going home forgotten. "I'm listening."

Santiago considered whether he should tell her

the truth, then shrugged, thinking it might be wise to let her know what they were up against.

Taking hold of the chair across from hers, he straddled it, then folded his arms across the back. "Vasile killed someone I cared for," he began slowly. "I hunted him down and we fought. During the battle, I bit him. He shifted and he bit me. The taste of his blood was like acid on my tongue. It left me feeling weak, sick. I can only guess that my blood had the same effect on him because he ran away. I am guessing that ingesting my blood drained him of strength, at least for a time. I found a new lair and . . ." He grinned wryly. "If you will pardon the pun, I slept like the dead for several days." He did not tell her of Marishka or of the nights he had spent holding her lifeless body in his arms. "When I woke, it was morning and I discovered I was no longer held captive by the Dark Sleep."

"So you can go out during the day?"

"No, but the rising of the sun no longer renders me powerless."

"Did your blood affect Vasile?"

Santiago nodded again. "I believe it is my blood that allows him to shift during the day. I have hunted him for centuries. And now he is here."

"And you think he's looking for you?"

"Why else would he have come here?"

"I don't know. Maybe he's not looking for you at all. Maybe his being here is just a coincidence. It's a small world, after all."

"Perhaps, but it does not matter. He is killing in my territory and it has to stop."

"What does any of this have to do with me?"

Santiago leaned back in his chair, wondering what she would say, what she would do, if he told her the truth.

Chapter 9

In spite of Santiago's suggestion that she wait until dusk, Regan put on her shoes, dropped her gun into her handbag, and after thanking him for letting her spend the night, she headed for home, one eye on the rearview mirror the whole way. Thankfully, there was no sign of a silver-gray Mercedes.

She breathed an audible sigh of relief when she was safe inside her own apartment. After the glaring white and sparse furnishings of Santiago's condo, her home seemed even more colorful and cluttered than usual, but that was the way she liked it, thank you very much. She liked the living room's dark green walls, the off-white sofa, the flowered red and orange sling-back chair. Modern art decorated the walls; a tall hand-blown vase held a bouquet of dried red, orange, and gold flowers. The kitchen was painted a cheerful yellow, her bedroom was a bold lilac. She knew her décor was out of fashion. The trend today was earth tones or high-contrast colors, like black and white, but she didn't care. She had never been one to follow trends in either furniture or fashion.

She went into the bedroom and changed her

clothes, combed her hair and brushed her teeth, and felt a hundred percent better.

Going into the kitchen, she checked her messages. There was one from her mother, another from her older brother, Kevin, and two from Flynn, one "just to say hello" and one inviting her out to dinner that night.

After calling Flynn to accept his offer, she threw a load of clothes in the washer, then went into her bedroom and turned on her computer. She spent two hours reading about werewolf mythology before weariness overcame her. Kicking off her shoes, she stretched out on the bed and was instantly asleep.

Santiago paced the living-room floor, a distant part of his mind wishing he was in his lair in the Byways. He rarely stayed at the condo in the park. Perhaps it was time to redecorate the place so that it would be more to his liking. The white walls made him feel like he was living in a padded cell. A few paintings would relieve the monotony. He glanced disdainfully at the brown furniture, left over from the previous tenant. Perhaps it was time to get rid of that, as well.

Pausing in front of the door, he swore softly. He didn't give a damn about the condo's furnishings. The whole place could burn down, for all he cared. The only reason redecorating the place had even occurred to him was because Regan didn't like it as it was. Ah, Regan, he couldn't help worrying about her. It had been years since his inability to walk in the sun had bothered him, but Regan's life hadn't been in danger before. She was home now, alone and vulnerable— and Vasile was somewhere in the city.

Santiago resumed his useless pacing. Regan had insisted she would be safe enough, that Vasile only killed after dark, but Santiago knew better. Marishka had been killed while the sun was high in the sky. He closed his eyes and his mind filled with horrific images . . .

He had awakened to the sound of Marishka's terrified cry. Fighting the Dark Sleep, Santiago had lifted up on his elbows and looked toward her resting place. Vasile loomed over her casket, his lips drawn back in a feral snarl as he drove a wooden stake into her heart and gave it a cruel twist.

Horror, anger, grief, and disbelief had spiraled through Santiago. With a murderous roar, he had leapt from his resting place and flown toward Marishka's attacker. Santiago would have torn Vasile limb from limb had he been able, but Vasile had escaped into the sun's light. Santiago had yearned to give chase but he dared not leave the protection of his lair while the sun was high in the sky. After closing the door to the crypt, he had gathered Marishka into his arms. He had withdrawn the stake from her limp body and tried to revive her. He had gashed his arm and forced his blood past her lips, but it was too late. Everlastingly too late. Perhaps she would have responded had she been older in the life, or had he been able to get to her sooner.

At dusk, he had found a new lair. Clutching Marishka close, he had surrendered to the Dark Sleep, all the while wishing that he had let Vasile destroy him, as well. He woke several nights later, his physical wounds healed, though his pain at Marishka's death burned as bright and clear as the night she had been destroyed. Lost in his grief, he had remained in his lair, Marishka's body cradled in his arms. He had lost count of how many nights he had held her wasted, mutilated body and wished for oblivion.

Reluctant to put her outside and let the sun destroy her remains, he had kept her with him until the stench of her decomposing body became unbearable. When he could put it off no longer, he had carried her out into the woods, covered her body with flowers, and left her where the dawn's light would find her.

It had taken Santiago over a year to find Vasile. No words were needed between them. They had fought a long and bloody battle and in the midst of it, Vasile had shifted. Santiago's fangs had pierced the werewolf's neck. The werewolf had savaged Santiago's throat. The resulting wounds had left both of them too sick and weak to continue the fight.

It wasn't until months later, when his grief at Marishka's death had begun to pale, that he realized the full implication of the change Vasile's bite had wrought: he was no longer rendered powerless by the rising of the sun.

Thinking perhaps the sun's light no longer had any effect on him, he had decided to put it to the test. That was a mistake he never made again. It had taken almost a year for the burns caused by the sun's light to heal.

And now, after all this time, Marishka's killer was here, in the city. His presence begged the question: Was Vasile here by design or coincidence? Santiago had counted Vasile as his enemy for centuries, always plagued by the mystery of why Vasile had killed Marishka. Had it been a random act? If Santiago hadn't awakened when Vasile attacked Marishka, he would likely have been the werewolf's next victim. But the question remained. Why had

Vasile attacked Marishka? It was a question that had haunted him from the day of her death, and remained a mystery to this day. He had searched the world over for Vasile, his need for answers and his lust for vengeance driving him onward until, after more than three centuries, he had decided the werewolf was dead. Convinced that revenge would forever be beyond him, he had returned here, to the country where he had been born, and forged a new existence.

And now Vasile was here. Santiago smiled, his fangs lengthening in anticipation. Sooner or later, they would meet again and he would have his revenge at last.

Regan woke from a troubled sleep. Her dreams had been peppered with fangs and claws and hideously deformed bodies—and awash in blood. It had poured from wounds and water faucets and dripped from the sky like crimson rain.

With a grimace, she went into the bathroom and rinsed her face with cold water, then went into the kitchen for a soda. She popped the top of the can and took a long drink. If meeting a vampire was going to subject her to such vivid, horrifying dreams, then she wished she had never met Joaquin Santiago!

But there was no time to think about the master of the city now. She had a date with Flynn and he was going to be here in less than an hour.

She took a quick shower, then spent ten minutes fussing with her hair, only to shake it out and let it fall around her shoulders. She dressed in a pair of jeans and a comfy sweater, pulled on a pair of low-heeled boots, brushed her teeth and applied a touch of lipstick, and she was ready to go.

Flynn knocked at the door a few minutes later.

She smiled up at him. "Right on time."

"You know me," he said with a wink. "I never keep a beautiful lady waiting. You ready to go?"

With a nod, she grabbed her handbag, dropped her gun into her jacket pocket, and left the apartment, making sure to lock the door behind her.

"So," Flynn said, handing her into the car, "where would you like to go for dinner?"

Food was the furthest thing from her mind, but some perverse demon made her suggest Sardino's.

Flynn gave her a funny look as he pulled away from the curb. "Are you hoping to run into that bloodsucker you were having a drink with the other night?"

"Of course not, they just have really good food. We can go somewhere else, if you like."

"No, Sardino's is fine."

"Any news on the killings in the park?" she asked.

"Hey, I'm off duty," Flynn admonished lightly. "No shop talk tonight." He looked over at her and smiled. "Did I tell you how pretty you look?"

"No."

He winked at her again. "That's my favorite sweater."

"That's why I wore it," she replied, though she realized that was only a half-truth. It was her favorite sweater, too, but she had worn it with Santiago in mind. Chiding herself for even thinking of the vampire, she turned on the radio, and there was Hunter Double D singing about the danger of falling in love with a fanged female.

*"The lovin's good, mister, don't get me wrong, she can
woo you and love you all the night long, but by and
by, just between you and me, her beast will break out
and her fangs you will see . . ."*

Muttering, "sheesh," she switched off the radio.

"What's the matter?" Flynn asked with a grin,
"don't you like Double D?"

"The music stinks and the lyrics are ridiculous."

Flynn laughed out loud. "I can't argue with that."
He pulled into the parking lot behind the restaurant and cut the engine.

As he helped her from the car, Regan realized
coming here really wasn't a good idea. She hoped
Mike wouldn't mention Santiago again. Her relationship with the vampire was something she didn't
want to talk about with Flynn or anyone else until
she herself had figured out what it was.

They had no sooner been seated than Santiago
entered the restaurant from the vampire side. He
chose a table where she couldn't miss seeing him.
He inclined his head in her direction and then sat
down. Moments later, a beautiful young vampire
with short, curly red hair and long, long legs joined
him. The woman kissed his cheek, then sat down.

Regan was perplexed by the sharp stab of jealousy that pierced her when she saw Santiago with
another woman. There was no reason for her to
be jealous. Sexy looks and devastating kisses aside,
he was nothing to her.

Dragging her gaze away, Regan spent the rest of
the evening trying to concentrate on what Michael
was saying, but time and again she caught herself
staring at Joaquin Santiago and his date, found her-

self wondering what synthetic blood tasted like, and if he drank it warm or cold.

"Regan?"

Blinking, she looked at Mike. "I'm sorry, did you say something?"

"I asked if you wanted dessert?"

"No, I don't think so."

Mike looked up at the waitress. "Just the check, please."

"I guess I haven't been very good company," Regan said. "I'm sorry."

"You seem a little distracted," Mike said, reaching for her hand. "Is anything wrong?"

"No, I just . . . it's the killings in the Park. I guess they bothered me more than I thought."

"I didn't want to talk shop," Flynn said, "but there was another killing last night. I tried to call you . . ." His voice trailed off.

She knew he was wondering where she'd been, but their relationship hadn't reached the point where he had the right to ask or she had the responsibility to tell him.

"I'm sorry, I wasn't home," she said, and then frowned. She never turned her cell phone off. Why hadn't it rung last night? Reaching into her handbag, she checked the phone. Sure enough, it was off. She glanced over at Santiago. He was the only one who could have turned it off; she hadn't been with anyone else. She dropped the phone back into her bag. "Who was the victim this time?"

"Another middle-aged man, same M.O. as the last one."

She wondered if she should tell him about the murders Santiago had mentioned, then wondered why she was even questioning herself about it. The

police needed to know. Then again, there was no
evidence of the murders and, thanks to the vampire
community, no bodies. She bit down on the inside
corner of her mouth. If she told Flynn about the
other deaths, she would have to tell him how she
knew and she was suddenly, unaccountably, reluctant to do so.

They talked of the case for a few minutes, then
Flynn paid the check and drove her home.

"Would you like to come in?" she asked as he
pulled into the driveway.

"You know I would, but I've got to be in court
early tomorrow morning."

"All right."

He walked her to her door, drew her into his arms,
and kissed her good night. Some tiny imp inside her
couldn't help comparing Flynn's kiss with Santiago's.
To her dismay, the vampire's kiss was far and away
the more sensual and satisfying of the two.

Flynn gave her a quick hug. "I'll call you during
the week."

"I'd like that." She stood in the doorway, watching his car until it was out of sight, her fingertips
sliding over her lower lip. What was wrong with her,
that Flynn's kisses, while warm and sweet, didn't
excite her the way Santiago's did, didn't leave her
yearning for more than just kisses? How perverse
was she, to prefer the kiss of a vampire to that of a
nice, normal, handsome man?

She was still pondering that when she went inside
and closed the door.

Even before she switched on the light in the
living room, she knew there was someone else in
the house.

Chapter 10

The man standing in her living room was tall and lean. There was nothing particularly frightening about his appearance. Dressed in faded jeans and a flowered shirt, with his long blond hair falling to his shoulders, he looked like a California surfer, until you looked into his eyes. Dark brown eyes. Feral eyes.

She didn't have to ask who he was. In the deepest part of her being, she knew.

For a moment, she couldn't move, couldn't think, and then she whirled around and bolted for the front door.

She had just wrenched it open when he reached her.

She screamed as he grabbed a handful of her hair and flung her across the room, cried out when the back of her head struck the wall. Lights danced in front of her eyes as she slowly slid to the floor.

He closed the front door, then came to stand over her.

Regan slid her hand into her jacket pocket, her

fingers curling around the butt of her pistol. "What do you want?"

"Santiago."

For a moment, she considered denying that she knew the vampire, but one look into the intruder's eyes changed her mind. "He's not here."

"Where is he?"

"Turn around, Vasile. I am right behind you."

Regan glanced past the werewolf to see Santiago standing in front of the door. She had never been so glad to see anyone in her life.

The werewolf's lips drew back in a predatory grin. "I knew I would find you here."

"The woman has no part in this."

"No?" Vasile took a step back, his hand once against fisting around a handful of Regan's hair. "I think she does."

"She is nothing to you," Santiago said, his voice cool and detached. "And nothing to me."

Regan looked up at Santiago, chilled to the bone by his words. *He doesn't mean it,* she told herself. *He can't mean it.*

Vasile laughed. It was an ugly sound, like dry bones scraping together. "Then you won't care if I kill her."

"Do what you will to the woman," Santiago said impatiently. "It will change nothing between us."

Uncertainly flickered in the werewolf's eyes; then, with a low growl, he gathered Regan into his arms. "You say the woman means nothing to you. We shall see."

Knowing that Vasile could move almost as fast as he could, and knowing that any attempt to interfere would only make things worse, Santiago remained where he was, hoping against hope that the werewolf was bluffing. He should have known better.

Santiago let out a cry of rage when Vasile buried his fangs in Regan's neck. The werewolf bit down hard, then threw her away from him. She slammed into the far wall, fell to the floor, and lay there, limp and unmoving, like a rag doll.

Santiago lunged toward her, but Vasile sprang forward, murder in his eyes as he placed himself between Santiago and Regan.

"Before I kill you," Santiago said, every fiber of his being fixed on the werewolf, "I want to know why you attacked Marishka."

Pausing, Vasile looked over his shoulder. "You don't know?" he said with a sneer. "You expect me to believe she never told you?"

Santiago frowned. "What are you talking about?" He glanced at Regan, his senses surrounding her. Her heartbeat, though erratic, told him she was still alive. "What was Regan supposed to tell me?"

"Not her! Marishka. She was mine! We were to be married. And then she met you. I warned her that I would kill her before I let her go. She should have believed me."

"You killed Marishka because she left you?"

"And now I intend to kill you, and the woman, as well," Vasile snarled. He sprang forward, his body shifting in midair.

In the same instant, Santiago called upon the beast that dwelled within him, reveling in the rush of preternatural power that flowed through him as he, too, shifted into wolf form.

Regan stirred, her eyelids fluttering open. She stared at the scene before her through eyes that refused to focus while a distant part of her mind wondered if she was having another nightmare. Vasile and Santiago were gone and two wolves—one yellow haired, one black—were at each other's throats, claws and fangs slashing and ripping. Blood sprayed through the air in a fine crimson mist. It was an eerily silent battle, and all the more frightening because of it. She wanted to run away but when she tried to move, pain exploded through her limbs, crawled up her neck, and lodged in the back of her head. It couldn't be a dream, she thought. The pain she felt was all too real.

Helpless, she could only watch the deadly dance in morbid fascination. The creatures were both wolves, yet they looked nothing the same, and it wasn't just the difference in their coloring. The fair-haired one seemed distorted somehow, its arms and legs seeming out of proportion to its body; not only that, but its ears were too small, its head too big.

In a sudden rush, the black wolf managed to knock the other wolf off balance. With a victorious howl, it buried its fangs in the yellow-haired wolf's shoulder.

The injured wolf let out a bloodcurdling cry that was almost human, its fangs snapping wildly at the other wolf. Its jaws locked on the black wolf's neck. With a low growl, the black wolf shook himself free. In an instant, the yellow-haired wolf gained its feet and with a wild cry, it leaped through the front window and disappeared into the night in a shower of broken glass.

The black wolf stared after it for a moment, then turned and padded toward Regan.

She took one look at the bloody muzzle and glowing eyes, and slid into welcome oblivion.

Santiago glanced at the window. The urge to

follow Vasile and end the feud between them once and for all was strong within him, but he couldn't leave the woman here alone. Though slim, there was always a chance Vasile would double back and try to finish what he had started. It wasn't a chance Santiago was willing to take.

Shifting back to his own form, he knelt at Regan's side and gently examined her from head to foot. He could detect no broken bones but she was badly bruised, and there was a sizeable lump on the back of her head. As expected, the worst wound was the hideous bite in her neck. Just how bad it was would be determined at the next full moon.

Lifting Regan into his arms, he carried her into the bedroom, drew back the covers on the bed, and lowered her onto the mattress. He was certain she would not be pleased to have him undress her, but he couldn't leave her lying there covered in blood. Moving quickly, he stripped off her soiled garments and tossed them aside. In spite of his concern for her well-being, he couldn't help noticing that her body was as lovely as her face.

After washing and bandaging the wound in her neck, he searched the dresser drawers until he found a nightgown. He slipped it over her head, pulled it over her breasts, and smoothed it down over her hips, all the while thinking it was a crime to cover such perfection. Rummaging through her closet and dresser, he picked out a change of clothing for her, then went into the bathroom and scooped up her comb and brush and all the other feminine doodads on the counter.

He stuffed everything into a pillowcase and carried it into the living room.

Pausing, he glanced around the room. The side

window was broken. There was a thin spray of blood on the hardwood floor. Muttering an oath, he wet a towel, found a bottle of liquid soap and a towel, and scrubbed the floor clean.

Now, what to do about the window? He was tempted to worry about it later, but a broken window was an invitation to any thief in the neighborhood. Moving quickly, he searched the grounds and when he found nothing useful there, he searched the garage where he found a piece of plywood. A further search turned up a hammer and nails.

Returning to the house, he checked on Regan, then covered the window with the plywood and nailed it in place.

When that was done, he picked up the pillowcase, gathered Regan into his arms and carried her outside. He locked the door behind him and then, traveling at preternatural speed, he soon arrived at his underground lair in the Byways.

In the bedroom, he held her close for a moment before he drew back the blankets and put her to bed. She looked as pale as death against the black sheets. The bandage on her neck was dotted with fresh blood. As he drew the covers over her, he couldn't help wondering how she would feel if the worst happened, but perhaps he was worrying for nothing. He had never heard of anyone being turned into a werewolf when bitten by a werewolf in human form. But then, Vasile was no longer an ordinary werewolf.

Santiago brushed a lock of hair from Regan's forehead, his fingertips sliding lightly over her brow. Her skin was baby soft and smooth, warmed by the blood flowing through her veins. It called to him, singing an ancient song of life. He had known her only a short time, yet he could no longer imagine his world without her in it.

He ran his knuckles over her cheek. Long ago, he had heard it rumored that a shaman in the Black Hills of South Dakota possessed a cure for lycanthropy. Of course, over the years, Santiago had heard rumors that there was a cure for vampirism, too, only that cure was supposedly obtained from a witch somewhere in the hill country of Tuscany. He had spent a dozen nights contemplating what it would be like to be mortal again, to eat solid food, to move about in the daylight, to sleep only when he was tired.

Finally, driven by boredom and curiosity, Santiago had traveled to Italy and scoured every inch of the country looking for the witch or a cure, only to come to the conclusion that neither the witch or the cure had ever existed. To this day, he didn't know what he would have done had he found a cure for the Dark Trick while in Italy. Today, he would not have to think about it twice. He had no wish to return to mortality. His current lifestyle suited him just fine.

For Regan's sake, he hoped that, should a werewolf antidote become a necessity, it would prove to be more than a myth.

He stayed at Regan's side until late morning and then, after writing her a quick note, he closed himself in his lair. Though he could be active during the daylight hours, sooner or later he was compelled to surrender to the Dark Sleep.

He was on the brink of oblivion when he remembered that when she woke, there would be nothing in the house for her to eat or drink, but there was no help for it now.

Closing his eyes, he succumbed to the darkness.

* * *

With a low groan, Regan turned onto her side. She ached in places she had never known she had; there was a really bad taste in her mouth. Why hadn't she brushed her teeth last night before she went to bed? Slowly, it occurred to her that the mattress beneath her didn't feel like her mattress, the sheets didn't feel like her sheets, and the pillow beneath her head wasn't as soft as the one she was used to. And why was her neck so sore?

Opening her eyes a crack, she stared, uncomprehending, at the unfamiliar sight of windowless blue-gray walls.

Fear came quickly, and with it, a rush of panic. Where was she? Sitting up, she saw that she was in her own nightgown. But in whose bed? Had Vasile carried her off to his lair?

She lifted a hand to her neck, her fingers tentatively exploring the bandage swathed around her throat. So, it hadn't been a terrible dream, after all. The horror of what had happened the night before returned in a rush. She had been bitten! By a werewolf! Nausea rose in her throat and she bolted from the bed, one hand covering her mouth as she searched for the bathroom, her stomach heaving. Bitten by a werewolf!

Later, weak and shaken, she sat on the floor, her back against the tub, her arms wrapped around her middle. She had been bitten by a werewolf. The thought made her stomach clench anew. Would she grow fanged and furry with the next full moon? She was shaking now, horrified beyond words.

Bitten by a werewolf. The realization struck with

icy certainty and with it came the realization that her life as she knew it was over.

Still trembling, she dragged herself to her feet and moved toward the sink to rinse her mouth, only there was no paper cup or drinking glass.

Moving slowly, she went looking for the kitchen, only there wasn't one. Where was she? Returning to the bathroom, she turned on the faucet, cupped her hands under the water, and rinsed her mouth as best she could.

Forcing herself to remain calm, she went back into the bedroom and sat down on the edge of the bed, noting, as she did so, that the sheets were black satin. It was then that she saw the note on one of the pillows. Picking it up, she read:

Regan,
I know you have questions. Stay here and rest. Try not to worry. I will come to you at sunset.

JS

JS. For Joaquin Santiago? She glanced at the black sheets again. It had to be him. She glanced around, wondering where he was—wondering where she was. She had been to Santiago's condo and this definitely wasn't it.

Feeling like an old, old woman, she rose from the bed and hobbled into the living room where she dropped down on the sofa.

Whatever this place was, it was a lot nicer than his other place, she thought, gazing at her surroundings, and far more suited to the man who owned it than the condo in the park. She studied the paintings, thinking it was touching and a little sad that all his paintings were of sunrises and sunsets.

Leaning forward, she perused the items displayed under the glass top of the coffee table, wondering if they held any special meaning for Santiago, then grimaced as a horrible thought crossed her mind. Maybe they were mementos taken from people he had killed. He was, after all, a vampire.

With a shudder, she leaned back and closed her eyes. Once, she had thought that being a vampire was the worst thing in the world. Now, contemplating the possibility that she might become a werewolf, she wasn't so sure. Closing her eyes, she took a deep breath. Maybe she was worrying for nothing. Vasile had been in human form when he bit her. As far as she knew, werewolves had to be in wolf form to create another werewolf.

She clung to that thought as bits and pieces of what she had read on the Internet flitted through her mind. Throughout the mythology of the known world, there were stories of humans transforming into animal shapes. Odin had changed himself into an eagle. Loki had taken on the form of a fish. The Greek gods had often transformed into beasts, the better to move among men in secrecy. Jupiter had changed into a bull, Hecuba into a dog.

It was believed that werewolves didn't age and were immune to most human diseases. Not only that, but their bodies were constantly regenerating, which made them pretty much immortal. And since they also healed rapidly, the only way to kill one was to inflict a mortal wound to the heart or the brain.

There were various ways to become a werewolf, such as through sorcery, being bitten by a werewolf, being cursed by a witch, or being born to a werewolf. People who were turned into werewolves against their will weren't considered damned until they tasted human blood; once that happened, they were forever cursed.

Regan thought briefly of Vasile and the people he had killed and mutilated. Surely he deserved to be damned for all eternity . . .

She lifted a hand to the bandage on her neck, her stomach churning as she imagined herself transforming into a wolf and prowling the moonlit streets of the city looking for prey. A wave of hysterical laughter rose in her throat. Maybe she could go hunting with Santiago! He could drink the blood and she would eat the flesh. She shuddered at the thought. She didn't want to be a werewolf. She didn't want to be cursed forever.

Thinking to dispel her morbid thoughts, she turned on the Satellite Screen, grateful for the sound of human voices. She found an old Tom Hanks comedy, hoping it would distract her, but to no avail. The word "werewolf" whispered in her mind over and over again and with it came the horrific images of the mutilated bodies in the park.

Huddled in a corner of the sofa, she stared at the television screen and waited for sunset.

Chapter 11

Santiago rose at dusk. He paused at the door between his lair and the bedroom closet, listening. Only when he had ascertained that Regan wasn't in the adjoining room did he leave his lair.

He found her in the living room, curled up in a corner of the sofa, asleep. He studied her face a moment, noting that her complexion was still pale. There were dark shadows under her eyes, hollows in her cheeks. She looked worried, even in sleep. He supposed he couldn't blame her. Given a choice, he knew he would rather be a vampire than a werewolf. He wondered if, given the choice, Regan would feel the same.

Sitting beside her on the sofa, he gently brushed a lock of hair from her cheek.

She woke with a start, her body tensing, her eyes widening with fear.

"Do not be afraid," he said quietly. "It is only me."

She blew out a sigh of relief as she slumped back against the sofa once again. "How do you feel?" he asked.

"Fine, now, but . . ." She looked up at him, her

eyes haunted. "Joaquin, I don't want to be a were-wolf. If . . . if it happens . . ." She shuddered. "If I start to turn furry, I want you to . . ." She took a deep breath. "I want you to do whatever you have to."

"Let us not worry about that now. It is rumored that there is a cure."

She sat up, her eyes alight with interest. "A cure? Where?"

He told her quickly of the little he knew about the shaman in the Black Hills.

"I have to go there," she said, her voice rising with excitement. "Will you . . . never mind."

"Will I what?"

Her gaze slid away from his. "Nothing."

"Were you perhaps going to ask me to go with you?"

"Yes, but . . . I have no right to impose on you. We hardly know each other, and . . ."

Santiago took her hand in his, turned it over, and lightly kissed her palm. "Did you really think I would let you go alone?"

She shook her head. "No," she said. "No, I guess not."

She sat back, suddenly having second thoughts about the whole thing. Maybe she wouldn't turn into a werewolf. Maybe she should wait and see how Vasile's bite affected her before she took off on a wild goose chase to the Black Hills. She considered putting the trip off, then decided against it. Better to go now. If she found the cure and Vasile's bite hadn't affected her, no harm would be done. And if she was infected, well, she wanted to be cured as soon as possible.

Just worrying about the possibility of turning into a creature like Vasile made her head ache. Better to think of something else. She looked at Santiago. "Can I ask you something?"

"Anything."

"When were you born? What was your life like before you became a vampire?"

Leaning back on the sofa, he slipped his arm around her shoulders. "I was born in the time of the conquistadors in what is now New Mexico. My mother was Apache. My father was a conquistador who deserted his post. He was found wandering in Apache land, half out of his mind from exhaustion and lack of water. The People took him in and nursed him back to health. He died in a hunting accident a few years after I was born. My mother soon followed. My grandfather raised me to be a warrior."

"Joaquin Santiago is a funny name for an Apache warrior."

"My Apache name is Nepotonje."

"Ne-pot-on-je? What does it mean?"

"Bear Watcher."

"So, how did you go from being a warrior to a vampire?"

"I had left the village in search of buffalo. The third night, as I sat by my fire, a woman came to me, she asked if she could warm herself. I had never seen anything like her before. She had silver hair that reached past her waist and dark eyes that sometimes looked red in the light of the fire. She was not Apache, yet she spoke my language as if she had been born to it. I offered her food and drink but she refused.

"She said very little but suddenly I was aware that she was sitting close beside me, and then she placed her hand on my thigh. In spite of the heat of the fire, her skin was cool, yet her touch burned like fire itself.

"I started to ask her if she was ill, but she placed her hand over my mouth, silencing me, and then she kissed me. I remember very little after that. When I could think again, she told me she had given me the gift of eternal life. I would have to drink blood to survive, and because the gods would be jealous of my immortality, I would only be allowed to live by night.

"I wanted to question her but I was suddenly wracked with pain. She stood over me, watching dispassionately while I writhed in agony in the dirt at her feet. There was nothing to be afraid of, she said, it was just the death of my old body and the birth of my new one.

"When the worst of the pain had passed, she knelt beside me, her lips cool as she kissed my cheek. 'Find a place to hide from the sun,' she whispered. 'Or your new life will be over before it begins.' And then she disappeared."

"She left you out there, alone?"

"Yes."

"Just like that? Where did she go?"

"I have no idea. I never saw her again. I never knew her name or where she came from."

"It must have been awful for you."

He nodded. "The next few weeks were filled with confusion and self-loathing. I craved blood the way an addict craves cocaine. Because I was afraid that I would prey upon my own people, I left the Apache and preyed on our enemies.

"I had been roaming the land like a wild animal for about a year when I attacked a man who turned out to be a man of learning." Naveen had been a short, slender man with long brown hair and the face of a saint. He had been an old man, even then.

"He begged me to spare his life," Santiago said after a moment. "He promised that he would do whatever I asked. I kept him as a slave for several years, feeding off him at my leisure. In return, I made sure that he had the best food and drink I could steal. At my request, he taught me to speak English and French and Latin. He taught me of the world, and how to read and write. When he had taught me everything he knew, I let him go. I spent the next seventy-five years traveling the world."

And what a world it had been! Especially for a man who had been raised with the Indians. He had visited every continent, every country, marveling at what mankind had accomplished—the art, the literature, the inventions of the time. So much to see, so much to learn. He had spent years reading every book he could get his hands on. He had toured palaces and cathedrals old and new and wandered through museums and zoos, awed as much by the works of the masters as he was by the strange animals that he saw. If he had to enter such places by night and by stealth, then so be it. Silent as a ghost, he had walked the dark halls of the world's art galleries and museums, admiring the works of Picasso and Chagall, Goya and da Vinci, Michelangelo and Cézanne, Raphael and van Gogh.

Santiago expelled a deep breath. "Eventually, I grew weary of wandering and I settled in the hill country of Romania. It was there that I met Marishka."

"Ah, a woman, at last," Regan murmured. "I should have known there would be a woman sooner or later."

He made a soft sound of assent, remembering

the beauty of Marishka's smile, the warmth of her flashing brown eyes. "She was a wild Gypsy woman with the body of a temptress and the soul of a saint."

"You loved her, didn't you?"

"Yes."

"And she loved you?"

"Yes."

"Did she know what you were?"

He nodded.

"And she didn't care?"

"She never knew until it was too late."

"You made her a vampire against her will?"

He nodded again, his expression shuttered, leaving her to wonder if he had regretted bestowing the Dark Trick upon her. As much as she wanted to ask, she didn't have the nerve to probe into something that was still painful even after such a long time.

"Where does Vasile come into all this?"

"Marishka and I settled in a little village outside of Transylvania. Vasile found us there six months later. He killed Marishka while she slept. It wasn't until Vasile came to your apartment that I learned he had been in love with her. He had killed her for leaving him."

"I'm so sorry," she murmured, though the words seemed inadequate.

Santiago nodded. Vasile was here, in the city. It had been Santiago's intent to hunt the werewolf down and kill him for destroying Marishka, but now that would have to wait. Revenge would not restore Marishka's life. It was Regan he must think of now. It was her life that was in danger, and only he could save her. Choosing between revenge and saving Regan's life was no choice at all. Regan had to come first. Avenging Marishka's death would have to wait.

"What about other vampires?" Regan asked.

"What about them?"

"I don't know. I mean, don't you have any vampire friends here in the city?"

"No."

"Why not?"

"I do not trust any of them."

"Why not? I mean, you're like them."

"It is not normal for vampires to gather together. Werewolves run in packs. Vampires are by nature solitary creatures."

"Really? I didn't know that." She looked thoughtful a moment. "What about women? You must have known a lot of them in your long life."

"Yes," he replied, looking past her, "but I have loved only one."

She looked at him, her eyes wide with surprise, or perhaps disbelief—it was hard to tell. He wondered what she would say if he told her he was very much afraid he was falling in love with her, and that he feared his growing fondness for her would only bring about her death. No doubt the best thing he could do for Regan Delaney would be to leave her, and yet that was something he could not do. If he left her now, alone and defenseless . . . no, it was out of the question. He could not leave Regan at the werewolf's mercy; he could not let her face the next full moon alone.

"What of you?" he said, stroking her cheek with the tip of one finger. "Tell me of you."

She shrugged. "There's nothing to tell. I was born in Chicago, the youngest of three children. My parents still live there. My younger brother, Josh, is a test pilot. My older brother, Kevin, is married."

"And you are not."

"No. I guess I'm still looking for Mr. Right."

"Why were you at the scene of the murder in the park?"

"Oh, didn't I tell you?" she said with forced aplomb. "I used to be a vampire hunter, before your kind became an endangered species and put me out of a job."

Santiago looked at her, one brow raised. She had surprised him that time, Regan thought, and wondered, somewhat apprehensively, what his reaction would be. It was entirely possible that she had just made the biggest mistake of her life. Vampires and vampires hunters were like oil and water. They just didn't mix.

"I do not believe you," he said at last.

"Well, it's true!"

He shook his head. "Why would you pursue such a distasteful career?"

She took a deep breath. His hand, resting on her shoulder, seemed suddenly heavy. "A vampire killed my best friend, Amy."

"Ah." He understood the need for revenge all too well.

"We were seniors in high school when she met Dante. Of course, we didn't know he was a vampire. He just seemed like a nice guy. Amy fell for him really hard. The summer we graduated, she spent practically every minute of every night with him. And then one night she didn't come home. The police found her body two days later."

"I am sorry for your loss."

"It was a long time ago."

"But the pain is still there. How does one become a hunter? I always thought it was like a rite of passage, passed on from father to son."

"I took classes from a school in Los Angeles." Rigorous classes, she recalled. At the time, she had thought she had learned everything there was to know about vampires—how to detect them, how to render them helpless, how to destroy them. Only after meeting Santiago did she realize she still had a lot to learn. "I passed the test and received my credential as a hunter. A year later, I was hired as an investigator for the police department."

"A test?" he asked, his eyes glinting with wry amusement. "What kind of test?"

"Nothing like what you're thinking," she replied tartly. But close. Students had practiced staking and beheading on dummies that were all too lifelike. Three students had fainted the first time they had to take a head. She prided herself on the fact that she hadn't been one of them.

Santiago looked at her through heavy-lidded eyes, the weight of his gaze like a physical caress as it moved over her face, touching on her lips before moving down to her throat, sliding downward to linger on her breasts before returning to her lips.

"Ah, Regan," he said, his voice low and enticing, "you have no idea what I'm thinking."

To the contrary, she knew exactly what he was thinking. It was there, in the sudden heat of his eyes, in the lazy sensuality of his voice, in the way his arm tightened around her shoulders.

He laughed softly as her breathing became erratic. "Perhaps I was wrong." He leaned toward her, his intentions clear. "Perhaps you do know."

She stared at him, confused by the conflicting

emotions that plagued her. He was a vampire, Nosferatu, Undead. She shouldn't want his kiss or his caress. Why didn't he disgust her the way others of his kind did? Why didn't she find his very existence repulsive? She had met other vampires. They had all been handsome and charming, and yet their very nature had repelled her. She didn't know why Santiago should be any different, but he was. He enchanted her with a look, mesmerized her with a smile, and enraptured her with a kiss. Why was he the exception to the rule?

All her questions and confusion were wiped away when his mouth closed over hers. His tongue seared her lower lip and she opened for him, hungry for the taste of him. Her tongue met his, tentative and uncertain, but only for a moment. Desire unfurled deep within the very innermost part of her, unleashing a shiver of pleasure as he kissed her again, and yet again, each kiss deeper and more intimate than the last. His hand moved up and down her back, massaged her nape, tangled in her hair. His thigh pressed intimately against her own.

There was a roaring in her ears. Images flitted through her mind. Images of the two of them locked in a torrid embrace. Images that were so real, she felt herself blushing.

He drew back, his eyes hot. "Isn't that what you were thinking about?" he asked, his voice husky with desire.

She nodded, her cheeks burning under his probing gaze. She only hoped he didn't know that she had been thinking of something far more intimate than kisses. She took a deep breath. It was time to end this now, before things got entirely out of hand.

Taking another deep breath, she said, "How soon can we go look for the shaman in the Hills?"

His look said he understood her tactics all too well. "We will go to your house tomorrow night so you can pack whatever you need. We will leave the night after that."

"But how . . . I mean, it's a long way to the Black Hills. What will you do during the day?"

"Sleep, I should imagine."

"But . . . Are we going to fly?"

"No, drive." He could cover short distances at remarkable speeds, but South Dakota was beyond even his ability. Planes made him claustrophobic. AirTrains and AutoBuses were overcrowded and offered no protection from the sun. Behind the wheel of his own car, he was in control. "There will be motels along the way." He looked at her, his expression sober. "I am trusting that you will watch over me while I rest."

"Watch over you? You don't mean you want me to watch you . . . sleep?"

"No. Only to stay inside and make sure no one disturbs my resting place."

She didn't like the idea. A blind man could have seen that. But she didn't argue, and he hadn't expected her to. She had a great deal at stake.

They left at dusk two nights later. Regan felt a rush of excitement as Santiago handed her into his car, a sleek black convertible Speedster equipped with every possible luxury one could imagine, and then some.

She sank back in the remarkably soft leather seat as he pulled away from the curb. They were going to look for a shaman who reportedly had a cure for lycanthropy. If they didn't find him, or if they found him and he had no cure, what then? She had asked Santiago to take her life if she turned fanged and furry, but she didn't want to die. She tried to imagine herself as a werewolf, her life revolving around the phases of the moon. She couldn't conceive of such a thing, couldn't picture herself as a wolf, couldn't imagine what it would be like to hunt for prey or to rend human flesh. Who would have thought that her whole life could turn upside down in such a short time? It seemed too bizarre to be real. If only she would wake up and find it had all been a bad dream.

She looked over at Santiago as he pulled onto the highway. "Do you like being a vampire?"

He glanced at her, one brow raised. "Are you thinking of embracing the Dark Trick?"

"No, of course not! I was just wondering . . ."

"What it is like to be different from the rest of the world? To prey on mankind?"

"Yes." It sounded much worse when it was put into words.

"I have been a vampire far longer than I was a mortal man," he said. "I scarcely remember my other life."

"If you could choose, would you rather be a vampire or a werewolf?"

"A vampire, to be sure."

Glancing out the window, Regan considered the similarities and differences between the two. Werewolves were ruled by the pull of the moon; vampires were repelled by the sun. Both killed indiscriminately. Both had remarkable powers of regeneration and healing. Both were, for all intents and purposes, immortal. But werewolves were living creatures. Vampires were not.

She looked at Santiago again. "Doesn't it bother you, that you're . . . you know? Dead."

"Do I look dead?" he asked, a note of amusement in his voice.

"No, but . . ."

"Do I act dead?"

"No, but . . ."

"Did you think I was dead when I kissed you?"

She swallowed hard at the memory, which was all too vivid in her mind. "No." She didn't care for the direction their conversation was going at all. "So, how will we find this shaman?"

"He is said to live in a cave at the top of the Black Hills."

"A cave?"

Santiago shrugged. "Some say he is a werewolf himself, and that he lives in the cave as a penance for the lives he has taken."

"But if he has as cure . . . why wouldn't he use it?"

"Perhaps he likes being a werewolf."

"No," she said vehemently. "I'm sorry, I can't believe that. I can't believe anyone would want to be a werewolf, or a . . ."

"Or a vampire?"

"Or a vampire."

"And if you had to choose between the two, Regan Delaney, which would you be?" he asked quietly.

"Have you killed a lot of people?"

"Define a lot."

"One is a lot," she said, her voice sharp.

"Then I have definitely killed a lot."

"How many?"

"I have not kept a record." The only kills he remembered were the first ones, when the hunger had been excruciating, the pain overpowering, and the hunt exhilarating.

"Ten?" she prodded. "Twenty? Fifty? A hundred?"

Telling himself to be patient, Santiago took a deep breath. He couldn't blame her, he supposed, for being worried and afraid, or for trying to find out all she could about him. He was, after all, a stranger, and a vampire.

"As I said, I haven't kept a record, but I would guess the number to be rather high. I have regrets, of course," he remarked. "Do I wish those I killed were alive? Yes. Would I wish to be dead in their place? No." He stilled her next question with an upraised hand. "Not all the people I have killed have been prey. Some were killed in self-defense. And some . . ." He met her gaze. "Some were vampire hunters."

Her face paled a little at that admission. "What about Vasile? Do you know how many . . . ?"

"I have no idea."

She fell silent, her thoughts turned inward as she watched the moonlit countryside rush by. After a time, Santiago turned on the radio. Regan closed her eyes, lulled to sleep by the car's movement and the music.

Santiago felt himself relax. Not that he minded answering her questions. He couldn't blame her for being curious, couldn't fault her for wondering about his past or how many people he had killed. She had known him less than a month and her life was, after all, in his hands.

It was a beautiful night for a drive. The sky was clear, shimmering with a multitude of stars. There were only a few other cars on the highway. On the radio, Brooks and Dunn were singing an old song about a neon moon. That was how the moon had looked when he had first seen it as a new vampire, he recalled with a wry grin, like a fiery ball of silver neon.

He had awakened after sunset that first night, wondering if the mysterious woman and everything that had happened after she had wandered into his camp had been some kind of fever dream.

Rising, he had emerged from the small cave where he had spent the day in oblivion. After the pain of the night before, he was surprised to find that he felt better and stronger than he had ever felt in his life. Though it was full dark, he could see everything clearly. His nostrils filled with a myriad of smells and odors—the feral odor of animals, the fecund scent of plants and grass and dirt, the stink of a decaying animal in the distance.

His puzzlement at his increased senses was soon swallowed up in a sharp slash of pain that engulfed his whole body. It took him a moment to realize that what he was feeling was hunger, but a hunger unlike any he had ever known before. He felt as if his insides were being shredded with hot knives, shrinking, shriveling.

Frantic to alleviate the pain, he had pulled a piece of dried venison from his war bag. He ate it quickly, then doubled over in pain, retching violently as his body rebelled. Blood, he thought dully. She had told him he would need blood.

When his nausea passed, he wiped his mouth, then walked the short distance to where he had left his horse. At his approach, the mare's nostrils flared, her ears went flat, and she turned and bolted across the prairie.

He had known, in that instant, that his life had been forever changed.

Santiago looked over at the woman sleeping in the seat beside him and knew his entire existence was about to change again.

Chapter 12

The ringing of her cell phone woke Regan. Grabbing her handbag, she fished the phone out. "Hello?"

Michael Flynn's voice came over the line, loud and clear. "Hey, Reggie, where the devil are you?"

"What?" She sat up, momentarily disoriented until she glanced out the car window. She remembered where she was then, who she was with, and where they were going.

"I stopped by your place," Michael said. "Your car was there but you didn't answer the door or the phone." He paused and she visualized him running a hand through his hair. "I was worried."

"I'm fine, Mike. I just decided to take a short vacation."

"Kind of sudden, isn't it?"

"I guess so. I'm sorry, I should have let you know."

"Where are you going?"

"South Dakota."

"South Dakota!" he exclaimed, disdain evident in his voice. "Why on earth would you want to go there?"

She glanced at Santiago. He was watching the road but she was sure he was listening to every word, not only hers, but Flynn's, as well. Vampires were known to have a remarkably acute sense of hearing. "I . . . it's just a place I've always wanted to see and . . ."

"Go on." It was obvious from Flynn's tone that he didn't believe a word she was saying.

"I've been a little on edge lately, that's all. I just wanted to get away for a while. I thought a change of scene might do me good, you know?"

"Uh-huh."

"I'll call you when I get back."

"There's been another killing."

She glanced at Santiago again. "Same M.O. as the others?"

"Yeah. This one was a woman." He cleared his throat. "At first . . . at first I thought it might be you."

When she looked over at Santiago this time, he was watching her.

"Why did you think that?" she asked.

"I heard the report at the station. The victim's general description matched yours—same height, same hair color."

"Where was she found?"

"In the park. Funny thing is, she was wearing a blue jacket just like the one I gave you last Christmas. If I didn't known better, I'd swear it was the same one. Hang on a minute." She heard him speak to someone, though she couldn't make out the words. "I'm back. Listen, I've got to go. Call me when you get home."

"Yes, I will." She broke the connection and dropped the phone back in her bag, then turned in her seat to face Santiago. "Flynn said they found another body."

"I heard."

So he had been listening.

"The body," Santiago said. "It was a warning."

"What do you mean?"

"I would be willing to bet that the blue jacket is yours. It is Vasile's way of telling me that he has not given up."

"He means to kill me to get even for Marishka, doesn't he?"

Santiago nodded. "I will not let that happen."

She wanted to believe him, but how could she? He had loved Marishka but he hadn't been able to protect her from Vasile.

Regan dozed again, waking when the car's motion stopped. Opening her eyes, she saw that the sky was growing light and the Speedster was parked in front of a nice motel. She noticed there was a restaurant across the street, an ice cream parlor, a strip mall, and a gas station.

A few moments later, Santiago emerged from the motel office. He slid behind the wheel, handed her a keycard, and drove around to the west side of the building. Pulling up in front of room number 13, he switched off the ignition and got out of the car.

Regan muttered, "Thirteen, bad luck," as she opened the door and went inside, leaving Santiago to retrieve their luggage from the trunk.

It was a nice room, actually two rooms and a bathroom. The walls were papered in a slick green print, the bedspreads and curtains were off-white, the carpet was a dark shade of green. The bathroom had both a tub and a shower. The larger of the bedrooms had a Satellite Screen; the remote was on the table beside the bed. A robot coffeemaker stood in one corner, ready to brew a fresh pot; cups of various sizes sat on the tray atop the robot's head.

Regan blew out a sigh. She was going to spend the day in here, keeping watch over a vampire while he slept in the next room. And what if he woke up hungry? She lifted a hand to her throat. In her years as an investigator with the police department, she had seen her share of vampire kills. Some of the victims died smiling. Most had died in pain and terror. Whatever had possessed her to agree to make this journey with Joaquin Santiago? She should have asked Flynn to go with her, or gone alone. She slipped her hand into her pocket, her fingers caressing the cold, smooth barrel of her gun. She had carried the weapon since becoming a hunter but, thankfully, she had only had cause to use it a few times. Her parents were less than enthusiastic about their only daughter's choice of a career. She had lost a steady boyfriend when she refused to quit her job.

Startled, she whirled around, the gun in her hand, when Santiago stepped into the room. "Sorry," she muttered. "Guess I'm a little on edge."

He grunted softly as he dropped their bags on the floor. He shut the door and punched in the lock code. He couldn't blame her for being twitchy, what with a vampire sharing her quarters and a werewolf trying to kill her.

"I am going to take a quick shower." He pulled a change of clothes from his bag, then headed for the bathroom. "Do not answer the door for anyone."

"Who would be . . . oh, right."

"Just so," he said, and going into the bathroom, he shut the door.

Regan put her suitcase on the bed and rummaged around inside for her nightgown and robe. She should get some sleep, too, she thought, if they were going to be driving at night and resting during the day. As long as she was hanging around with a vampire, her days and nights were going to be topsy-turvy.

She paused when the shower came on. Unable to help herself, she imagined Santiago standing under the spray, water sluicing through his long black hair, streaming over his smooth, copper-colored skin, dripping over his broad shoulders, cascading over his muscular chest, down his hard flat belly and . . .

"Quit that!" she admonished, but the image wouldn't go away. She took a deep breath when the shower went off. Thank goodness. Maybe now she could concentrate on what she was doing.

And maybe not. Her heart did a somersault when Santiago stepped out of the bathroom wearing nothing but a pair of soft gray sweatpants. His upper torso was magnificent, taut and powerful. Had he always been that way, she wondered, or had he spent the last few hundred years pumping iron? He wasn't bulky. His muscles were corded and well-defined, hinting at the kind of strength she could only imagine.

He lifted one brow in wry amusement as she continued to stare at him. "Do you like what you see?"

"I've seen better," she retorted, embarrassed to be caught staring.

"Have you?"

She shook her head, unable to maintain the lie. "No."

"I thought not."

There it was again, she thought, that touch of

smug masculine arrogance. Of course, in his case, it was well-deserved.

"If anyone comes to the door, wake me immediately."

"Will I be able to? Wake you?"

He nodded. "You understand that you are not to leave the room?"

"Yes."

"If you need anything, order it on the phone and be sure to ask for the name of the person who will be bringing it to you."

"All right." It was like being in a spy movie, she thought. All she needed was a password and a cyanide capsule. "What time do you, ah, get up?"

"An hour or so before sunset." He started toward the other bedroom, then paused and glanced over his shoulder. "If you need to wake me before then, speak before you approach the bed."

Her eyes widened, the question unspoken.

"It would not be wise for you to wake me without warning."

"Ah," she murmured. "I understand."

He smiled faintly, then, picking up his suitcase, he went into the small bedroom and closed the door behind him.

Regan stared at the door. She had seen sleeping vampires before. It was a creepy sight. They didn't breathe, they didn't move, and they had no heartbeat. Nor did they look like they were sleeping. They just looked dead. Did Santiago look like that? Or had the blood of the werewolf altered that, as well?

Thrusting all thought of Santiago and werewolves from her mind, she went into the bathroom and locked the door. Stepping into the shower stall, she switched on the controls and punched in the temperature of the water and the kind of bubbles she wanted, as well as the soap and shampoo she preferred. She took a long shower and then washed her hair. Later, after drying her hair, she pulled on her nightgown and went to bed.

She had certainly been sleeping in a lot of strange beds lately, she mused as she slipped under the covers and most of them were Santiago's. Taking a deep calming breath, she closed her eyes and waited for sleep. But sleep wouldn't come. Instead, she found herself thinking of Santiago, wondering again what he looked like when he was caught up in the Dark Sleep. Wondering if he slept in his sweats. Or in nothing at all . . .

Regan woke a little after three in the afternoon. She lay there, her thoughts drifting. She should have called her parents before she left home. She should have let the department know she was leaving town. She should have cancelled the Internet Daily News and asked her neighbor, Polly, to pick up her mail, but everything had happened so quickly. At least she was working again, though she had no idea how long this case would last, or if the department would keep her on once it was solved.

She glanced across the room to the closed bedroom door. Santiago wouldn't be rising for a while yet. She had plenty of time to make a few phone calls. Instead, she let her mind conjure images of Santiago the vampire. Of them all, she decided she favored the memory of the first time she had seen him, that night in You Bet Your Life Park. At the time, he had reminded her of the angel of death. It was still an apt description, she mused. But, coming a close second was the memory of the last time she had seen him, when he had been wearing nothing but a well-worn pair of gray sweatpants. He really had a magnificent build, all smooth tawny flesh and rippling muscle.

She wondered if vampires dreamed when they were trapped in the Dark Sleep, or if it was truly like death. Would he know if she opened the door and peeked inside? Was he aware, on some subconscious level, of what went on around him, or was he really dead to the world?

She sat up when her stomach growled. Rising, she programmed the coffee robot, choosing something dark and rich with a faint hint of chocolate. In moments, the air was redolent with the aroma of fresh-brewed coffee. Carrying the cup with her, she went to the window and drew back the curtains. Dark gray clouds hung low in the sky. She saw a faint flash of lightning in the east and heard a distant rumble of thunder.

Her stomach growled again. Letting the curtain fall back into place, she sat on the edge of the bed and reached for the menu on the table. Picking up the desk phone, she called the restaurant across the street and ordered a bacon, lettuce, and tomato sandwich, a double-thick chocolate shake, and an order of curly fries. Just before she hung up, she remembered to ask for the name of the person who would be delivering her order.

After getting dressed, Regan went into the bathroom and washed her face and brushed her teeth. She was combing her hair when someone knocked at the door.

"Who is it?" she called.

"Jerry, from the diner."

She grabbed her handbag. "How much do I owe you?"

"Sixteen credits for the meal and two for the delivery."

Regan shook her head. Two credits just to carry her order across the street. Prices were getting higher every day. She dug her wallet out of her handbag and found her credit card, then released the lock on the door and opened it a crack. A young man with a cowlick stood outside, a sack in one hand and her malt in the other.

Taking a step back, Regan opened the door. The young man handed her the sack and the malt, which Regan carried inside. Returning to the door, she handed the young man her credit card and signed the receipt.

Murmuring her thanks, she closed and double-locked the door.

Carrying the sack over to the bed, she grabbed the remote and switched on the Satellite Screen, surfing through the online guide until she found an old Reese Witherspoon romantic comedy that she had seen only ten or twelve times. With her back propped against the pillows, she opened the sack and ate her lunch, which turned out to be surprisingly good—or maybe she was just really hungry.

She was finishing the last of her malt when Santiago emerged from the other room. Tonight he wore black jeans, a dark green shirt with the sleeves rolled up to his elbows, and black boots.

Regan glanced at her watch. It was only a little after five. "I didn't expect you up so soon."

He shrugged. "The sky is overcast."

"I thought it didn't matter anymore, whether the sun was up or not."

"I am not at my full strength when the sun is high in the sky. Once I succumb to the Dark Sleep, I usually sleep until sunset, though not always."

She didn't know what to say to that, so she didn't say anything.

"We will leave after I have . . ." He paused.

She knew he was trying to think of a tactful way to say he needed to hunt. She saved him the trouble. "I understand."

A faint smile tugged at his lips as he sat down in the chair across from hers.

"What's it like?" she asked. "Hunting for prey, I mean." Although she couldn't imagine such a thing, there was a good possibility that she would be hunting prey herself if she turned fanged and furry at the next full moon.

He regarded her through narrowed eyes for a moment. "I do not think I can explain it to you," he replied slowly. "There is nothing in the human experience with which you can compare it. The scent of fresh prey in your nostrils, the scent of fear when they realize they cannot escape, the rapid beat of their heart, the rich coppery taste of hot blood flowing over your tongue . . ." He stopped abruptly. "Forgive me, I did not meant to be so . . . descriptive."

She swallowed the bile rising in her throat. Descriptive was right. "I thought you didn't kill anymore."

"The thrill of the chase is the same, only the manner of it has changed." Where he had once hunted his prey with single-minded intent, he now seduced them, oft times with flowers and sweet words. The latter lacked the rush of the former, but the results were the same and, in some ways, seduction was more satisfying.

His gaze slid over Regan, from the top of her

blond head to the tips of her dainty toes. She would be sweet indeed, he mused. He would like to woo her and win her, then start at her feet and nibble his way up to her mouth, sampling all her feminine delights along the way.

From the sudden blush in her cheeks, he suspected she might be reading his mind.

He glanced at the window. The sun was down. It was time to go.

"I will not be gone long," he said. "Remember to keep the door locked."

She nodded. Though she tried not to show it, he could see the revulsion in her eyes.

That look stayed with him as he stalked the shadows. He had not given any regard to what others thought of him in hundreds of years. Why did this woman's opinion, from a woman he hardly knew, have the power to make him feel guilty for what he was about to do? He snorted softly. He had nothing to feel guilty about! He was a vampire. It wasn't a lifestyle he had sought, but he had made peace with what he had become and everything it involved years ago.

It didn't take long to find what he was searching for. Every town had a dive where people went to be alone and forget, or to seek companionship for the night, and this place was no different. He found the bar on the outskirts of town, a seedy-looking red brick tavern located at the end of a long dirt road. Cars were parked haphazardly in the lot. The sound of one of those someone-done-her-wrong songs poured from the open windows. A man and a woman stood in the shadows by the front door, their bodies so closely entwined it was impossible to tell where one began and the other left off. They didn't look up when he passed by.

The inside of the tavern was dimly lit. The air was pungent with cigarette smoke and sweat that no amount of cologne or perfume could mask. He wrinkled his nose as he made his way to the bar. There were times, like now, when having a preternatural sense of smell was a curse and not a blessing. Several couples were slow-dancing, if you could call it dancing. It was more like vertical foreplay.

Santiago took a seat near the end of the bar and ordered a glass of red wine. The allure of the vampire was no myth, and while he wasn't sure how it worked, he had only to sit there and wait. In a short time, three women gravitated toward him.

Santiago smiled inwardly. It was like choosing a fine wine for dinner, he mused. Should he have the blonde, the brunette, or the redhead? Or a taste of all three? In the end, he decided on the brunette, since the blonde reminded him of Regan and the redhead simply didn't appeal to him.

He smiled at them all, chatted with them for a few moments, and then asked the brunette to dance.

Smiling smugly at the other two, the brunette put her hand in his and let him lead her onto the dance floor.

"Do you come here often?" she asked as he drew her into his arms.

"No. I am just passing through."

"That's too bad." She made no protest as he drew her closer. "You don't look like the other guys that come in here."

"Indeed?"

She nodded, her brows drawn together in a thought frown. "They seem like boys next to you," she remarked. "Not that you look old," she said quickly, "but there's something about you . . ."

"I am older than I look." He grinned inwardly, thinking how shocked the woman would be if she knew just how old he really was.

"I'm Lilith." She smiled in a way that told him she had played this game many times before.

He inclined his head. "Joaquin."

"I've never known anyone by that name. It's kind of sexy. Are you sure you can't stay in town a little longer, maybe just overnight? I don't live far from here."

"Alas, I cannot." He gazed deep into her eyes. "Relax, Lilith. I need something from you." He listened to the sound of her heartbeat, heard it slow as she succumbed to his enchantment. He bent his head over her neck, his tongue laving her skin. To anyone watching, it would appear he was kissing her throat. And indeed he was, but only for a moment before his fangs pierced the tender skin. He drank deeply, quickly, his arm tightening around her waist as she went limp in his embrace.

He licked his lips before lifting his head and guiding her back to the bar. He eased her onto the stool, ordered her a glass of orange juice, and compelled her to drink it.

"Lilith?"

"Hmm?" She looked at him as if she had never seen him before.

"I am going to leave you now," he told her. "You will not remember this night or anything that happened."

"No," she said, blinking at him, "I won't remember."

He patted her arm and muttered, "good girl," and then he was gone.

* * *

Regan sat on the edge of the bed, her gaze fixed
on the Satellite Screen, though she had no idea
what she was watching. She was thinking about Santiago, wondering where he had gone, who he was
with, and, morbidly, what it would be like to drink
blood to survive. Did a person's normal revulsion
at drinking human blood magically disappear when
one became a vampire? Was it something you got
used to gradually, like the taste of champagne? Or
was it just something you had to accept and learn
to live with?

She swallowed the bile rising in her throat. She
might be able to get used to drinking blood if she
had to, but eating human flesh? No way! She tried to
imagine herself turning fanged and furry, howling
at the moon as she ran through the night searching
for prey. Human prey . . .

"No!" She had to think positive. She had to believe that everything would be all right or she would
never get through this. Think positive. They would
find the shaman and he would cure her, if necessary, though she clung to the faint hope that Vasile's
bite had been benign.

For the tenth time in as many minutes, she went
to the window and looked out, but there was nothing to see except the lights from the businesses
across the street. She stared at the blinking sign
above a soft-serve ice cream parlor. How dangerous
would it be to run across the street and buy a cone?
It wouldn't take more than a minute or two, five at
the most . . .

She had her hand on the door when her yearning for ice cream was overcome by her good sense.
She had always hated movies where the foolish
young woman went into the basement or up the

stairs and walked right into the killer's arms. She didn't know if Vasile was outside the door, but she knew he was out there somewhere.

With a sigh, she sat down on the bed again. She hated waiting. Everyone in her family knew that. It was a family joke that Regan had hated waiting even before she was born and that was why she had emerged from the womb a month early and had been hurrying through life ever since.

Lost in thought, she looked up, startled to discover that she was no longer alone in the room.

"How did you get in here?" she asked, glancing at the door, which was still closed and locked.

Santiago shrugged negligently. "I slid in beneath the door when you weren't looking."

She stared at him, wondering if he was kidding, and then shrugged. Vampires were supposed to be able to squeeze through tight places by dissolving into mist, though she had never seen it done. Apparently, it was more than a myth.

She couldn't help feeling relieved that he was back. Even if she hadn't known where he had gone, she would have known, just by looking at him, that he had fed recently.

"Do you like it?" she blurted. "Drinking blood, I mean?"

He regarded her through fathomless midnight blue eyes. Although his expression remained impassive, she could almost see him trying to decide whether to tell her the harsh truth or a gentle lie.

After a moment, his voice devoid of emotion, he said, "Yes, I like it."

"Did you always like it? I mean, from the very first?"

"Yes."

Even hearing it from his own lips, she found it hard to believe. How could anyone possibly like it?

"Is there anything about being a vampire that you don't like? Anything that you miss? I know I asked you that once before and you said no, but . . ."

"I miss my people," he said quietly. He missed their way of life, missed the rhythm of the changing seasons, the sight of horses running across the prairie, the lonesome howl of the coyote, the throbbing heartbeat of the drum. "I miss listening to the Old Ones relate the ancient tales." He missed hearing the language of his childhood, missed the thrill of hunting the buffalo, and the feasts that followed. "I miss watching the sun rise over our stronghold in the mountains."

She heard the wistful note in his voice and thought how unhappy she would be if everything and everyone she had ever known was gone. It must be a terribly lonely feeling, she thought, knowing that there was no one left in all the world who shared your memories, your experiences, and your childhood.

"So, if there was a cure for being a vampire, would you take it?"

He considered it a moment. Would he give up his preternatural powers if he had the chance? Would he want to be mortal again, his senses limited, his body weak and vulnerable? Would he want to be subject to disease and death?

He shook his head slowly. "I do not think so. In the beginning, perhaps, but now I am content as I am." He glanced at her suitcase. "Are you ready to go?"

"Yes."

He quickly gathered their luggage.

She unlocked the door and followed him out of the room.

Moments later, they were on the highway heading west, toward the Black Hills.

Chapter 13

Regan looked out the window. She had never seen the Black Hills except in movies and photographs, and she was anxious to see the place for herself. It was a land with a lot of history. When Santiago told her about the shaman, she had researched the area on Joaquin's computer. Now, she tried to recall what she had learned.

For centuries untold, the Sioux and Cheyenne had considered the Hills to be sacred ground. The Sioux had tried to regain possession of the Hills for hundreds of years, but with no success. Then, about the same time vampires had been declared an endangered species, the Indians had scored a great victory when legislation had been passed granting the Great Sioux Nation ownership of the Black Hills, which consisted of millions of acres of land. In addition to reclaiming ownership of the Hills, the Lakota had reasserted their right to be a sovereign nation, with their own constitution, their own laws, and their own army.

It was said that the Hills, which rose high above the great plains, were the very heart and soul of the

Lakota people. Pine trees grew in such rich abundance on the hillsides that the sacred Hills looked black from a distance, thus giving them their name. It was a colorful land—green with pines and red with shale and sandstone cliffs. Wildlife was plentiful in the Hills. Bear Butte, another place the Indians held sacred, was also located in the Hills, along with the Devil's Tower, which rose thousands of feet above the surrounding prairie.

Regan glanced at Santiago, wondering if being in the Hills would make him yearn for his old life. She had no idea if the Apache and the Sioux had anything in common other than the fact that they were both Indian nations. She tried to imagine what Santiago had looked like back in the old days, when he had been a young warrior living wild with the Apache. Though he seemed to have been born to wear the black clothing and black duster that was his customary attire, she had no trouble at all picturing him in a deerskin loincloth and moccasins, an eagle feather tied into his long black hair, a slash of war paint across his cheek, and a quiver of arrows slung over his shoulder. The image was not only far too appealing, but far too arousing, as well.

She shook her head, banishing the image from her mind.

As he had the night before, Santiago drove with single-minded purpose, stopping only when Regan expressed the need to stretch her legs, relieve herself, or get something to eat or drink.

Santiago never tired. She often wondered what he thought about as the miles slipped past. Sometimes he seemed like a class H-1 robot, programmed to do nothing more than drive and answer questions.

Discomfited by the silence, she switched on the

radio. Moments later, she wished she hadn't. There had been another murder in You Bet Your Life Park. A young man, nineteen years old, had been found dead at the bottom of the park swimming pool.

"I should be there," she remarked, though she didn't know what good her presence would do. She hadn't given the police much in the way of useful information. She wondered if she should call Flynn and tell him about Santiago's theory that a werewolf was responsible for some of the murders, or if that would just complicate things and make matters worse—or if Flynn would think she was out of her mind, since everyone believed werewolves were extinct.

"There is nothing you could have done," Santiago replied.

His words only reinforced her own thoughts. She felt like a fraud for being on the department payroll. As of yet, she hadn't done a thing to earn her pay. "I should have told Flynn about Vasile."

"He would never believe you."

Once again, his words reflected her own thoughts. She was about to tell him so when her cell phone rang.

It was Flynn. "You picked a hell of a time to go on vacation," he said brusquely. "There's been another death."

"Yes, I know. I just heard about it on the news."

"This one hasn't made the news yet," Flynn said, his voice tight.

Something in his tone sent a chill down her spine. "Who's the victim?"

"A woman." He paused and when he spoke again, she heard the strain in his voice. "I'm the one who found her. I thought . . . dammit, even though I knew you weren't in town, I thought it was you."

Heart pounding, she asked, "Why would you think that?"

"She looks like you," Michael said. "And I don't mean someone who just resembles you. I mean, she looks . . . looked . . . exactly like you."

Regan's grip tightened on the phone until her knuckles went white. "That's not possible."

"I didn't think so either, but she's a dead ringer for you. Sorry, bad choice of words. The M.E. thinks it might be a clone of some kind."

"Why . . ." She swallowed past the lump in her throat. "Why would anyone go to all that trouble?"

"I don't know, but promise me you'll be careful. And call me the minute you get home."

"All right, I will."

"Night, Reggie."

"Good night, Mike."

Regan slipped the phone back into her bag, then stared out the window, shivering convulsively.

"He is only trying to frighten you," Santiago said.

"Why would Mike want to frighten me?"

"Not Flynn," Santiago said. "Vasile."

She glanced at Joaquin. "Are you going to tell me that werewolves are making clones now? Anyway, that kind of thing was outlawed years ago."

"I do not think Vasile has much use for the law."

She couldn't argue with that.

"Even though he is trying to frighten you, the message was for me."

"What do you mean?"

Santiago looked at her. "I think you know."

She did know. Fear tightened its grip on her as

she stared out the window again. Killing a woman who could be her twin was Vasile's way of telling Santiago that he intended to kill her.

The next two nights on the road passed pretty much the same as the first one. They traveled after sunset and they rested during the day.

Now it was night again. Tomorrow night they would reach the Black Hills. Regan glanced up at the sky, at a moon that all too soon would be full, then looked down at her hands, trying to imagine them turning into paws. She ran the pad of her thumb over the ends of her fingernails, trying to imagine them as claws . . .

"Regan."

She looked over at Santiago, blinking rapidly to keep from crying.

"We will find the shaman."

"What if we don't? What if there isn't any cure?" She clenched her hands in her lap. "I'm afraid."

Reaching across the space between them, he folded his hand over hers. His touch was soothing, comforting. She felt her fears melt away. He would protect her, and would risk his life to do so. "Thank you for coming with me."

"You asked me once if I would rather be a werewolf or a vampire," he said. "Do you remember?"

"Yes."

"What would you rather be?"

"Neither! But if I had to choose, I guess I'd want to be a werewolf. I don't want to hide from the sun. I don't want to drink blood. I don't want to be dead and yet not dead."

"We are dead but not dead. We are Undead.

There is a difference, though it is hard to explain. Vampires can learn to control the craving for blood. And now, with synthetic blood, there is no need to hunt."

"But there are still vampires who hunt for prey, vampires who would kill if they could."

"Yes, but humans also kill, and for far less reason than the need to survive."

"That's true, I guess."

"Werewolves, on the other hand, have no control over the urge to kill. When the moon is full, they must shift. Any animal or human that crosses their path when the moon is full is doomed."

"Are there other werewolves besides Vasile?"

"Yes, though no one knows how many. Some say the number must be small. Others disagree."

"So they're not extinct," she murmured. "Damn."

"Long ago, werewolf packs roamed every country in the world, but they were hunted to near extinction. Now it is believed that there are only thirteen packs remaining out of a hundred or more."

"Thirteen," Regan murmured. "Unlucky."

He grunted softly. "Most of them are located in Europe. There is evidence that their numbers are growing. Last I heard, Vasile's pack was located in the forests of Romania, which makes me wonder again what he is doing here, and if he came alone."

Regan nodded. She knew she should be worried about Vasile and what evil he might be concocting, but at the moment, right or wrong, she was more worried about her own future.

"If we cannot find the shaman," Santiago said, "if he has no cure, I can bring you across if we do it before the full moon."

"You mean, make me a vampire?"

He nodded. "Think about it, just in case."

Fanged and furry, or fanged and Undead? It was, she thought glumly, one heck of a choice.

Before sunup, Santiago found a motel where they could spend the day. Regan ate breakfast in the restaurant across the street while Santiago secured their room and then went in search of prey.

She was on her second cup of coffee when he slid into the booth across from her. As always, she couldn't help noticing how attractive he was, or that he moved with a kind of fluid grace that defied description.

"Were you . . . successful?" she asked, wondering if she really wanted to know.

"Of course. I took what I needed and sent her happily on her way, none the worse for the experience."

"Why don't you just drink the synthetic stuff?" she asked. "I'd think it would be easier. On everyone."

He snorted derisively. "Have you ever tasted it?"

"Of course not."

"If you had, you would know the answer."

"I thought it was supposed to taste just like the real thing."

"Not even close."

"Then why do you keep some in your refrigerator?"

He shrugged. "For emergencies. For an occasional guest." He glanced out the window. The sky was turning light in the east. "Are you about through?"

Regan followed his gaze. "Yes, let's go."

Santiago paid the bill and darted across the street

to their motel room. Grabbing her handbag, Regan hurried after him.

It was pretty much like every other motel room she had ever seen—a queen-sized bed flanked by matching nightstands, a dresser, and a portable Satellite Screen bolted to the wall. The carpet was an unremarkable shade of brown. The bathroom had a combination tub and shower. The counter-top was puke green.

Regan glanced around, dismayed when she realized there was only one room.

She looked over at Santiago, and quickly looked away.

"It troubles you that there is only one room."

"Yeah."

"Afraid I might want to share your bed?"

She stared at him, wondering why the thought wasn't as repulsive as it should have been. She really was losing her mind, she thought, to even consider sleeping in the same bed with a vampire, no matter how sexy he was, or how attracted she was to him.

"Not to worry," he said dryly. "I will sleep on the floor under the bed."

"*Under* the bed? Wouldn't it be easier to just get another room? I mean, I haven't noticed anyone following us, have you?"

"No, but I will not leave you alone."

"I admire your sense of chivalry, I really do, but . . ." She lifted one shoulder and let it fall. "I don't know what help you'll be if Vasile happens to show up while you're asleep."

"If you need me, I will know it. Self-preservation is very strong in my kind, as is the instinct to protect those we . . ."

Regan's heart skipped a beat as she waited for him to finish his thought.

"Those we care about."

"And you care about me?"

"More than is good for either of us."

"I care for you, too," she murmured, and wondered how and when it had happened. She had known him only a short time. They had shared little more than a few kisses and yet, in spite of the danger that threatened her and the nagging fear that she might be a werewolf, she couldn't think of anywhere else she would rather be, or anyone else she would rather be with.

As if sensing her thoughts, Santiago closed the distance between them and drew her into his arms. "Do you know how beautiful you are? So incredibly beautiful." His hand moved in her hair, lightly massaging her scalp.

A shuddering sigh escaped Regan's lips. How could such a simple touch feel so erotic?

"Your spirit is so strong," he went on, his voice low and whiskey smooth, "and yet you are so fragile. So desirable . . ." His lips brushed hers lightly. "I never intended to love anyone again."

She blinked up at him. "You . . . you love me?"

"It does not please you?"

"I didn't think vampires were capable of love." But even as she uttered the words, she remembered the woman he had told her about. The Gypsy girl, Marishka.

Santiago looked down at her, amusement dancing in his dark eyes. "Do you think we are only capable of hatred?"

"I . . . I sort of thought all those human emotions

were, I don't know, wiped out when you became a vampire."

He grunted softly. "It would be easier if they were."

"I find it hard to believe that the vampire who killed those teenagers was harboring any tender feelings."

"Like anything else, what is not nourished gradually withers and dies."

"So you have to make a conscious effort to hang onto your human emotions?"

He nodded.

"I'm glad you did."

"As am I," he said, his eyes glowing with an intensity that sent a shiver down her spine.

Regan's heart began to beat a little faster. Hardly aware of what she was doing, she tilted her head back a little, hoping he would kiss her.

But it wasn't her mouth he was looking at. His gaze was focused on the hollow of her throat—and the pulse beating there.

"Joaquin . . ."

"One taste?" he asked, his voice almost a growl. "A sip, no more."

"Don't, please," she whispered. "You're scaring me."

His arm tightened around her waist. She had often heard of a man's arm feeling like a steel band. Usually, it was just an exaggeration, but not in this case. She saw the change in his eyes, saw the internal struggle as he fought down the urge to take what he wanted by force, if necessary. She had never done drugs, but she thought being a vampire must be a little like being an addict, the craving for blood a constant clamor for one more hit, one more taste, one more . . .

She had always admired his ability to be in control of the hunger that lurked forever just under the surface. She only hoped he didn't lose hold on that control now.

She stood quiescent in his embrace, afraid to move for fear any movement on her part would be mistaken for flight, arousing the vampire's instinctive urge to hunt. She could feel her heart beating erratically in her chest, hear it roaring in her ears, and knew that, with his preternatural senses, he could hear it, too. He was still staring at her throat.

"Santiago," she implored. "Please, don't . . ."

"Ah, Regan, you tempt me almost beyond my power to resist."

Hardly daring to breathe, she clung to the word "almost," felt her whole body go weak with relief when his arm fell away from her waist and he backed away from her.

"Rest well," he said, and before she could reply, he turned and slid gracefully under the bed, hidden from her sight by the overhang of the bedspread.

She stood there a moment, her heart still beating wildly, unable to think clearly. So much had happened in the last few days, she feared she was on sensory overload. Too many dead bodies. Learning that werewolves weren't extinct. Being bitten. Living with the fear that she would become a werewolf at the next full moon. Meeting Santiago. Kissing Santiago. How much more could one girl take and remain sane?

She stared at the place where he had stood only moments before. Vampires had amazing powers. Could he see through the bedspread? Would he watch if she undressed for bed, or, rather than take that chance, should she just sleep in her clothes?

Maybe he was already unconscious, trapped in the Dark Sleep of his kind, but how was she to know?

And how was she going to get any sleep, knowing he was in the same room?

Grabbing her overnight case, she went into the bathroom and locked the door, then stood at the sink, staring at her reflection in the mirror. What would she look like as a werewolf? Would she have blond fur and green eyes? What would it be like to run on all fours? To have a tail? And sharp white teeth, the better to eat you with, my dear?

She had told Santiago she would rather be a werewolf. For one thing, vampires were vampires every day, or night, of the year, whereas werewolves were compelled to change only during the full moon. True, Vasile could shift whenever he wished, but he was a rare exception. If she went into the woods or some other unpopulated place before she shifted, perhaps she could avoid killing anyone.

As for being a vampire, except for Santiago and perhaps a few other ancient vampires, the Undead were helpless during the day, every day of the year, dragged down into the darkness of oblivion whether they wished it or not. They had to drink blood to survive. They had to live in protected areas, and if someone came along and changed the law and that protection was lifted, they would again be hunted because they were different and therefore to be feared and destroyed.

"Eeny, meeny, miney, moe . . . werewolf or vampire, which way should I go?"

She was losing it, she thought, stifling the urge to laugh. No doubt the men in white coats would show up and haul her off to the funny farm long before she and Santiago reached the Black Hills.

And wouldn't the attendants be surprised when they discovered they had a werewolf in their midst?

"Stop it!" Undressing, she took a quick shower, pulled on her nightgown, and brushed her teeth, all the while refusing to think of anything but the task at hand. There was no Santiago. There were no werewolves. She was getting ready for bed. Soon she would be asleep.

She switched off the bathroom light and hurried across the floor to the bed. She slipped under the covers, turned off the bedside lamp, closed her eyes, and took several deep, calming breaths.

They would find the cave. They would find the shaman. He would help her with the cure. And everything would be all right.

Santiago loved her . . . it was her last conscious thought before sleep found her.

The following evening they stopped at a small sporting goods store to buy suitable clothing and footwear for climbing. Santiago had chosen—what else but black, of course. Black T-shirt, black jacket, black pants, black boots. Regan picked a pair of blue jeans, a red T-shirt, a denim jacket, and brown boots. She also bought a pair of white shorts and sneakers in case the weather was warm during the day.

The store also sold groceries. Santiago followed her up and down the aisles. She looked at him inquiringly when he told her to buy enough food for two.

"The extra food is for the shaman," he explained. "It is customary to take a gift when one is asking for a favor."

Regan nodded. That made sense. In addition to

the food, Santiago tossed a small sack of tobacco into the cart. "Also a gift."

When the clerk at the check-out counter found out they were going into the Hills, he admonished them to be careful, warning them to be on the alert, not only for wild animals, but also for wild Indians.

"The Sioux don't take lightly to trespassers these days," he said somberly. "It's almost like we're back in the eighteen-hundreds, when a man was putting his life on the line every time he entered Indian territory. I've heard things." He shook his head, then, after looking around to make sure they were alone, he whispered, "There's been some killings up in the Hills. It's all hush-hush, but word gets around, you know?"

"Thank you for the warning," Santiago said.

The man nodded. "You, ah, might want to think about buying a gun, if you don't have one already."

Santiago smiled faintly. "That will not be necessary." Regan already had a pistol. He knew she carried it with her at all times and slept with it tucked under her pillow. The scent of the weapon was a part of her, a very tiny, rather disagreeable part which, perversely, added to her allure. He had never been with a woman who possessed not only the knowledge but also the means to destroy him.

Gathering their purchases, Regan and Santiago left the store.

"Hope to see you again," the clerk called after them.

A sentiment with which Regan heartily agreed.

At the car, Santiago stowed all the food into his backpack, so that all Regan had to carry was her sleeping bag and her extra clothing, and the six candy bars she had added to the cart at the last minute.

"Comfort food," she had told Santiago with a shrug, thinking that on a trip like this one, chocolate was the one thing she didn't want to be without.

Bathed in the light of the moon and stars, the sacred Black Hills rose up from the plains like some mystical mountain of legend. It was here that the Sioux and Cheyenne Indians had roamed for hundreds of years, here that General George Armstrong Custer had found gold, thereby sealing the fate of the Indians who had lived there at the time.

The Hills belonged to the Sioux now, and members of the tribe from all over the world had come home. Large herds of buffalo foraged in the Hills again. Deer and elk grazed in the deep grasses, bears roamed the timbered hills, wolves and coyotes stalked the land, birds nested in the trees, fish filled the rivers and streams, beavers built dams, and the spotted eagle again soared over the tops of the sacred mountains.

Santiago drove as close to the Hills as he could and then he pulled off the road and parked the car. He shouldered his backpack, helped Regan with hers, and started walking.

Regan followed close behind, hoping she could keep up. She considered herself to be in pretty good shape, all things considered. She worked out from time to time, and she jogged around the department track on a regular basis, but she was afraid hiking to the top of the Black Hills was out of her league.

The landscape was beautiful and eerie in the darkness. Regan knew it was her imagination, but as they started their trek up the mountain, she was certain she could feel the spirits of all those who had inhabited the Hills in years gone by hovering nearby. Their voices called to her, muffled by the evening breeze, so that she wasn't sure if the mountain's ghosts were singing a welcome or chanting a warning. She listened to the sounds of the night—the rustle of the leaves on the trees, the lonely wail of a coyote, the cautious hoot of an owl.

Beside her, Santiago swore softly.

"What is it?" she asked.

"The owl," he said, and she heard the faint note of self-mockery in his voice. "The Apache believe the call of an owl is a harbinger of death."

"Maybe he knows there's a vampire nearby," Regan said with a wry grin.

"Perhaps."

"You can't be afraid of dying," she remarked, "since you're already dead."

He looked at her, his eyes glowing like a cat's in the darkness. "But you, my lovely little mortal, are not."

His words sent a cold shiver racing down her spine.

They walked for hours, steadily climbing higher and higher. When Regan grew weary, Santiago carried her. At first, she protested, but then, seeing how effortlessly he managed it, she rested her head on his shoulder and went to sleep.

Santiago gazed down at the woman in his arms. Seeing her, holding her, only seemed to emphasize how empty his life had been. For centuries, he had been content to drift through his existence, always keeping his distance from those around him, never becoming involved in the world or its affairs.

But Regan . . . there was something about her, an

air of strength and vulnerability he found endearing. Of course, it didn't hurt that her skin was smooth and baby soft, or that her body was young and supple, or that her hair was like a shimmering river of gold where it fell over his arm.

He loved her. And he wanted her, wanted her with a single-mindedness such as he had not known since he became a new vampire drunk on the scent and the taste of blood. He ached with wanting her, not just her blood, but her love, as well. How had he existed all these centuries without her? And how would their relationship, new and tenuous as it was, change when she did?

He rubbed his cheek against her hair. No doubt she would make a beautiful wolf.

He walked until he sensed the coming dawn, then searched for a place where Regan could spend the day. He settled on a small clearing surrounded by tall trees. Holding Regan in one arm, he shook off his backpack, then unrolled her sleeping bag and spread it on the ground. He removed Regan's backpack and gently lowered her onto the sleeping bag, drawing half of it over her. When that was done, he dug a pit and laid a fire.

His skin tingled, the minor discomfort turning to pain as the sun began to climb higher in the sky.

"Regan." He shook her shoulder. "Regan, wake up."

With a sleepy sound, she opened her eyes. "What's wrong?"

"It is morning. I must go find a place to rest. Stay here until I return."

She glanced around. There were trees everywhere. The sky was still dark, though a faint light glowed in the east. "Where will you stay?"

"Do not worry. I will find a place."

"But where . . ."

"I do not have time to explain." He kissed her quickly on the cheek, then vanished from her sight.

Yawning, Regan sat up, wondering if she would ever get used to his coming and going so quickly. And where the heck was he going? As far as she could see, there was no place where he could hide from the sun. Reminding herself that he had existed for hundreds of years, she slid back into her sleeping bag and closed her eyes.

The sun was high in the sky when next she woke. Rising, she stretched the kinks from her back and shoulders, wondering what she was going to do while Santiago slept. He had told her to stay where she was, though there was little need, since there was nowhere to go. A glance at her watch told her it was almost two o'clock. How was she going to pass the hours until sundown?

Rummaging in her backpack, she found a box of matches and lit the fire Santiago had laid, then filled a blue-speckled coffee pot with water and put it in the coals. While waiting for the water to heat up, she found a convenient tree to hide behind while she relieved herself, though she didn't know why she was hiding. There was no one to see her.

Breakfast was a cup of instant coffee, a peach, and an enormous piece of coffee cake, which she figured she would walk off come nightfall.

When she finished eating, she put out the fire, brushed her teeth, changed her underwear, again behind a tree, and then, with nothing else to do, she decided to take a short walk. Taking her gun from her handbag, she dropped it in the pocket of her jacket.

The scenery was breathtakingly beautiful. The

hills were covered with trees and shrubs and wild-flowers. The sky was a clear, brilliant blue. There were birds and squirrels and chipmunks every-where. She spent the better part of an hour watching two gray squirrels chase each other from tree to tree. Must be nice, she thought, to be so carefree, with nothing more worrisome than finding your next meal.

Returning to her campsite, she fixed a quick lunch; then she sat down on her sleeping bag and turned on her MBox, hoping that listening to some soothing music would help relax her. With her back against a tree, she gazed at the countryside, trying to imagine what it must have been like back in the 1800s, when the whites were moving westward and the Indians were fighting to hang onto their land and their way of life. She had never been much for old Western movies, but she had watched a few in her time. Her favorites had been films like *Windwalker* and *Dances With Wolves* and *Winterhawk,* and even the more contemporary *Thunderheart,* movies where the Indians had been portrayed as real people who were trying to survive in a harsh environment instead of mindless savages who killed indiscriminately and spoke in broken English. She had to admit, most of those films had also featured darkly handsome heroes, like Michael Dante in *Winterhawk.* She had watched that one over and over again, imagining herself as the innocent young white girl who had been kidnapped by Winterhawk and had refused to be rescued when her uncle found her.

With a sigh, Regan closed her eyes, imagining Santiago as a wild savage and herself as the young white girl he kidnapped. For a time, she let herself get lost in the fantasy. She could see it all so clearly, the two of them riding across the sunlit prairie, stopping beside a ribbon of blue water, making love on a buffalo robe under the stars, standing on a high bluff to watch a herd of horses running across the plains. It took her a moment to realize that the sound of hoofbeats growing ever closer wasn't in her mind.

With a sense of foreboding, she opened her eyes.

Three mounted warriors clad in breechclouts and carrying bows and arrows stared down at her.

Chapter 14

Regan looked up at the Indians, her heart in her throat. Was she dreaming? Please, she thought, let me be dreaming! She blinked and blinked again.

They were still there.

A warrior with an eagle feather tied in his long black hair urged his horse forward a few steps. "Who are you?" he demanded. "What are you doing here? This is Lakota land. The *wasichu* are not allowed. To cross our border without permission is punishable by death."

Fear knotted in the pit of Regan's belly, and with it the urge to laugh. Mortals who strayed into You Bet Your Life Park did so at their own peril. Apparently that was true for whites who wandered, uninvited, into the Black Hills, as well.

"I'm . . . that is . . ." What should she say? That she was lost? That she was looking for a shaman? She slipped her hand into her jacket pocket, her fingers curling around the butt of her gun, and then, slowly, she withdrew her hand. She couldn't just shoot them, not when she didn't know if they meant her any harm. Besides, she had a feeling any one of them could put an arrow into her before she could draw and fire her own weapon.

The three warriors spoke to each other in a language Regan assumed was Lakota, then Eagle Feather dismounted and stalked toward her.

She shrieked when he grabbed her by the arm and hauled her to her feet. "Let me go!"

The warrior didn't respond. Instead, he lifted her onto the back of his horse, then vaulted up behind her. Reaching around her, he took up the reins and urged his horse down the hill. The other two warriors followed.

"Wait!" Regan cried. "My things. I need my purse and my . . ."

But the Indian wasn't listening.

She told herself there was no reason to be afraid. These weren't uncivilized savages and this wasn't the nineteenth century. In spite of what Eagle Feather had said, she couldn't believe they would kill her just for trespassing! But maybe she was just fooling herself. Hadn't the clerk at the sporting goods store warned them to be on the lookout for wild Indians? What had he said? *The Sioux don't take lightly to trespassers these days?*

They could kill her, she thought, and no one could do a thing about it. They had their own land now, their own laws, and she was trespassing.

That thought was uppermost in her mind as they rode through a stand of tall timber that opened onto a flat meadow, and she beheld an Indian village for the first time. What looked like hundreds of tepees were spread alongside a slow-moving river. Horses grazed in the tall grass. Men and women, all dressed in Native attire, could be seen going about their daily tasks. Children ran among the conical hide lodges. Several old men were playing a dice game. Dogs slept in the shade. She couldn't help grinning at the sight of two teenage boys clad in buckskin leggings tossing a football back and forth.

Eagle Feather reined his horse to a stop in front of a large tepee decorated with stars and half-moons. Regan checked her watch. It was three hours until sundown. She only hoped she was still alive when Santiago came looking for her.

The warrior riding behind her slid off the rump of the horse, then lifted her from its back.

Regan glanced around, her apprehension growing as dozens of men, women, and children gathered around her, their expressions ranging from merely curious to openly hostile. Angry voices rose on the wind, some of them in English, some in Lakota.

She clenched her hands at her sides, determined to keep her face impassive lest they see how frightened she was.

A sudden stillness fell over the crowd as a bent old man came into view. He leaned heavily on a wooden staff as he slowly made his way to the center of the group. His skin was the color and texture of old saddle leather. An eagle feather was tied into one long gray braid.

The old warrior stopped in front of Regan, his dark eyes moving over her from head to foot. "Who are you?" he asked. "Why have you come here?"

One look into his eyes and Regan knew she didn't dare lie to him. "My name is Regan Delaney. I came here looking for a man, a shaman."

The old man's eyes glowed with interest. "What is this shaman's name?"

"I don't know."

"Then how will you find him?"

"I'm traveling with a friend. He knows the way."

"Where is he, this friend of yours?"

"I don't know. He was to meet me this evening."

"Why do you need a medicine man? Are you sick?"

"No. Yes. Well, not exactly, but I might be. I was told the shaman in the Black Hills could help me."

The old man grunted softly. Turning to the man beside him, he spoke a few words in his native tongue, then walked away.

Before Regan could call after the old man to ask what was going on, a grim-faced warrior led her to a small lodge and pushed her inside.

"Stay here," the warrior said brusquely, and dropped the door flap into place.

Regan glanced around the dim lodge. It was empty. No blanket. No firepit. Nothing to eat or drink. Nothing to do but pace the dirt floor while her imagination conjured up one horrible scenario after another, each one worse than the last. The Indians would kill her and take her scalp. They would leave her in here to starve to death. They would skin her alive. They would bury her up to her neck in an ant hill and cover her head with honey. They would . . .

Muttering, "Stop it!" she sat down on the hard-packed earth and forced herself to take slow, deep breaths. Santiago would be rising soon, and he would come for her. Of that, she had no doubt.

* * *

Santiago rose as soon as the sun slid behind the horizon. For a moment, he simply stood there, basking in the beauty of his surroundings. It was a wild and beautiful land painted in vivid hues, from the rusty reds and earth tones of the shale and sandstone cliffs to the deep green of the pines. Animals were plentiful—buffalo and elk, beaver and muskrat, white-tailed deer and mule deer, bighorn sheep and mountain goats, eagles and hawks.

Standing there, his face lifted to the sky, he could feel the ancient power sleeping deep in the heart of the sacred Hills. He had felt similar vestiges of power at Stonehenge, in Chaco Canyon, at the Mayan pyramids, and at the pyramids at Giza, but nothing as strong as the power he felt here, in this place. For hundreds of years, mystics and shamans had come to the Black Hills seeking visions. The Lakota believed that the sacred *Paha Sapa* were the heart and soul of their people, and although Santiago was not Lakota, he was Indian enough to understand why the Lakota revered this place above all others. He knew of their unending struggles to regain the land through the centuries. He knew of the battles they had fought against the whites in the past, remembered their victories and their defeats. He had met some of their leaders. Men like Crazy Horse, Red Cloud, Sitting Bull, Two Hawks Flying, and Black Elk. All had been brave warriors, proud of their heritage, willing to sacrifice everything they possessed to preserve their way of life. He wondered if those ancient warriors knew that the Hills again belonged to their rightful owners.

Santiago blew out a sigh as the sun sank further into the west, splashing the horizon in vivid blood red hues, reminding him that he had not fed, but

there was no time to search for prey now. He had
left Regan alone long enough. He smiled at the
prospect of seeing her again, and then frowned as
a sense of foreboding rose up in his mind.

It took him only moments to return to where he
had left her.

Less time than that to realize she was gone.

He scanned the ground, his preternatural sight
easily picking up the tracks of three unshod ponies
and the moccasin prints of a Lakota warrior. He
read the story quickly. Three Indians had ridden
into Regan's camp. One had dismounted, put her
on his horse, and carried her away.

He glanced briefly at the hoofprints cut into the
ground, but it was Regan's scent he followed through
the gathering dusk.

Regan lifted one corner of the door flap and
peeked outside. The sun was setting in a splash of
crimson. Plumes of blue-gray smoke rose from a
multitude of smoke holes and cook fires. The scent
of roasting meat reminded her that she hadn't had
anything to eat or drink since early afternoon.

Looking at the activity in the camp, it was difficult
to believe that she hadn't been transported back in
time to the early 1800s. Except for the boys she had
seen playing football earlier, there were no visible
signs of civilization. No cars. No houses. Nothing
but a vast untamed land, tepees, horses, and dogs.
And people wearing native dress. If she wasn't being
held prisoner, she might have thought she had
stumbled onto an old Western movie set, only these

people weren't actors, and there were no lights, and no cameras. And no sign of the Seventh Cavalry!

She watched the sun sink further behind the Hills, her anxiety growing as she wondered what was taking Santiago so long. Surely he was awake by now!

Nearing the outskirts of the village, Santiago heard the slow, steady beat of a drum, smelled the slightly nauseating scent of roasting buffalo meat and the acrid odor of smoke curling from numerous cookfires.

He paused at the tree line, his gaze sweeping the lodges spread along the river. Seeing so many tepees took him back in time, back to a large Lakota village camped along the Little Big Horn in the summer of 1876.

What a day that had been! It was a day still discussed in some places, a day made famous by the death of George Armstrong Custer and his command. Santiago had been unable to fight in that epic battle, but he had gotten his licks in after the sun went down. Impervious to enemy fire, he had slipped into the ranks of the soldiers under Reno's command. The soldiers had taken refuge on a hill now known as Reno's Hill. He had counted coup on a dozen bluecoats, killed a handful, and fed off a few others. His only regret was that he had been unable to fight alongside Crazy Horse.

Shaking the memories aside, Santiago ghosted past the sentries, strode into the center of the camp, and called for the peace chief of the village.

Moments later, a tall warrior carrying a feathered lance strode into view. "Why have you come here?"

"You have my woman. I have come to claim her."

"She is trespassing. The penalty is death."

"She is with me, and you will not touch her."

The warrior stared at Santiago. "How are you called?"

"I am Joaquin. Crazy Horse called me Rides in Darkness."

A collective gasp rose from the crowd that had gathered around Santiago and the chief. As one, the people took a step backward. It might have been respect. It might have been fear.

"Your name is well known to us," the warrior said, his voice tinged with awe. "I am Hunonpa Luta. It has been many years since you walked among us."

"If you know who I am, then you know of my power."

Hunonpa Luta nodded. "It is said that you have great magic."

Santiago nodded. "Release my woman."

Hunonpa Luta spoke to the man at his right, who immediately ran off in the direction of a small lodge near the edge of the camp circle.

Santiago waited, his face impassive as he watched the warrior duck into the lodge. He emerged a few moments later, pulling Regan along behind him.

Santiago's gaze quickly moved over her from head to foot. As near as he could tell, she was scared but unhurt.

Her relief at seeing him was a palpable thing. With a cry, she wrenched her arm from the warrior's grasp and ran the remaining few feet to where Santiago waited.

He caught her to him, one arm slipping around her waist. "Are you all right?"

"I am now that you're here."

"Did they hurt you?"

She shook her head no just as her stomach growled.

"When did you eat last?"

"This afternoon."

Santiago looked at the chief. "My woman is hungry. What has happened to Lakota hospitality, that a guest is not offered food and drink?"

A muscle twitched in the warrior's cheek. "I will have my woman prepare something immediately," Hunonpa Luta said, his voice brittle. "Will you stay the night?"

"It is not possible, but I thank you for the offer."

"Then we will have a feast to honor your return to our people."

Santiago nodded. It would have been rude to refuse the chief's hospitality. He gestured toward the lodge where Regan had been held prisoner. "We will wait there."

Inclining his head, the chief went to his own lodge. Seeing that there was to be no further confrontation, the crowd dispersed.

Taking Regan by the hand, Santiago led her back to the lodge at the edge of the village.

Inside, he drew her into his arms, his hands running lightly over her hair, her face, her arms. "I should not have left you alone."

"I don't know what else you could have done," she replied, then frowned. "Where did you spend the day?"

Santiago considered his answer for a moment, wondering what her reaction would be. For all that she was a hunter—and he had no doubt she was a good one—she still had a lot to learn about the vampire way of life.

"I slept in the earth," he replied.

"In the earth? Like, under the ground?"

He nodded.

"Sounds, um, dirty."

He laughed, charmed as always by her candor. "Do I look dirty?"

She frowned. "No, you don't. Why don't you?"

"I cannot explain it, but the earth does not cling to us."

"Interesting. I suppose you go down six feet?"

"Ah, Regan," he exclaimed, "you are an endless delight. It is only necessary to go down deep enough to hide from the sun."

She shuddered at the thought. All those bugs and worms . . .

"As always, you see only the worst," he remarked.

"I'm sorry, I just don't see anything good about it."

"I suppose it depends on your perspective. Personally . . ." He fell silent as four women entered the lodge. The first one carried a clay bowl filled with soup. The second carried a plate heaped high with roasted meat in one hand and a tin cup of coffee in the other. The third carried a pair of backrests and a blanket, which she spread on the floor. The fourth carried a flat piece of wood and a candle.

It was amazing, Regan thought, how a blanket and a candle transformed the tepee from a prison to a comfortable abode.

Santiago nodded at the women. "*Pilamaya.*"

"Do you require anything else?" asked the first woman.

Santiago looked at Regan. She shook her head.

"Someone will come for you," the woman said. Gesturing for the other women to follow her, she left the lodge.

One woman stayed behind. She was younger than the other three, tall and slender, with sleek black hair and large brown eyes. She looked at Santiago expectantly.

"Is there something you want?" he asked.

With a hand that trembled slightly, she pushed her hair away from her neck. In a voice that also trembled, she said, "I am for you."

"What does she mean?" Regan asked.

"You have your food," he replied, gesturing at the meal spread on the blanket. "And I have mine."

"She's your dinner?" Regan asked in disbelief.

"So it would seem."

"You're not going to . . . are you?"

"It would be an insult to refuse."

Slipping his arm around the girl's waist, he drew her close. He could feel her body trembling. "Relax," he said quietly, "I will not hurt you." He gazed deep into her eyes for a moment. Capturing her mind with his, he assured her once more that there was nothing to fear, and then he bent his head to her neck. He took only a taste, and then released her from his spell. "*Pilamaya.*"

Looking vaguely disoriented, she smiled and left the lodge.

Regan stared at him, her own hunger forgotten. "I can't believe you did that."

"You did not have to watch."

"How could I help it? Watching a vampire feed is something you don't see every day."

"I would not call that feeding," he said with a wry grin. "I took only a drop, to be polite." He would have taken more had he not been aware of Regan's horrified reaction at watching him.

"Polite," she repeated. "Yeah, right." She tilted her head to the side. "So, that little bit filled you up?"

"No, but it is not necessary for me to . . . dine every night."

"Oh. How long can you go without, ah, you know?"

"As long as necessary."

"I always heard vampires went a little bonkers if they didn't feed regularly."

He lifted one brow. "Bonkers?"

"You know, crazy. Off the deep end. Nutters."

"I know what it means," he said dryly. "Though I confess I have never heard anyone use it before. But you needn't worry. I am old enough to control my passions." His gaze touched her lips, her throat, moved down to linger on her breasts before returning to her face. "All of them."

"That's . . . ah, good to know."

He gestured at the food spread on the blanket. "I thought you were hungry?"

"I was."

"Sit," Santiago said. "Eat."

"I'm not sure I can now."

"Do not make it more than it was," he said with a laugh. "She has no doubt lost more blood cutting her finger than what I took."

He was probably right, but it was still disconcerting to see him actually feed off of someone. When her stomach growled again, she sat down. Since he had "eaten" in front of her, she didn't feel the least bit self-conscious eating in front of him.

Sitting cross-legged on the blanket, she picked up a piece of meat, her expression dubious as she took a bite. Hungry as she was, she couldn't help wondering what kind of meat she was eating. In the old days, when food was scarce, the Indians had eaten their horses and their dogs. But food wasn't scarce these days. The Black Hills were thick with game. She had never eaten venison or buffalo, but either one was preferable to eating a dog or a horse. She took another bite, hoping it was buffalo or venison. Whatever it was, it was delicious.

Knowing that his presence made her nervous, Santiago went to the door and peered out into the darkness. They would leave as soon as possible after the feast.

He tried to concentrate on something other than the woman behind him, but it was impossible. In a remarkably short time, Regan Delaney had become the most important thing in his life. Now, all he had to do was decide what to do about her.

After what seemed like hours but was probably no more than forty minutes, a young boy summoned them to the feast.

Regan didn't know what she had expected, but she was somewhat taken aback to find what must have been the whole village gathered outside. Men, women, and children sat in a large circle. Several large fires provided warmth and light.

The chief of the village rose to meet them, inviting them to sit at his side. As the honored guest, Santiago would ordinarily have been served first, but since it was known that he shunned food, Regan was served first. The chief and camp leaders were served next, and then the rest of the tribe.

All Regan's qualms about what might be served were swept away when she was handed a large plate heaped with what she hoped was a steak, potatoes, and corn on the cob.

"They prepared your meal especially for you," Santiago told her. "Everyone else is eating buffalo tongue and hump. And dog. Among the Lakota, it is highly prized."

Regan glanced at her plate in horror. "This is dog meat?"

"Only that one small piece," he said, pointing at a tiny morsel. "Courtesy demands that each one present have a piece."

"But . . . I can't eat a dog."

"It will be seen as an insult if you refuse."

Regan swallowed hard, suddenly aware that all eyes were watching her. Taking a deep breath, she swallowed the tiny piece of meat and quickly washed it down with a drink of coffee.

"How was it?" Santiago asked.

"I don't know. I ate it so quickly, I couldn't taste it."

He laughed softly. "Well done."

Now that she'd eaten the dog meat, she was glad to see that she was no longer the center of attention.

After a while, the low beat of a drum could be heard above the hum of conversation. Without intending to eavesdrop, she overheard snatches of conversation. One woman was lamenting the fact that her little boy still sucked his thumb. One of the men was griping about the price of fuel. Another was wishing he didn't have to go back to work the following week.

Regan couldn't help smiling. They might dress

and live like their ancestors, but it seemed they had the same problems and concerns as everybody else.

When the feast was over, an enormous drum was brought into the center of the circle. Four men sat around it. As they began to beat the drum, a number of men got up to dance. When they were through, the women danced.

Regan was about to ask Santiago why the men and women didn't dance together when they formed two lines facing each other.

"Come on," Santiago said, taking her by the hand.

She started to protest, then thought better of it. The steps looked simple enough, and she might never get another chance to dance with the Lakota.

She couldn't take her eyes off Santiago. He moved like a cat, his feet hardly touching the ground, his every movement supple and sensual. The heat of his eyes speared through her when his gaze met hers.

When the dance was over, they returned to their seats.

"We should go," Santiago said.

Regan nodded, though she was reluctant to leave. There was something hypnotic about watching the flames, listening to the beat of the drum, feeling the evening breeze feather through her hair. As she had once before, she seemed to hear the spirits of those long dead whispering to her.

Santiago was about to get up when an old man stepped into the circle. As soon as he sat down, a group of children surrounded him.

"What's going on?" Regan asked.

"He is going to tell them a story."

"Can we stay until it's over?"

Santiago nodded. "If you wish."

"What is he saying?" Regan asked, unable to understand the storyteller's language.

"It is a story about Old Man Coyote and his brother. It seems that one day, Old Man Coyote and his brother, who were bored and hungry, went out walking together. After a time, they came upon a chipmunk and a frog who were sunning themselves on the banks of a river. 'Ah,' Old Man Coyote said to his brother, 'here is our dinner.' But before they ate them, Old Man Coyote decided to see if the chipmunk or the frog could entertain them."

"Dinner and a floor show," Regan remarked dryly.

"Indeed." Santiago said, smiling. "'Can you sing or do a trick?' Old Man Coyote asked the chipmunk. 'If you can sing or make us laugh, we might not eat you.' The chipmunk didn't believe Old Man Coyote because everyone knew Coyote was a trickster. But the chipmunk was a smart fellow. 'I can't sing, but I can spin in circles,' the little chipmunk said. So Old Man Coyote said, 'show me,' and the chipmunk began to spin around and around. He spun around Old Man Coyote and his brother until they were both dizzy, and then the chipmunk ran up the trunk of a nearby tree and hid in the branches.

"This made Coyote's brother angry. 'Let us build a fire and throw the frog into it so he doesn't run away,' he said. So Old Man Coyote gathered some wood for a fire.

"Now the frog was also a clever young fellow and before Old Man Coyote or his brother could throw him into the flames, the frog hopped toward the fire as if that was where he wanted to go. Confused by the frog's odd behavior, Old Man Coyote and his brother stared at each other. Then Old Man Coyote said, 'Maybe this one belongs to the fire clan. If so, he will hide in the fire and it will not hurt him.'

"'Let us put him in the river then,' said Old Man Coyote's brother. 'We will drown him and then we will cook him and eat him.'

"So Old Man Coyote dropped the frog into the river and the frog swam away, leaving Old Man Coyote and his brother still hungry but much wiser."

When the story was over, Santiago thanked the chief for his hospitality.

Twenty minutes later, Santiago and Regan rode out of the village. The chief had gifted each of them with a horse. Regan's was a lovely chestnut mare with one white stocking.

"I didn't know the Indians lived like that," Regan remarked when the village lay behind them.

"Some do," Santiago replied, "though only a handful live in the old way all year long. Most return to their homes in the city when winter sets in."

"They seemed very . . . fierce," she said, thinking of the three who had found her. "At least at first."

Santiago grunted softly. Many of the Lakota had gone back to living in the old way, some full time, some only during the summer. They hunted the deer and the buffalo. They performed the Sun Dance ceremony. They lived in hide lodges. The women tanned hides and gathered wild fruits and vegetables, the old men told the ancient stories. Fathers and grandfathers taught their sons to follow the path of a warrior, to value generosity and bravery, to defend those who were helpless, and to provide for those who could not provide for themselves.

Thinking back to his own days among the Apache, Santiago had to admit that it was a good way to live.

The breeze shifted, carrying Regan's scent to his nostrils. She smelled of perspiration and the meal she had just eaten. Fainter, but just as easily identified were the lingering scents of her shampoo and the soap she used to wash her clothes. The warm, heady fragrance of the woman herself called to him, as did the siren call of her life's blood.

He slid a glance in her direction. His fangs pricked his tongue as his gaze caressed her neck. While it was true that he didn't have to feed every night, that didn't mean he was immune to the scent of prey, especially when it was wrapped up in a package as tempting and beguiling as that of the woman riding beside him.

"Joaquin, is something wrong?"

He dragged his gaze from her throat. "No, my lovely one."

She didn't miss the taut line of his shoulders, the glow in his eyes. She wondered just how much control he really had over his passions. All of them.

After a few hours, she was no longer worrying about Santiago's passions. She had never been on a horse before and while she rather enjoyed the sensation of riding, she ached in places she'd never known she had.

They made a brief stop at their old campsite to gather her handbag and their sleeping bags and supplies, and then they were riding through the darkness again, climbing steadily upward.

Regan looked up sharply when the melancholy howl of a wolf rose on a vagrant breeze. A chill went down her spine as the cry was picked up by another wolf and then another. Gazing into the darkness, she had an almost overwhelming urge to peel off her clothes and run wild through the night, to lift her face to the heavens and howl along with the wolves.

Her aches forgotten, she glanced up at the sky. A shiver coursed through her body when she saw the moon. It rode high in the night sky, a bright white sphere that was almost full.

Santiago glanced from Regan to the moon and back again. He could feel the tension radiating off her, sense her uneasiness, her fear. He didn't have to be a wise man to know what was troubling her. The moon was almost full. But there was nothing to worry about. They had almost reached their destination.

The cave was located near the crest of a mountain top. A gray horse grazed near the entrance. It looked up, ears twitching at their approach.

Santiago paused, his senses testing the wind and the surrounding area. The smell of violent death hung heavy in the air.

Dismounting, he handed his horse's reins to Regan. "Wait here."

"What's wrong?"

He shook his head. "Wait here," he repeated, and stepped into the cave. He felt a shimmer of preternatural power as he crossed over the threshold of the cavern.

The inside was as black as night but he was able to see clearly, even in the dark. A number of boxes and sacks lined the walls. The floor of the cave was covered with buffalo robes. A fire pit filled with cold ashes occupied the center. A raised altar made in the old way was located behind the pit. A bow, a quiver of arrows, and a rifle rested on a narrow shelf

that was cut into the cave wall. A brown leather re-
cliner, looking ridiculously out of place, was the only
piece of furniture in evidence.

Santiago moved deeper into the cave. Here, he
found a rough-hewn wooden table, a bowl made
of birch bark, an eagle feather, a pipe, and several
clay jars filled with herbs.

The scent of blood and death was stronger here.
There were signs of a scuffle in the dirt, the marks
of a body dragging itself deeper into the cave, and
the tracks of a wolf following.

Santiago followed the trail. The ceiling grew
lower, the passageway narrower as it gradually
curved to the left to form a small chamber that
ended a few feet further on.

It was here that he found the bodies. The shaman
lay on the floor inside a circle that appeared to be
made of pure silver. A knife, the blade of which was
also made of silver, protruded from the heart of the
second body. Santiago knew, from the smell that
lingered on the second corpse, that he had been a
werewolf.

Muttering an oath, Santiago knelt beside the old
shaman. There were numerous bite marks on his face,
neck, chest, arms, and hands. As near as he could tell
from the evidence at hand, the old man had been attacked by the werewolf, then had dragged himself
into the back of the cave and crawled inside his sacred
circle for protection.

Santiago examined the bite marks on the medicine man's body, but it wasn't the bites that had
killed him. In and of themselves, none of them
would have been fatal. Instead, the old man had

slowly bled to death, either too frightened or too weak to leave the circle and tend his own wounds.

Rocking back on his heels, Santiago stared at the old Indian. Why would anyone want to kill the reclusive medicine man? And how was he going to tell Regan that the old man was dead, and that the cure, if indeed one had existed, had died with him?

Regan shifted in the saddle. Where was Santiago? What was taking him so long? Had he found the old shaman?

She glanced from side to side, her nerves strung tight. Were those eyes glowing there, just beyond the trees, or was her imagination playing tricks on her?

She felt warm all over, constricted, as if her skin was shrinking. She looked down at her hands, imagining them turning into paws, her nails into claws.

She practically jumped out of the saddle when a wolf howled somewhere in the distance.

The moon would be full tomorrow night. She could feel herself changing already. Her body felt different, alien, and she was plagued by a restlessness she had never known before.

She knew in the deepest part of her being that if the shaman couldn't help her, she was doomed to become what she feared most.

She wrapped her arms around her waist as the first wolf's mournful howl was picked up by another, and then another. Her horse tossed its head, its ears twitching nervously as it pulled on the reins. Santiago's horse pawed the ground, its eyes showing white. Regan didn't know much about horses but she knew exactly what the animals were feeling.

She had almost decided to dismount and go into the cave in search of Santiago when he stepped outside.

"Did you find him?" she asked anxiously. "Can he help me?"

Santiago didn't say anything. Instead, he lifted her from the back of her horse and drew her into his arms.

Regan stared up at him, her gaze searching his, and then, with a sigh of resignation, she rested her cheek against his chest and closed her eyes.

There was no need for questions. His silence said it all.

There was no cure.

Chapter 15

With her cheek resting against Santiago's chest, Regan listened quietly as he told her what he had found inside the cave. She didn't know how long they stood like that. It could have been minutes, it could have been days. She couldn't move, couldn't think of anything to say. The word "werewolf" played over and over again in her mind. She was going to be a werewolf. Tomorrow night, when the moon rose in the sky, she would transform into a beast. Her hands and feet would turn into paws, her body would be covered with fur, and she would be compelled to run though the night in search of prey . . .

She shook the thought aside. Lifting her head, she looked up at Santiago. "Remember what I asked you before?" She took a deep breath. "I want you to do it now, before it's too late."

"Regan . . ."

"Please, Joaquin. I can't live like this, knowing that I'll become a monster when the moon is full. Please, if you care for me at all."

He cupped her face in his hands. "Let me bring you across."

"No! I don't want to be a vampire, either. Just do it now . . . but, please, don't hurt me."

A muscle throbbed in his jaw. "Regan, do not ask this of me."

"Why not? You've killed before."

His arms tightened around her. "Dammit, Regan, I cannot take your life. Let me bring you across. You will not have to hunt. I will feed you. We can have a good life together."

"Life?" She twisted out of his arms. "What kind of life is that? You'll keep me like a pet, you'll feed me! And it's not just the blood thing, it's all of it. I don't want to live only at night. I don't want to give up all the things I enjoy. I want to get married and have children, and . . ."

"I love you, Regan Delaney. I will cherish you and look after you for as long as I live. You will want for nothing, I swear it on all that I hold dear."

As it had before, his declaration of love left her speechless. He loved her. Joaquin Santiago, the most feared vampire in the city, loved her.

"Joaquin . . . I don't know what to say." She wanted to tell him that she loved him, too, but, once spoken, the words could not be taken back, and loving a vampire was a complication she didn't need in her life just now.

"There is no need for you to say anything. I tell you only so you will know why I cannot take your life."

Regan shook her head. "If you really loved me, you'd do as I ask."

"I will do anything but that."

"Please . . ."

He cut her words off with a slash of his hand. "We will spend the night here."

She glanced at the cave. "Here?" She shivered with revulsion. Two people had died inside the cave. She told herself there was nothing to fear. The dead couldn't hurt you. Unless they were vampires, she thought morbidly.

"It is the only shelter for miles."

"I don't mind sleeping outside. We did it last night."

"It is going to rain."

"It is?" She glanced up at the sky. "There aren't any clouds."

"There will be."

"How can you possibly know that?"

"I can smell the rain."

Regan sighed heavily. She wasn't crazy about sleeping out in the rain, but she was less thrilled with the idea of sleeping in a cave with two dead men.

Santiago's hands squeezed her shoulders reassuringly. "Wait here. I will take the bodies out and bury them."

She wrapped her arms around her middle. She didn't believe in ghosts. Still, she had never spent the night in a place where someone had died a violent death only hours before. She had read somewhere that the spirits of those who died violent deaths sometimes lingered on Earth, refusing to move on. She shook off her fanciful thoughts. Unless you were a vampire, dead was dead.

"You will be more comfortable here," Santiago

said, stroking her cheek. "There is an easy chair and a fire pit. And food."

"All right." She stood by her horse, her face turned away from the cave's entrance, while Santiago went inside to retrieve the bodies. Standing there, in the stillness of the night, she realized her senses were expanding. She could detect the scent of death in the air, smell the sweet, coppery tang of the blood that had been shed.

She was already changing, she thought. Her sense of smell was sharper, her vision clearer, her hearing more acute.

Staring into the darkness, she absently stroked the mare's neck. Her life had certainly taken a turn she had never expected. How could she be a werewolf? What kind of changes would she have to make in her lifestyle, other than the obvious? Would people take one look at her and know what she had become? What would her parents think? Not that she could tell them. Her folks were liberal thinkers, at least on the surface, but they had been opposed to any and all laws protecting vampires. She could only imagine how they would react to having a daughter who was a werewolf.

She laughed harshly. She would be one hell of a vampire hunter now! She blinked back her tears. Her parents weren't the only ones she couldn't tell. She couldn't tell her brothers, either. And she certainly couldn't tell Michael! He would never understand.

And then there was Santiago. What would he think when she went furry? Of course, he would probably be sympathetic, being one of the monsters himself.

She blew out a sigh. How could she be a werewolf? Would she remember who she really was when she was running wild? When she was human again, would she remember being a wolf? And what if she killed someone? Would she remember? Or would the memory be mercifully erased from her mind?

She pressed her face to the horse's shoulder. How could she live with herself if she killed someone? Oh, lord, what if she killed someone she knew?

It was a nightmare, she thought, sniffing back her tears, a horrible nightmare from which she would never awaken.

She slipped her hand into her jacket pocket. The butt of the gun felt icy in her hand as she withdrew it. If Santiago wouldn't put an end to this nightmare, she could. She stared at the pistol. The barrel was smooth, shiny in the moonlight. Her finger curled around the trigger. One shot to the head and it would all be over. She looked into the black maw of the barrel, stared at it until she couldn't see anything else. All she had to do was put the gun to her head and squeeze the trigger. Would she feel it? Would it hurt?

"Regan." Santiago's voice wrapped around her like soft black velvet. "Give me the gun."

She looked up to see him standing in front of her, one arm outstretched.

"Regan, listen to me," he said quietly. "You do not want to do that."

"I have to," she said dully. "What else can I do since you won't help me?"

"I will." He took one step toward her, and then another. "Trust me, Regan."

She lowered the gun, her hand trembling, and now the weapon was aimed in his direction.

Santiago paused, his attention focused on the pistol. If she pulled the trigger now . . . His gaze captured hers again. "Trust me," he repeated.

Time stilled as she stared at him, and then her hand fell to her side. "I'm so afraid."

"I know." He plucked the gun from her grasp and shoved it into the waistband of his jeans, then drew her into his arms. "I will be here with you tomorrow night," he promised, one hand stroking her hair. "You will not be alone."

"Stay with me tonight."

"Regan . . ."

"Please."

"I will stay until dawn."

"Will you hold me until morning?"

How could he refuse?

Santiago lit a fire in the cave so that Regan could have a cup of hot chocolate. He hoped it might help relax her. For a cave in the Black Hills, it was remarkably well stocked. A large trunk held numerous cans of fruit, meat, and vegetables, bottles of water, and juice.

"Will you be all right for a few minutes?" he asked.

"I guess so, why? Where are you going?"

"Outside to look after the horses."

"All right. You won't be gone long?"

"No."

Leaving the cave, he unsaddled the horses and turned them loose. They moved away from the entrance, then began to graze.

Santiago stared into the distance. Why had a werewolf killed the old medicine man? It made no sense, especially if the rumors were true and the shaman himself had been a werewolf. He shook his head. If the medicine man had been a werewolf, the bites he had received would have healed before he bled to death. There was always a chance the old man had been a threat to the werewolf community . . . Santiago shook off that line of thinking. What kind of threat could a medicine man who lived like a hermit in a cave have been? He shook his head again. None of it made any sense.

"Joaquin?" Regan's voice called him back into the cave.

He found her sitting in the overstuffed leather chair, a blanket across her knees. She looked very young—and very afraid.

He placed the gun on the shelf; then, lifting her into his arms, he took her place in the chair and settled her on his lap.

"What took you so long?" she asked.

He shrugged. "I was just outside, looking at the view."

She was quiet a moment, and then she said, "Tell me about your life. How did you get to be master of the city?"

"By being stronger and more powerful than all the rest, of course," he said with a faint grin.

"Did you frighten them all into submission?"

"You could say that."

"And what makes you so powerful?"

"Age, for one thing." He stroked her back absently, thinking how soothing it was to hold her, to touch her, to breathe in her very essence. "We grow stronger as we get older."

"You don't look old," she remarked, snuggling against him. "But then, I guess you never will."

"No, I never will." Neither would she, he thought, but this didn't seem like the right time to bring that up.

She sat quiescent in his arms for so long, he thought she had fallen asleep until she said, "You know a lot about werewolves. Tell me what to expect. Will it . . . will it hurt when I . . . ?"

"I am no expert. I cannot tell you if it will hurt. I have heard that it does. I have heard that it doesn't. I suspect it will be less painful if you do not fight it."

"And I'll have to change, whether I want to or not?"

"Yes."

"Will I still be me, inside?"

"That I do not know."

"Will I remember being a wolf?"

"Again, I do not know."

"You must have some idea!" she insisted.

"I have heard the change is painful the first time, but that it gets easier as time goes on. I do not know if you will remember being a wolf, or if you will remember what you do when you are in that form. Vasile is the only werewolf I know and we have never discussed his condition."

With a sigh, Regan settled back into his embrace, her trepidation growing with each passing moment.

"Maybe I'll write a book about werewolves," she muttered. "You know, something like *The Were-wolves' Guide for Complete Idiots, Everything You Always Wanted to Know but Never Had a Werewolf to Ask.*"

Santiago smiled at her, thinking it was a good sign that she could find humor, however grim, in her situation.

"Perhaps I will write a companion book about vampires," he remarked with a wry grin.

"I don't know what I'd do if you weren't here with me." Lifting her hand, she caressed his cheek. "You must be . . . what do you call it? Hungry? Thirsty?"

"Either," he said, stroking her cheek. "Both."

"Does it hurt terribly when you haven't fed for a long time?"

"Yes. It is a pain worse than anything you can imagine. Far worse than mortal hunger."

"Have you ever had to go without feeding for a long time?"

"Once."

"How come?"

"It happened when I was still a newly made vampire. A hunter found my resting place. He would most likely have destroyed me if he hadn't been a young hunter. He poured holy water over me and then put a stake to my heart. He pierced the skin of my chest and the muscle beneath but at the first sight of blood, he backed off. The pain roused me. When I sat up, he dropped everything and fled. The holy water weakened me and I fell back, the stake still buried in my flesh. It took all my strength to pull it free. I left the crypt as soon as I was able and sought a new resting place. My skin was badly burned from the holy water. It took several weeks for me to regain my strength."

"And that's the longest you've gone without?"

He nodded, his thoughts turned inward. He had been almost mad with hunger when he recovered enough to hunt. Even now, so many years later, he felt regret for the first mortal he had seen that night. He had taken the young man quickly, savagely, and cast the body aside, the only thing on his mind the need to ease the pain that engulfed him like a living flame.

But that had been long ago. He was older now, wiser, more in control of his passions and his needs. If it were not so, the girl lying so trustingly in his lap would have more to fear than the full moon. He stroked her hair lightly.

"Go to sleep now, my lovely one," he said. "You will need your strength for tomorrow."

"I don't think I can sleep." She paused, her head tilted to one side. "Listen. You were right. It's raining."

He nodded. "Why are you surprised?"

"I've never known anyone who could predict the rain. Maybe you should become a weatherman."

He snorted softly. "No." He rubbed his knuckles over her cheek. "Go to sleep now."

"Will you kiss me good night?"

Murmuring, "What do you think?" he lowered his head and claimed her lips with his.

The cave and its meager furnishings faded away. The morrow and its uncertainty ceased to exist. His hellish thirst was no longer uppermost in his mind. There was nothing in all the world but the woman in his arms, the touch of her skin, the scent of her hair, the fire in her kiss. His tongue swept her lips, seeking entrance. She opened to him at once, as eager and hungry as he. His body reacted immediately and predictably.

His hands delved into her hair, softly kneading her scalp as his tongue explored the soft inner recesses of her mouth. She tasted of the soup she had eaten earlier and the cocoa she'd had to drink. He rained kisses over her cheeks, her brow, her eyelids, the sweet curve of her throat. His tongue mated with hers again. The scent of her blood tantalized his nostrils, stirring his other desire. Her tongue brushed his fangs, just the slightest touch, but it was enough to draw blood.

He groaned with pleasure as her sweetness slid down his throat. For a moment, he forgot everything but the taste of her life's blood and the fact that he hadn't truly fed for several days. But this was Regan. He had sworn to protect her.

She made a soft sound of protest when he withdrew his lips from hers. "Don't stop."

"This is not a good time," he said, keeping a tight rein on the thirst burning through him. "You are far too tempting, and I am far too hungry, and not just for your sweet flesh."

She blinked up at him, one hand kneading the muscle in his arm. "But I want you."

"As I want you, but . . ." He paused, trying to find just the right words.

"But what?" She ran her tongue across his lower lip. "I want you. You want me. We're both over twenty-one."

"One of us is way over," he muttered.

"Joaquin, I need you."

He knew the attraction between them was real, just as he knew that her sudden urge to make love was influenced more by the pull of the moon than her own desire. Somehow, it didn't seem honorable to take her now.

"Regan." He held her gaze with his. "It is late and you are weary. Close your eyes. There is nothing to fear tonight. I am here with you. I will be with you tomorrow night. Sleep now."

She looked up at him, her gaze becoming unfocused as he gently bent her will to his. Her body slowly relaxed. Her eyelids fluttered down. In moments, she was asleep.

Santiago stroked her hair, his body humming with desire. It must be love, he thought with a wry grin, else he never would have refused such a welcome invitation.

Chapter 16

Vasile stood in the shadows, his gaze fixed on the heavens. Tomorrow night the moon would be full and the Delaney woman would shift. He had originally intended to kill her, seeing it as the perfect revenge against the man who had stolen Marishka away from him. But in the very act of biting the Delaney woman, he had come up with a better use for her and so, instead of delivering the coup de grace, he had thrown her away from him, careful to make sure he didn't hurt her too badly. He would need her later, after the revolution.

The werewolves were tired of lurking in the shadows, hiding like sheep. They were meant to be predators, not prey. It was time to reclaim their rightful place in the scheme of things. Vasile had spent the last few years bringing the packs together, urging them to increase their numbers while foolishly neglecting to ensure that his own pack did the same. That was something he intended to rectify immediately. Then, when the time was right, he would be the one to lead them to victory, with Santiago's woman at his side.

Vasile had called on the pack in South Dakota and ordered them to kill the old shaman in the Black Hills. Foolish old man, offering a cure to those who were misguided enough to want one. In the past, Vasile hadn't cared. He wanted only the strongest of their kind at his side, but there could be no cure for Regan Delaney. No, he had plans for her. Every king needed a queen, and she would be his. And if Zina objected, well, he would worry about that when the time came.

He could have followed the Delaney woman into the Black Hills, killed the old medicine man himself, and brought her back, but there had been no need.

She would return to her home, and she would bring Santiago with her.

He would kill the meddling vampire when the time was right—and he would make the woman watch.

Though in human form, Vasile threw back his head and howled at the moon.

"What are you doing here?" Regan wondered aloud. "Where did you come from? And why do you have hazel eyes?"

The wolf smiled at her, its tongue lolling out of the side of its mouth.

"This is too weird," Regan muttered, shaking her head. She glanced up, surprised to see the sun was no longer high in the sky. "Stick around," she said, "should be quite a show later tonight."

With a wave of its tail, the wolf turned and disappeared into the trees.

Regan remained where she was for a long while, feeling as though she was caught between two worlds and not sure if she belonged in either one. Tonight she would know if Vasile's bite had cursed her to become a werewolf or not, and all she could do until then was wait and wonder and worry, though deep inside, she was afraid she already knew the answer.

As the sun slipped behind the mountains, she began to tremble uncontrollably. Nerves, she thought, it was just a bad case of nerves. And yet it was more than that. She felt as though her skin no longer fit, as if she had woken up wearing someone else's body.

She was trying to summon the strength to rise and return to the cave when Santiago found her.

There was no need for words. He took one look at her pale face, the tremors that wracked her slender frame, and pulled her to her feet and into his embrace.

She wrapped her arms around his waist and held on tight. Shaking so badly she could hardly speak, she said, "I'm . . . so . . . afraid."

"I know." He stroked her hair and her back, all

the while promising her that it would be all right, that he would be there with her through the night, that there was nothing for her to be afraid of.

"I'm sorry to be . . . such a coward."

"You are not a coward."

She buried her face against his chest. "I've faced vampires. I've staked vampires. I should be able to handle this."

"You are handling it just fine."

She looked up at him, her face drawn, her eyes brimming with tears. "Were you afraid, when you were turned?"

He nodded. "Afraid does not quite describe what I felt."

She sniffed back her tears, comforted somehow by the knowledge that he had once been afraid. "I talked to a wolf today."

"Indeed? And what did you talk about?"

"You're making fun of me, aren't you?"

"No. I believe you."

"You do? Really?"

"In the old days, the animals were not as they are today. They were bigger and stronger and had mystical powers. In those days, they were friends to the Indians and often spoke to them."

"But I'm not Indian. Anyway, I think I imagined the whole thing." She laughed self-consciously. "He told me his name was Pahin Sapa."

She didn't think she had ever seen Santiago looked surprised, but he was definitely flabbergasted now.

"You are sure that is what he said?"

"Yes, I think so, why?"

"Pahin Sapa is the name of the shaman we came here to see, the one who was killed."

* * *

The moon had taken command of the sky by the time Santiago and Regan returned to the cave.

Anxiety rolled off Regan in waves so strong it was palpable, almost visible, provoking an answering tension in Santiago. The only werewolf he had ever seen shift had been Vasile and, due to the werewolf's age, the transformation had happened in an instant.

Inside the cave, Regan began to pace. She couldn't sit still, couldn't stop shaking. She kicked off her shoes and removed her jacket as heat built inside her. Then she paced some more. Time and again, she reached up to explore her face with her hands, as if to reassure herself that nothing had changed, then, uttering a harsh cry of dismay, she came to an abrupt halt. She was trembling uncontrollably now.

Eyes wide, she stared at Santiago. "It's happening," she whispered. "Oh, lord, it's happening now. Make it stop! Please, make it stop!"

"Try to stay calm," Santiago said. "Listen to the sound of my voice."

Regan saw his lips move but his words had no meaning. She clutched her stomach, doubling over as a burning sensation spread through her, as if all her internal organs were on fire, melting and reforming. There was a buzzing inside her head. Her skin rippled, her bones popped and cracked as they realigned themselves. With a hoarse cry, she dropped to her hands and knees, staring in horror at the thick coat of fur that sprouted from her arms, the strong claws that replaced her fingernails.

Looking up at Santiago, she cried, "Help me!"

He shook his head, helpless to do anything for

her now except watch as the transformation pro-
gressed. Her shirt and jeans ripped at the seams
and she shook them off.

Speechless, Santiago could only stand there,
completely engrossed at what he was seeing as
Regan Delaney disappeared and a beautiful blond
wolf with bright green eyes stood in her place.
Throwing back her head, she whined softly, and
then, with a mournful howl and a twitch of her tail,
she ran out of the cave.

In the blink of an eye, Santiago changed into a
wolf and followed her into the night.

Panic chased Regan through the darkness. Unbe-
lievable as it seemed, she was a wolf, and she knew
it. The earth was cool beneath her paws. A hundred
different scents inundated her nostrils, among
them the fecund smell of the forest and the animals
that dwelled within it, from the jackrabbit trembling in the underbrush to the owl that swooped
overhead. She knew there was water nearby, and
somewhere in the distance, a dead animal.

She ran blindly, tirelessly, amazed at the way the
world looked through her wolf eyes. Only when she
slowed did she become aware that she was being
followed.

Coming to an abrupt stop, she spun around, her
hackles rising, a growl rumbling deep in her throat
when she saw the black wolf. She walked toward it,
stiff-legged, ears and nostrils twitching.

Recognizing Santiago's scent, she whined softly.

With a low *woof,* he rubbed his body against hers,
and then ran off into the night.

With a joyful bark, she followed him.

It was a strange feeling. She knew, on some deep
level, that she was Regan Delaney, but it didn't

seem to matter. For now, for this night, she was a wolf, as wild and unfettered as her feral brothers and sisters. She was a wolf, and she loved it. She saw things, heard things, and smelled things, that the human part of Regan Delaney would never experience or understand.

When the black wolf flushed a rabbit from the underbrush, she bounded after it, jaws snapping. There was no revulsion in the kill, none when she sank her teeth into the soft, still-warm flesh.

She wagged her tail when the black wolf trotted up to her side, snarled a warning for him to back off when he nosed the kill. It was hers and she wouldn't share.

Later, they ran side by side through the night, playing tag, jumping deadfalls, and splashing through a shallow stream. Why had she been afraid of this? She had never felt so alive, so free!

Hours later, she was following Santiago back to the cave when the unmistakable scent of man reached her nostrils. In that instant, the beast rose up within her and Regan Delaney ceased to exist, swallowed up in the sudden, overwhelming need for flesh—human flesh.

She veered sharply to the right, following the scent to a campfire where two warriors sat sharing a pipe.

Dropping to her belly, she crept closer to the campsite, her heart pounding in anticipation, her mouth watering. Power swelled within her, thrumming through every fiber of her body. The moon was high in the sky and she was invincible.

She drew in a deep breath, her nostrils filling with the scent of prey. The rabbit she had consumed had been sweet. The taste of human flesh would be sweeter still.

In an instant, Santiago shifted back to his own form. He sprang forward when the wolf did, his arms closing around her, bearing her down to the ground.

Jaws snapping, she turned on him, her only thought to dine on human flesh. His or that of the other two men, it didn't matter. She needed it, wanted it, could think of nothing else.

She growled her anger as she attempted to tear out Santiago's throat, but even as a werewolf, she was no match for his ancient preternatural speed or strength. He clamped one hand around her jaws, rendering her helpless as he carried her back to the cave.

Inside, he held her imprisoned in his arms until the sun chased the moon from the sky.

She cried out in pain as her body assumed its own shape once more and hid her face against his shoulder in shame as her humanity returned and she found herself naked in Santiago's arms.

"You should have killed me," she murmured.

"Was it that bad? What do you remember?"

"I remember all of it." She recalled her initial joy as she ran through the forest, all her senses alive. She had received stimuli through her eyes, ears, nose, and the pads of her feet. But then the darkness had come, blinding her to everything but the impulse to kill the Indians sitting at the campfire. It had been an urge she could not resist. Worse, she hadn't wanted to resist it. Had she been able, she would have killed the Indians and savaged their flesh. Had she been able, she was afraid she would have killed Santiago, as well.

She sighed. So it hadn't been all bad. In fact, some of it had been enjoyable. If it wasn't for the overpowering urge to kill, she might have embraced being a werewolf. But the bad far outweighed the good.

"I can't live like this," she said dully. "What am I going to do when you're not around to stop me?" She remembered all too clearly what she had read about werewolves; how, once they had tasted human blood, they were beyond redemption, their souls dammed for all eternity. While she had never been big on religion, she did believe in heaven and hell.

"You can come to my lair when the moon is full," he said. "I will lock you inside from moonrise to sunrise."

"I don't want to be locked up once a month, like some kind of . . . of . . ." Her voice grew very soft. "Monster."

"We can keep looking for a cure."

"And what if there isn't one? What if there never was one?"

"You will learn to control the change, in time, as I have learned to control my hunger."

"And how long did that take you?"

"A long time," he admitted ruefully.

She wriggled out of his arms. "I need to get dressed."

"Not on my account, I hope," he muttered with a wry grin.

Turning her back to him, Regan rummaged through her pack, then went into the back of the cave to dress. She would have to remember to undress in the future, she thought, or she would be spending a lot of money replacing the clothing she ruined during the change.

She didn't know what embarrassed her more, her actions of the previous night or finding herself naked in Santiago's arms. Of course, embarrassing was hardly the right word to describe what she had almost done last night. Horrifying was more like it. And what about tonight? Would she shift again, or did the moon have power over her only one night a month? That wouldn't be so bad, she thought, and then swore softly. Not so bad? What was she thinking? She could do a lot of damage in one night.

Her stomach growled as she pulled on her shoes. The fact that she was hungry surprised her. Returning to the main part of the cave, she opened a can of soup and warmed it over the coals.

Santiago regarded her through narrowed eyes as she sat down to eat. If being a new werewolf was anything like being a new vampire, then the worst was behind her. All things considered, she had handled it fairly well, although she was still unsettled by the experience. But then, who could blame her? Becoming a werewolf had to be a shock, physically and emotionally.

He didn't want to leave her alone but the sun was climbing high in the sky and the Dark Sleep was calling to him. He would have to rest sooner or later . . . and he would have to rest here. He had lingered too long, and the sun was too high for him to risk going outside.

He grunted softly, wondering what she would think when he told her he was going to have to spend the rest of the day in the back of the cave, then shrugged it off. She had shared a motel room with him; this was no different.

Regan muttered, "do whatever you have to," when Santiago told her he would be taking his rest in the back of the cavern. Truth be told, she was glad that he would be nearby. She didn't want to be alone and, even though he wouldn't be much company while he slept, it would still be nice to know he was there.

He drew her into his arms. "Will you be all right?"

She made a vague gesture with her hand. "Sure." What did she have to be afraid of now? Her worst nightmare had become reality.

He regarded her for a moment, then made his way to the back of the cavern.

Regan watched him until he was out of sight and then, leaving the cave, she sat down under a tree and let the tears fall.

Just when you thought life couldn't get any worse, it did.

For the first time in her life, she had fallen head over heels in love. Was he a doctor or a pilot or a lawyer? No, he was a vampire.

And now, if that wasn't bad enough, she was a werewolf.

The cosmic Fates must be rolling on the floor laughing their collective fannies off. She just wished she could find some humor in the situation. She had heard of life-altering experiences before, but this! She shook her head. How was she supposed to adjust to something like this?

She picked up a blade of grass and twirled it between her thumb and forefinger. She would never be able to have children now, and if she did, they probably wouldn't be children at all, but puppies. Maybe a whole litter of them!

A laugh bubbled up in her throat. She could tell Santiago she loved him now. She could even marry him. She wouldn't have to worry about getting pregnant, because vampires couldn't reproduce.

Life just kept getting funnier and funnier, she thought bitterly. Yes sir, her life must be the cosmic joke of the century.

She laughed and laughed, and then she buried her face in her hands and wept for what she had become, for all that she had lost . . .

She woke with a start. Not knowing what had roused her so abruptly, she sat up, a shiver of unease running down her spine. She wasn't alone. She knew it without knowing how she knew. It couldn't be Santiago. The sun was still in the sky. Afraid of what she might see, she glanced warily over her shoulder.

The spirit wolf stood a foot or so away, watching her.

Regan stared back. "Hello, Pahin Sapa. You have no idea how happy I am to see you."

The wolf barked, and then smiled a wolfish smile.

"Did you come to keep me company again?" she asked, scooting around so that she could see him better.

The wolf bobbed his head up and down.

"I'm glad," she said, wiping her eyes with the backs of her hands. "I could use some company."

With a low whine, the wolf trotted forward and dropped down beside her, its hazel eyes focused on her face. Once again, she heard the wolf's voice in her mind. *There is another cure, though you must be brave to obtain it.*

"At this point, I'm willing to do anything."

You must find the werewolf who bit you and destroy him with your own hand. His death will free you.

Kill Vasile? How could she accomplish what Santiago, with all his supernatural powers, had been unable to achieve? "Is there no other way?"

Not now.

"Then I'll just have to find a way to do it."

It will be easiest when the moon is not full.

"Thank you, Pahin Sapa."

With a low *woof*, the wolf bounded to its feet and disappeared into the trees.

Regan stared after the wolf. Destroy Vasile. That's all she had to do. All, she thought with a shake of her head. She could hardly wait to tell Santiago, and then she frowned. Santiago had been hunting Vasile for hundreds of years. How would he feel when she told him she had to destroy the werewolf? Surely Santiago would understand. Regardless of who killed him, Vasile would be just as dead. After all, what was more important? That she destroy Vasile and get her life back, or that Santiago destroy the werewolf to avenge Marishka's death?

Returning to the cave, she paused inside the entrance, her eagerness to go home momentarily overcome by her curiosity. Santiago was asleep in the back of the cavern . . .

Moving quietly, she went deeper into the narrow passage, her blood pounding in her ears. What did he look like when he was trapped in the Dark Sleep? Did he look like he was dead, or merely sleeping? Would he be angry if she spied on him? Would he even know she was there?

She stopped at the place where the cavern veered to the left, her heart in her throat. *Just one look*, she thought. *What could it hurt?*

Holding her breath, she peered around the cave wall, her eyes straining to see through the gloom—but there was nothing to see, no sign of Santiago. Frowning, she entered the small chamber. Where was he?

Returning to the main chamber, she looked outside.

The sun was low in the sky. Wherever he had gone, he would be rising soon—and so would the moon. How had she forgotten that?

A shiver of unease ran through her at the thought of shifting again. She had purposefully refused to think of it earlier, but now she couldn't put it from her mind. She recalled all too clearly the fear and the pain as her body transformed.

Tonight, if she felt herself shifting, she would ask Santiago to leave the cave so she could undress before the transformation began. Of course, he'd already seen all there was to see.

With that thought in mind, she turned away from the cave's entrance and let out a shriek of surprise when she found herself face to face with the master of the city.

"Damn!" she exclaimed, "where did you come from?"

"Back there," he replied, gesturing behind him.

"But I looked just a few minutes ago . . ."

"I did not wish to be seen."

"Oh." She stared up at him, frowning. Did that mean he had been there and she just couldn't see him, or did it mean he had hidden somewhere, although she couldn't for the life of her think where he could have hidden. And then she remembered that he sometimes hid in the earth. But none of that mattered right now.

Santiago listened quietly as Regan told him about the shaman's appearance. He wondered why it hadn't occurred to him that destroying Vasile would break the curse of the werewolf. Of course, he had always thought it was just a myth similar to the one that said if you destroyed a vampire, all those he had brought across would die with him. But perhaps Pahin Sapa was right, and they had nothing to lose by trying, since destroying Vasile had long been Santiago's goal. The one drawback was that Regan had to kill the werewolf. He told himself it didn't matter who destroyed Vasile as long as it was done, but he knew he was lying to himself. He had waited centuries to kill the werewolf. How could he let another, even Regan, accomplish what he himself yearned to do?

"So, I think we should head back home right now," Regan said. She moved through the cave, gathering her things together and stuffing them into her pack. She frowned when he didn't say anything. "Don't you?"

"No."

"Why not?"

"Some werewolves only change at the full moon, some also change the night before, as well, and some the night after. If you start to shift while we are riding down the mountain, it is likely to spook the horses, don't you think?"

"Very funny. I hate this! I don't want to change again. Do you think I'll change again?"

"We will know soon enough."

She began to pace back and forth. "Do you think we'll be able to find Vasile?"

"We will find him."

"What if he's left the country?"

"We will find him," Santiago repeated softly but emphatically. "Do not forget, he is also looking for me."

"I know but . . ."

"Regan," he murmured. "Worrying will solve nothing."

"But . . ."

Moving quickly, he put his arms around her and

drew her close. "I am with you," he said quietly. "Trust me."

She gazed up at him, everything else forgotten as she looked into his eyes, deep blue eyes that glowed with an inner fire, a fire that flared even hotter as he lowered his head and kissed her.

As always, the touch of his mouth on hers drove everything else from her mind until she saw only him, wanted only him. Her arms slid up around his neck, her body leaning into his like a lost lamb seeking shelter. A small, clinical part of her mind marveled that they fit together so well and then even that was forgotten as his hands moved over her—hot, eager hands that caressed her with exquisite tenderness. She moaned softly, her body writhing against his, yearning for more. Hungry for more. Why did he affect her like this? Why didn't Michael's kisses make her blood sing and her bones melt? She had tried to love Michael. He was a kind, decent, hardworking man. She had known him for several years, but the most she had ever felt for him was affection. Then, Joaquin Santiago showed up and all her good sense went flying out the window.

She slid her hands under his shirt, her greedy fingers moving lightly over his broad back. His skin was smooth and cool to the touch. Intoxicating. She had a crazy urge to rip his shirt off, to drag him down onto the floor of the cave, to explore the hard muscled length of his body pressing down on hers, to feel his mouth, hot and hungry, on hers.

He whispered her name, his voice filled with the same urgent longing that possessed her. Would it be so wrong to let him make love to her? They could never have a life together, but they could have this one night, this one fleeting moment in time. She needed him to make love to her, needed to know that this gorgeous man found her desirable, that she was still a woman and not a monster . . .

"Joaquin . . ."

"I am here."

She looked up at him, hoping he would see the desperate need in her eyes, that he would take her in his arms and make her forget . . .

Too late, too late. Groaning, she clutched her stomach as pain knotted her insides.

"Regan?"

"It's happening again!"

Twisting out of his arms, she quickly removed her shoes and began to shed her clothing.

Santiago stood back, watching, thinking what a rare and fascinating sight it was to watch her shift, her slight body shimmering like mist in the moonlight as the wolf emerged.

Hearing her cry out, he wished he could endure the pain for her, but he could only stand there, watching, marveling at the incredible transformation, until the woman was gone and the blond wolf stood in her stead.

She didn't bolt out of the cave this time, but looked up at him expectantly, her head cocked to one side. Waiting.

He smiled at her, and then he shifted. There was no pain for him. He had but to wish it and he became a wolf. Though he had, on occasion, assumed other shapes, the wolf form had always been his favorite.

Side by side, they trotted out of the cave.

As he had the night before, Santiago fell in behind her, content to follow her lead.

She ran for miles, effortlessly leaping over fallen

logs and branches, bounding across a shallow stream, chasing a deer she spooked from a thicket. He grinned inwardly as she howled her frustration when the buck eluded her.

A short time later, she caught a jackrabbit, and still later she brought down a young doe. He hoped the excitement of the chase and the two kills would satisfy her. It was a myth that all werewolves were ravening monsters, unable to control the beast within them. True, they had to shift when the moon was full, but before their numbers decreased, most werewolves had hidden out in unpopulated areas, living in small groups, content to prey on wildlife. It was only those that had tasted human flesh who turned into uncontrollable monsters. Having once tasted human flesh, they were no longer content with anything else. They lived for the thrill of hunt, the chase, and the kill. It was werewolves like Vasile that had caused them to be hunted to near extinction. Unlike vampires, who had needed human blood to survive until the synthetic kind had been invented, werewolves could survive without human prey.

Regan paused at a stream to drink, then playfully nipped Santiago on the shoulder. He retaliated by nipping her on the hindquarters and the game was on. Like puppies, they rolled on the ground, mock growls rising in their throats as they tussled. Gaining her feet, she attacked him again, knocking him into the water. With a joyful bark, she splashed in after him and they chased each other along the shore until a fish caught her eye. With a yelp of excitement, she plunged into the river, emerging moments later with a fat trout in her jaws. She dropped it on the ground, shook the water from her fur, and then, giving him a wolfish grin of triumph, she devoured the fish, bones and all.

After a time, she dropped down onto the grass and rolled onto her side. Santiago stretched out beside her, idly licking drops of water from her face. They rested there for a while, until she sprang to her feet. She waved her tail in his face and the game began once again, with her leading him on a merry chase that he was content to follow. The water was cool, the night warm as they splashed along the shore, leaping from rock to rock and jumping over boulders. She chased a bullfrog until it dove into deeper water and took shelter behind a rock. She spent several minutes trying to dig it out before she gave up.

Sensing dawn's approach a short time later, Santiago scrambled up the bank, his nostrils testing the breeze. She made as if to attack him yet again, but he growled a warning. The time for play was past. He needed to return to the cave before the sun came up. She looked at him askance a moment and then, when he glanced at the sky, she understood.

Shaking the water from her coat, she trotted toward the cave.

Santiago followed her, thinking that, woman or wolf, Regan Delaney was the most desirable creature he had ever known.

Chapter 18

Regan paced back and forth in front of the entrance to the cave, waiting, wondering if she would shift again. The moon had risen an hour ago; thus far, she hadn't felt the wolf stirring inside her.

"Do you feel anything?" Santiago asked.

"No."

"I think it is safe for us to leave."

With a nod, she helped him gather their gear together. The nightmare was over until the next full moon.

Riding down the mountain was much faster and more pleasant than walking up had been. Regan had been surprised to see the horses, thinking them long gone. When she asked Santiago about it, he told her he had called them to him. Another useful trick, she thought.

The trip home was uneventful. Regan had been worried about the horses when Santiago turned them loose, but he had assured her they would find their way back to Hunonpa Luta's camp.

It seemed odd to be riding in a car again, to see houses and stores, paved roads and street lights. It didn't seem right that everything in the city looked so normal, so unchanged, when her whole life had been turned upside down.

It was after midnight several nights later when Santiago pulled up in front of her apartment. "I do not think this is a good idea."

"I have to go home sometime. I need to change my clothes, and I want to sleep in my own bed and bathe in my own tub."

"Stay with me tonight."

Regan glanced out the passenger-side window. The streets were dark, the sky overcast. The thought of spending the night in her apartment alone when Vasile was on the loose sent a shiver down her spine. She was going to have to face Vasile sometime, but not tonight. She needed to come up with a plan, needed to get her emotions under control before she went hunting the werewolf. Perhaps she should go home with Santiago. She would be safer with him than she would be staying here alone.

"All right," she decided, "but I'm coming home in the morning."

He didn't say anything, but simply turned the car around and drove to You Bet Your Life Park. After unlocking the trunk, he gathered their bags.

Regan stayed close to his side as they entered the park. Few lights were visible inside the park. It was creepy, walking along the tree-lined path toward Santiago's apartment. From time to time, vampires appeared out of the darkness, seemingly from out of nowhere. It was disconcerting, having them appear and disappear like that. Some of them nodded at Santiago. Some of them looked at her as if wondering how she would taste. Here and there, they passed couples sitting on wooden benches, enjoying the evening air and the moonlight. A few of the vampires, both male and female, were with their mortal companions. There had been a time not so long ago when Regan had wondered how any man or woman could be seriously involved with a vampire, let alone live with one, but now, after spending time with Santiago, it was easier to understand the attraction, and easy to see why the vampires were trying to have a law passed that would allow vampires and mortals to intermarry. The fact that she didn't find that as disturbing as she once had was quite disturbing.

They took the elevator to Santiago's apartment. He tucked both bags under one arm, then unlocked the door and stepped inside ahead of her. Dropping the bags on the floor, he turned on the lights and muttered a vile oath.

Startled, Regan leaned to one side so she could see around him. She gasped at what she saw. The apartment was a shambles. The sofa and chair had been ripped to shreds, tables were overturned, lamps had been broken.

Santiago waited until Regan entered the apartment, then closed the door and set the lock. Hands clenched at his sides, he explored the rest of the apartment. Regan followed him from room to room. The bedding, mattress, and pillows were in shreds, the dresser and night stands were on their sides, the chair was in pieces. The refrigerator door had been ripped off; the bags of synthetic blood had been opened, their contents splashed across the floor and splattered over the walls.

"Who would have done this?" Regan exclaimed.

"Vasile."

"But . . . how did he get in here?"

Santiago shook his head. "I do not know, but I intend to find out."

"How?"

"Someone must have let him in."

"I didn't think anyone else had access to your apartment."

"Stay here. I will be right back."

"Where are you going?"

"Downstairs. To check with security."

"No way! I'm not staying here alone."

For a moment, it looked like he was going to argue with her, and then thought better of it. "Very well, come along," he said, picking up her bag.

The vampire at the desk, whose name was Lenny, denied letting anyone into Santiago's apartment and said that, as far as he knew, no one had come looking for him. When asked, Lenny replied that there hadn't been any killings in the park or in the city in the last week and a half.

Santiago thanked Lenny for his time and requested that someone be sent up to his apartment as soon as possible to clean up the mess.

"We can always go back to my place," Regan suggested as they left the office.

"No. We will go to my lair."

She was about to remind him it had been trashed when she realized he meant his other lair.

"Why do you keep two places?" she asked, and knew the answer before the question left her lips. She had seen the reason with her own eyes. "Do all vampires keep more than one place?"

"The smart ones do." Taking her by the hand, he led her to his car. He held the car door open for her, closed it, then rounded the front of the car and slid behind the wheel.

"You don't spend much time in the park apartment, do you?" Regan asked.

"Why do you ask?" Glancing over his shoulder, he pulled away from the curb.

She shrugged. "It's so bland. It doesn't look like you."

He glanced at her, obviously amused. "No?"

She grinned. "All that white. It just doesn't suit you."

"Perhaps I should paint the walls black," he mused, "to match my soul."

Regan's smile faded. "I didn't mean that."

"I know."

"Do you think Vasile left town? That vampire, Lenny, said there haven't been any killings recently."

"It is always a possibility."

"I'm going to have to go home sooner or later," Regan reminded him.

"But not tonight."

Knowing it was useless to argue with him, she sat back and made a mental list of the things she had to do when she got home—pick up her mail, call her parents, call Michael, call the department, check her e-mail.

Santiago pulled up in front of the dilapidated building ten minutes later. He parked the Speedster at the curb, then came around to open the door for her. Glancing around, she wondered why he didn't find a new lair, maybe in a nicer neighborhood where the surroundings weren't so run down. Most of the surrounding buildings had fallen into the same state of neglect and disrepair as the one he occupied.

She kept glancing over her shoulder as she followed him down the stairs to his lair. The building, with its broken windows and musty smell, gave her the creeps.

He opened the door for her and she preceded him inside. His apartment in the park was just a set of rooms, but this place, this was where he lived. His power washed over her as she stepped across the threshold. Why hadn't she felt it before? Even as she pondered the question, she knew the answer. She hadn't been a werewolf before. She hadn't wanted to acknowledge it, had tried to pretend it wasn't true, but her senses were sharper now. She had noticed the difference as soon as they entered the city.

"I'm like Vasile now," she murmured, thinking aloud. "Maybe he won't want to kill me anymore."

Santiago regarded her through narrowed eyes. "You may be right." He dropped the bag he was carrying beside the sofa. "It is against pack law for one werewolf to kill another. The penalty is death."

At last, Regan thought, a ray of hope. Vasile had intended to kill her to get even with Santiago, but now . . . She frowned. Would he defy the laws of his kind to exact his revenge? Or had he inadvertently given her back her life?

Regan sat down. "How do the werewolves live?"

Santiago sat down beside her, one arm draped across the back of the sofa. "What do you mean, how do they live?"

"Do they live like normal people when they aren't, you know, ravaging the countryside?"

"Ah. Yes. It is easier for them now that they are not as numerous as they once were."

"Are they . . . do they . . . ?"

"What?"

"Do they get married, have children?"

"Of the dozen or so that are rumored to be under Vasile's protection, six are mated pairs."

"Mated pairs? Does that mean they're married or just . . . mated?"

"They are married and live ordinary lives, at least for the most part, except when the moon is full."

"Are the married ones all werewolves?"

"Two of the couples are. The third couple is mixed, werewolf and human."

"Can they have children?"

Santiago nodded, his gaze intent upon her face.

"What kind of children do they have?"

He laughed softly. "The usual kind."

"And Vasile?"

"He has never married, nor had children, that I know of." He leaned toward her, his gaze caressing her. "It is important to you, having children?"

"Of course."

"Why?"

"Why?" She rose from the sofa and began to pace the floor. "Why? Because I'm a woman, that's why. Because I love children. Because I've always wanted to get married and have a large family."

Santiago sat back, his expression shuttered. "Hunting vampires and raising a family do not seem to be compatible."

"No, I guess not." She blew out a sigh. "I'm tired. I think I'll go to bed."

Rising, Santiago drew her into his embrace. "I love you, Regan. I wish I could give you the life you want."

"So do I." Standing on her tiptoes, she kissed his cheek. "Good night, Joaquin."

Blinking back her tears, she picked up her bag,

went into the bedroom, and closed the door. She had thought her life was complicated before she met Santiago. Now, she wished she could go back to those relatively quiet days, when all she had to worry about was finding a new job.

Opening her bag, she pulled out her toothpaste, toothbrush, and nightgown and went into the bathroom. She washed her face, brushed her teeth, put on her nightgown, and slid into bed. The satin sheets were cool beneath her. The pillow was redolent with Santiago's scent.

He loved her. The thought made her heart ache. In all his long life, he had loved only one other woman. And now he was in love with her. He had told her so on several occasions, asking nothing in return. Maybe he just needed to say the words.

She wiped her tears on a corner of the sheet. And she loved him. It would be so easy to succumb to him, to give in to the yearnings of her own heart, but she knew it would only lead to heartache.

Right now, she didn't have time for any kind of relationship. If she wanted to reclaim her humanity, she had to find Vasile and destroy him. It sounded so easy, yet she knew it would be difficult, perhaps impossible, to accomplish. She wondered if werewolves grew stronger with age, the way vampires did. She would have to remember to ask Santiago.

The thought had no sooner crossed her mind than there was a knock on the door. It could only be him. Her heart did a funny little quickstep as, sitting up, she bid him enter.

He loomed larger than life in the doorway. He had changed into a pair of black sweatpants and a black T-shirt. His feet were bare. Her mouth went dry as her gaze moved over his broad chest and muscular arms. She had a sudden urge to go to him, to run her fingers through his hair, to rain kisses over his cheeks, along the line of his jaw, across his brow.

Just looking at him made her whole body tingle with awareness. She felt very female, very alive. And very vulnerable.

"Is something wrong?" she asked, unable to keep her voice from trembling.

"No. I was . . ." He paused, then said in a rush. "I was lonely. Would you mind if I held you for a while?"

Remembering the way she melted whenever he kissed her, she shook her head. "I really don't think that's a good idea." Secretly, she thought it was a wonderful idea. Just not a smart one. Especially now, when her senses were more acute, when she could smell his need and his desire. Was he as aware of her yearnings as she was of his?

She saw the hurt in his eyes before he blinked it away.

He bowed from the waist in a courtly gesture. "I am sorry to have troubled you," he said, and turning around, he stepped through the doorway.

He even looked good walking away.

Did she really want him to go?

She reminded herself that he was a vampire, master of the city. He could take any woman he wanted.

And he wanted her.

"Joaquin, wait."

He stopped but didn't look back at her.

"I'd like to have you hold me." How could she turn him away when he had held her and comforted her in her darkest hour?

She saw his shoulders tense. "I do not need your pity, Regan."

"It isn't pity. I'm lonely, too. And worried about the future."

Slowly, he turned away from the door. He hesitated a moment, as if having second thoughts, and then he moved toward the bed, slid in beside her, and gathered her into his arms.

His nearness set her heart to beating double-time as she rested her head on his shoulder. It felt all too comfortable to be lying beside him, all too right when it was oh, so wrong! She closed her eyes when he began to stroke her hair. When had anything felt so good? His touch was tender, caring, sensual. His breath was warm against her neck, his body a temptation she didn't want to resist.

"Ah, Regan," he murmured huskily, "do you know what a treasure you are?"

She hoped he didn't expect an answer because she couldn't seem to find her voice.

"I have lived alone for so long," he went on. "I told myself it was better that way. It was not until I met you that I realized how empty my existence has been, how lonely I have been."

"Joaquin . . ."

He placed a finger over her lips. "Shh. I do not expect anything from you in return, my lovely one. I only wanted you to know that you have enriched my life. Anything you ask of me, save one thing, I will give you."

She knew what that one thing was. He wouldn't take her life, even if she wanted him to.

"I won't ask that of you again," she said. "I promise."

"Will you seal it with your blood?"

Her eyelids flew open. "What are you talking about? You mean, like a blood oath?"

"I will taste you. You will taste me."

"Taste how?" she asked suspiciously.

"Nothing like what you are thinking," he assured her. "I will prick your finger and taste a drop of your blood, and then you will taste mine."

"I don't know . . ."

"It will not hurt, nor will it bind you to me in any way, or make you as I am."

She wasn't worried about him bringing her across. She knew how vampires were made and it took more than a drop of blood. Still, a voluntary exchange of blood was . . . creepy. Intimate. Intriguing.

"All right," she agreed reluctantly.

Santiago sat up and settled her on his lap so that her legs straddled his thighs. She watched nervously as, using his thumbnail, he made a small cut in his little finger. A single drop of dark red blood oozed from the tiny wound.

Fighting down her revulsion, Regan leaned forward and licked the blood from the tip of his finger. It was warm and surprisingly sweet.

Taking her hand in his, he made a similar cut in her little finger. Instead of licking the blood, he took her finger into his mouth.

A shaft of liquid heat shot straight to her belly, then spread to every nerve ending in her body.

Still holding her hand in his, he said, "Was that so bad?"

"No," she replied hoarsely.

Slowly, deliberately, he wrapped his arms around her. His dark eyes glittered with desire; she could feel the male heat of him pressing against her belly.

She stared into his eyes—deep blue eyes, dark with hunger, not for blood, but for her.

Looking into those eyes, she was afraid that he was going to lay her down on the bed and make love to her, and even more afraid that she was going to let him.

"I thought . . ." It was suddenly hard to speak. Clearing her throat, she tried again. "I thought you said you just wanted to hold me."

"I am holding you."

She nodded. If he were holding her any closer, she would be behind him.

His hand slid into her hair, then, drawing her head toward his, he kissed her. He didn't close his eyes and neither did she.

His eyes . . . fathomless midnight blue eyes that burned with an inner fire. His tongue teased her lips, his hand massaged her back; his touch like nothing she had ever felt before. How could such a simple thing feel so provocative, so sensual? She squirmed against him and heard him groan. With pain or pleasure, she couldn't be sure. She only knew that she, too, was feeling aroused, and more so with every stroke of his hand, every stroke of his tongue.

Muttering an oath, he lifted her from his lap, stretched out on the mattress and drew her down beside him, one arm lightly draped over her waist.

"What are you doing?" she asked, feeling bereft of his touch.

"Keeping my word," he said, his voice ragged. "And believe me, just holding you is the most difficult thing I have ever done."

Chapter 19

Vasile stared at the body at his feet. Word of the girl's death had brought him home. Nadia had been one of the young ones, just entering her prime. She had been betrothed to one of their finest young men. Vasile had held great hopes for the pair of them, knowing they would produce strong progeny. Now that hope lay dead at his feet.

"Who did this?" He glanced at the men and women gathered around him. "Who did this!"

"A man from the village. She killed one of his sheep. He shot her while she was feeding."

A vile oath escaped Vasile's lips. The girl's loss was a huge blow. His gaze rested on the other single pack females. Two of them would not be of breeding age for another five or six years. The third, Zina, was approaching middle age. She should have been mated by now, but she had refused all offers, as was her right.

He swore again. He had never intended to mate. His heart had died with Marishka. For years, he had been content to be the leader of the mountain pack, to slake his lust on mortal whores. But now . . .

perhaps it was time to put the past behind him and take a mate. His thoughts immediately turned to Santiago's woman. He had intended to kill her but then, in one act of sheer stupidity, he had bitten her, thereby making her one of them. According to pack law, she was now under his protection. The irony of it did not go unnoticed.

He swore yet again. And then he smiled. He had made the woman, Regan, one of them. She was a healthy female in her prime, the perfect age to begin breeding. When he returned to America, he would make her his. He knew she would not be willing, which would make their joining that much more enjoyable. He did not want a mate who wouldn't fight, who wouldn't challenge him from time to time.

They buried Nadia's mutilated body in the family plot high in the mountains. When it was done, Vasile took Nadia's parents aside. "I will avenge her," he promised.

"I will go with you," Nadia's father said.

"No."

"It is my right."

Vasile nodded. He had not planned to stay here for more than a day or two, but now, looking into Stefan's eyes, he knew he couldn't refuse to let the man accompany him. Family ties ran strong in their kind, as did the need for vengeance.

"When the moon is full," Vasile said curtly, even though it meant staying longer than he had originally intended.

Nadia's father bowed his head. "When the moon is full."

* * *

Standing at the window of his house, Vasile gazed out into the darkness. He had not been back here in years. Guilt gnawed at him when he considered the decline of his people. Their spirits were low, their numbers decreasing, their hunting grounds growing ever smaller as civilization spread outward. Other packs were growing larger, stronger. Perhaps it was time to relocate the pack . . .

He turned as someone knocked at the door.

"Come," he called.

The woman who entered his dwelling was tall and fair skinned, with short brown hair and dark brown eyes. She inclined her head in his direction, a sign of respect from a member of the pack to its leader.

"What do you want, Zina?" he asked brusquely.

"Have you come home to stay?" she asked, her voice equally brusque.

"No."

"Your place is here, with us. The pack needs you."

"They follow you well enough."

She shook her head. "I am not their leader. Our young men are restless, they need your guidance." She lifted her chin, the gesture as defiant as her stance, her gaze intent as she met his. "It is time for you to take a mate."

Muttering an oath, he stalked toward her, his lips peeled back in an angry snarl. "You dare much, Zina," he warned. It was not the first time she had challenged his authority. She was a strong-willed woman. She had never mated and seemed content to remain single. Long ago, when the pack's number began to decrease, he had ordered her to mate. To Vasile's amazement, she had refused. Had she done so in front of the pack, he would have had no choice but to kill her for her insubordination. Instead, he had put her in charge of the pack when he was away.

She stood her ground without flinching. "You need a mate," she repeated. "It will bind the pack together. It will show them that you have not deserted us." She took a deep breath. "I offer myself."

Vasile stared at her, stunned by her audacity. Had she been waiting for him to return to the pack? Was that why she had never taken another as her mate? She was a strong female, the only one the pack would follow. Between them, they would produce strong, healthy offspring. Had he not been consumed with his desire to avenge Marishka's death, he might have considered taking Zina for his mate long ago even though he bore no love for her, no tender feelings. But he had always admired her courage.

Vasile frowned as he considered her proposition. Werewolves, like feral wolves, mated for life. "You wish to be my mate?"

"I will have no other."

He grunted softly. "Our pack will soon have a new female. She was blooded by me and as such, she is my responsibility. I intend to have her as my mate as well."

"She is an outsider."

Vasile shrugged. "Perhaps, but she will be mine."

"I will accept her among us," Zina said, a touch of arrogance in her tone, "but I will not be subservient to her."

Approaching the woman, Vasile rubbed his body against hers. He took a deep breath, drawing in her scent. She was still in her prime, strong and healthy. He could do worse. He grasped a handful of her hair and drew her head toward his. For a moment, he stared into her eyes and then he kissed her. There was nothing of warmth or tenderness in his touch. It was a token of possession, nothing more.

"Prepare yourself," he said, his voice rough. "We will join the first of the week."

"So soon?"

"Is that a problem?"

"No."

"Tell the others," he said. If they were going to do it, they might as well do it as soon as possible.

With a nod, she turned and left the house.

Vasile stared after her. Taking Zina for a mate would mean staying here, at least for as long as it took to ensure that she conceived. If they mated in human form, the child would be human; if they mated in wolf form, the child would be born a were-wolf, compelled to shift when it reached puberty.

For a time, he contemplated the prospect of fatherhood but, all too soon, his thoughts returned to Santiago's woman. She would soon learn to accept her new state of being. If she had survived the first change, she would grow stronger with each successive change, making her more suited to be his mate. As the days and weeks passed, Santiago would gradually relax his guard, making it easier for Vasile to take him unawares when next they met.

He grunted softly. Coming home had been the right thing to do. Feeling suddenly restless, he went to look out the window again as a familiar tingling, like the prick of a thousand needles, slithered down his spine.

The new moon was rising. It was time to hunt.

Chapter 20

When Regan woke in the morning, she was alone in the bed. Picking up the pillow Santiago had slept on, she took a deep breath, her nostrils filling with his scent. She knew he had held her all through the night because nightmares had awakened her three times. Each time, it had been Santiago's voice that had calmed her fears and his touch that had soothed her.

Sitting up, she glanced around the room. Where did he sleep? Was he close by?

Driven by her curiosity, she wandered through the house, hoping she would have some sense of his presence, but maybe that was impossible. When he slept, it was the sleep of the dead.

Her stomach growled loudly, reminding her that she hadn't eaten since the day before. She blew out a sigh. She wouldn't find anything to eat or drink here, she thought glumly.

Returning to the bedroom, she dressed quickly and gathered her things together. It was time to go home, time to check her messages, do her laundry, clean out her refrigerator, go grocery shopping, and get in touch with Michael.

Still, she hesitated. The only way to get home was to take Santiago's car. She didn't think he would mind. She didn't like taking his car without his permission, but walking through this neighborhood alone, even in the daytime, was out of the question. Besides, it was a long walk to her apartment, and Santiago wouldn't need the Speedster before nightfall. She would have it back by then.

She wrote him a quick note, grabbed her handbag and her suitcase, and left his lair. It was creepy, moving through the deserted warehouse by herself. Hurrying as fast as she dared, she picked her way through the gloom and the debris, breathing a sigh of relief when she stepped out into the sunshine. His car was parked at the curb.

She punched in the code for the lock, opened the door, and slid behind the wheel, thinking how amazing it was that he could leave his car parked in this part of town and expect it to be there, untouched, the following night.

She punched in the ignition code, glad that she remembered it, and pulled away from the curb. She had never driven anything as expensive or anything that handled so easily. No wonder he loved this car, she thought, it practically drove itself.

She pulled up in front of her apartment a short time later. Exiting the car, she retrieved her purse and her luggage, locked the door, and made her way across the sidewalk toward the entrance of her building.

The manager stood near the curb, watering the yard. He was a kindly old man, always admonishing her to find a nice young man and settle down.

He smiled as she approached. "Miss Delaney," he said. "I haven't seen you in donkey's years. I was beginning to worry about you."

"No need, Mr. DeLuca, I'm fine. I was called away on an emergency."

"Oh, right! I don't know where my head is these days. Miss Polly told me she was collecting your mail. I hope it wasn't anything serious that called you away."

"No, it was just a . . . a personal matter that needed my attention," she said, wondering what he would think if he knew he had a werewolf living in his building. Would he evict her?

"Oh, I fixed that broken window," Mr. DeLuca said.

"Broken window?"

"On the north side of the apartment. I replaced it while you were gone. I hope you don't mind."

Regan frowned inwardly. Broken window? What broken window?

"Ordinarily, I would have asked your permission before entering your apartment," Mr. DeLuca said apologetically, "but since I couldn't get ahold of you . . ."

"No, that's all right."

"You know I never intrude on my tenants."

She laid her hand on his arm. "Thank you for fixing it for me. I should have told her about it, but . . . I, uh, I was in a hurry when I left, and it was late. How's Mrs. DeLuca?" she asked, quickly changing the subject.

"Doing much better. The doctor says she'll be up and around in no time at all."

"I'm glad." Evelyn DeLuca was a tiny woman, hardly bigger than a minute, and perhaps the clumsiest woman Regan had ever known. Mrs. DeLuca was forever breaking things, usually crockery, but her latest mishap had resulted in a broken leg. "Tell her hello for me."

"I'll do that."

Entering the lobby, Regan took the elevator to her floor, turned left, and walked down the hallway to her apartment, noting, as she did so, that Mr. DeLuca had painted the hallway in her absence. The walls, once a rather stomach-churning shade of pea green, were now a pale and much more becoming shade of sky blue. She would have to remember to compliment him on his color choice.

Unlocking the door, she stepped inside and closed it behind her. For a moment, she just stood there, grateful to be home again.

Dropping her bags on the sofa, she glanced at the window Mr. DeLuca had replaced. No doubt it had been broken the night Santiago had confronted Vasile. She lifted a hand to the back of her head, thinking she was lucky to be alive.

Going into the kitchen, she filled a pitcher with water and then went from room to room, watering her wilted plants. When that was done, she returned to the kitchen. She decided on French toast and sausage for breakfast. It took only minutes to prepare. She put her plate on the table, poured herself a small glass of grapefruit juice and a cup of coffee, and then sat down. She ate slowly, savoring every bite. It felt good to eat without Santiago watching her every move, and yet she missed having him there.

He loved her.

She loved him.

With a sigh, she pushed her plate away, her

appetite gone. Why, out of all the men she had known, did she have to fall in love with a vampire? Talk about star-crossed lovers!

Rising, she rinsed her dishes and put them in the dishwasher. She took a shower, washed her hair, and then slipped into an old T-shirt and a pair of shorts. She turned on the radio, found a station she liked, and then spent the next hour and a half dusting, vacuuming, and sweeping—ordinary tasks to keep her from thinking of an extraordinary man.

It worked, until she changed the sheets on her bed, remembering that his were black satin, remembering that she had spent the night in his arms.

She pushed the memory away, gathered her dirty sheets, and shoved them in the washer.

Needing a distraction, she called Michael.

He answered the phone on the second ring. "Reggie! It's about time. How are you? Where are you?"

"I'm fine, Mike. I'm home. Anything new?"

"Nada. Things have been as quiet as a tomb."

She grimaced at his choice of words. "Thank God."

"Yeah. Whoever the killer is, he seems to have left town."

"For good, I hope," she said fervently.

"Yeah. Listen, I'm off duty tonight. How about dinner?"

She hesitated a moment, doubts running through her mind. She was a werewolf now. What if Michael suspected? No, that was silly. She looked the same as always. She knew Joaquin wouldn't like it, but he didn't need to know.

"Reggie?"

She took a deep breath. "Sure. What time?"

"Six? Six-thirty."

"All right. I have some errands to run before then. Why don't I meet you at Mr. Charlie's?" It was a small café on the other side of town, favored by cops and others in law enforcement of one kind or another.

"Okay by me. See you then."

"All right."

"And Reggie?"

"Yeah?"

"I missed you."

She hesitated a moment before replying, "Me, too, you. See you at six-thirty."

Regan stared at the phone in her hand, wondering what Santiago would say if she told him she had a date, and then she shook her head. She didn't have to tell him anything. Even though he had said he loved her, even though she loved him, that was as far as it went. Try as she might, she just couldn't see any kind of future for the two of them. She was a werewolf. He was a vampire. She lived by day. He lived by night. She was going to find Vasile and destroy him and when she did, she wouldn't be a werewolf anymore. Joaquin would always be a vampire.

Vasile. She had no idea where he was or how to find him. But she would.

She spent the rest of the day pretending nothing in her life had changed. She did her laundry. She picked up her overdue cleaning and then went grocery shopping, wondering all the while what people would think and say and do if they knew there was a werewolf in their midst.

Returning home, she went into the kitchen to put her groceries away, surprised to find that she had bought mostly meat instead of the fruits, vegetables and whole wheat bread that once made up most of her normal diet.

At five, she took another shower and shaved her underarms and her legs—were they hairier than usual? Standing naked in front of the mirror in the bedroom, she looked at herself critically. As far as she could tell, she looked the same as always. Needing to feel feminine, she decided to forego her usual slacks and a sweater in favor of a dress and heels.

At five forty-five, she picked up her handbag, checked to make sure her gun was inside and loaded, and left the house. If she hurried, she could drop off Santiago's car, catch a cab, and get to the restaurant by six-thirty.

Her heart began pounding a bit erratically as she pulled up in front of Santiago's lair. From the outside, the building was disreputable. The windows were boarded up and there was so much indecent graffiti scrawled across the walls, you couldn't see the color of the building's original paint. She wondered how long Santiago had lived there, and where he would go if some developer came along and bought the property out from under him.

After locking the car door, she picked her way across the sidewalk and ducked through the doorway.

She stopped just inside, wishing she had a flashlight. With the sun setting, what little light there was disappeared as she went deeper into the building.

She had almost reached the staircase at the far side of the building when she realized she wasn't alone.

Someone was following her.

She glanced over her shoulder, her gaze searching the shadows. "Who's there?"

Who's there, who's there, who's . . . ? Her voice echoed off the stone walls.

Had she imagined it? She was about to turn back toward the stairs when a man stepped out from behind a cement pillar. She couldn't see his face clearly in the darkness, but she could smell him. He reeked of old sweat and alcohol and some sickly sweet smell she didn't recognize.

"What are you doing in here, girlie?" he asked, staggering toward her.

She didn't answer. Instead, she reached into her handbag and withdrew her gun.

"Get out of here," she said. "You're trespassing."

"Trespassin'?" He barked a laugh. "You gonna tell me you live here?" He laughed again. It was an ugly sound, filled with menace.

"I mean it," she said. "Get out of here, or I'll shoot."

"Nah, you don't wanna do that," he said, and lunged toward her.

Heart pounding, Regan squeezed the trigger— and still the man came toward her. She couldn't have missed, she thought, not at this range. And then there was no more time for thought.

Before she could fire again, the man was on her. He yanked the gun from her grasp and tossed it away. She struggled against him, fighting with every ounce of strength she possessed, but he was impervious to her blows. Once, her fingers touched something warm and sticky and she knew then that she hadn't missed, and that he was high on something stronger than whiskey.

Muttering obscenities, he wrestled her to the floor.

She screamed when his filthy hands groped

under her skirt, inching up her calf to her thigh. Why had she worn a dress? She jabbed her knee into his groin but to no avail. He only laughed that awful laugh. She gagged when his mouth covered hers.

Ad then, suddenly, he was gone.

She heard a startled cry as he was lifted off of her, a sharp sound of pain, and then all was quiet. The air filled with the sharp stink of urine—and the scent of blood.

Scrambling to her hands and knees, Regan searched the floor for her gun, sobbing with relief when she found it.

Gaining her feet, her pistol clutched in a two-handed grip, she moved as silently as she could toward the doorway. If she could just make it outside . . .

She screamed as a hand closed over her arm.

"Regan."

Relief washed through her at the sound of his voice. Turning, she threw her arms around his neck.

"Are you all right?" he asked.

She nodded. "How did you know I was here?"

His hand stroked her hair. "I always know when you are near. Come."

Taking the gun from her hand, he slipped his arm around her waist and guided her down the stairs to his lair. Inside, he eased her down on the sofa, then dropped her gun on the coffee table.

"You are bleeding."

Regan glanced down at her legs. Blood was oozing from a cut just above her left knee. She looked up at Santiago, thinking that bleeding in front of a vampire wasn't a very smart thing to do.

Fear skittered down her spine when she saw the faint red glow in his eyes.

"Stay here," he said, and fled the room.

Returning a few moments later, he handed her a damp washcloth, then turned his back to her, his hands clenched at his sides, while she wiped away the blood, grateful it was just a scratch.

"Does it bother you that much, the sight of blood? I thought you could go a long time without feeding?"

"The need to feed grows less with age. The desire never goes away. Seeing your blood . . . you have no idea how tempting it is, or how it arouses me."

Quickly blotting the last of it, she wadded the bloody cloth up and placed it on the table beside her gun, then pulled her skirt down over her knees, glad that it was long enough to cover the wound. "I'm through."

He hesitated a moment before he turned to face her.

"I have to go," Regan said, getting to her feet.

"Then why did you come?"

"I borrowed your car this morning. I hope you don't mind. It's parked outside. I thought you might need it." She didn't realize how silly that sounded until she said it. He was a vampire, the master of the city. He didn't need his car to get around. Why not admit that she had wanted to see him again? The car had just been an excuse.

The look in his eyes told her he knew it, as well.

"Can I use your phone?" she asked. "I need to call a cab and I left my phone at home."

"There is no need. I will take you wherever you wish to go."

"No, I . . ." Her voice trailed off. She couldn't tell

him why she needed a ride. How could she have ever thought coming here was a good idea? Was she subconsciously hoping he would talk her out of her date with Michael? Why had she even agreed to go out with Michael when it was Santiago she wanted to be with? The words, *because Mike's not a vampire*, whispered in the back of her mind. Vampire or not, it didn't change how she felt about Santiago. "Just let me call a cab."

He looked at her, his eyes narrowed. "Regan, what is going on?"

She blew out a breath. She might just as well tell him the truth and get it over with. "I have a date with Michael."

"Indeed?" The word was clipped, cold. "Is that why you came here? To tell me you are going out with another man?"

"No, I . . ." She glanced at her watch. "I'm sorry," she said miserably. "I shouldn't have come here. I've got to go."

"Take my car," he said curtly.

"No."

"Cab drivers will not pick up fares in this part of town."

"Joaquin . . ."

"Go! I would not want you to be late."

"The body . . ."

"I will take care of it."

Afraid anything she said or did from that point on would only make matters worse, she grabbed her gun and hurried out the door. The scent of blood and death enveloped her when she reached the ground floor of the building.

She averted her eyes as she passed the dead man, thinking how differently things would have turned out if Santiago hadn't come to her rescue. Of course, she wouldn't have been there in the first place if it wasn't for him.

After unlocking the car door, she slid behind the wheel, locked the door, and punched in the ignition code, only to sit there, her hands trembling on the wheel as she fought the urge to cry.

Taking a deep breath, she pulled away from the curb, wondering what excuse she could give Michael for being late.

He was waiting for her inside the restaurant. He rose when she entered. Murmuring, "Hi, gorgeous," he wrapped his arms around her and kissed her cheek.

"Hi, Mike. Sorry I'm late."

"It's okay." Taking a step back, his gaze moved over her. "It was worth the wait."

"Thank you."

A hostess seated them a few moments later. Regan noted that most of the tables were empty, but that wasn't surprising. Mr. Charlie's was the kind of place that drew a late-night crowd.

"It's been a long time," Michael remarked. "And seems even longer."

"Yes."

He tilted his head to the side, his expression thoughtful. "You look . . . different somehow."

Regan's heart did a funny little flip-flop in her chest. "Different?" Could he tell that she had been bitten? Was it that obvious? "Different how?"

He sat back, his arms crossed over his chest. "I'm not sure."

"I don't know what could be different," she said, forcing a smile. "I haven't changed anything. Same hair, same perfume, same lipstick."

"Probably just my imagination. Whatever the difference is, I approve."

"So, how are things at work?" she asked, hoping to steer the conversation into another, safer direction.

"Same as always. Oh, Holloway was promoted to lieutenant on Friday."

"Holloway! I thought you were next in line?"

"Yeah, me, too."

"You deserved it more. Holloway's an ass."

"I can't argue with you there," Michael said, laughing. "Here comes the waitress. Are you going to have your usual?"

Her usual was a large Cobb salad and a glass of iced tea. "Not tonight. I think I'll have a steak. Very rare. And a glass of red wine."

Michael's eyebrows lifted in surprise. "Rare? Not well done?"

She shrugged. "I decided to try it your way tonight."

He looked at her oddly for a moment, then gave the waitress their order.

Regan fidgeted with her napkin. It seemed odd to be sitting there, though she wasn't sure why. Maybe it was just odd to be with Mike after spending so much time with Santiago. She asked Mike about work, her mind wandering as he told her about the case he was working on.

When their order arrived, Regan stared at the slab of meat on her plate for a moment before cutting into it. What on earth had possessed her to order it rare? It was blood red inside, more like raw than rare. Stabbing a piece with her fork, she took a bite. Heaven, she thought, pure heaven. Why had she ever ordered her steaks well done?

She was halfway through her meal when she had the unmistakable impression that she was being watched. Slowly turning her head to the side, she saw Santiago seated at a table near the window. She felt a sharp pain in her heart when she noticed that he was with the same red-haired female vampire she had seen him with once before.

She was wondering how the redhead had eluded the barrier when Santiago looked her way and caught her staring. Her first instinct was to lower her gaze; instead, she smiled faintly, as if it was of no concern at all that he was out with someone else. And why should it matter? Santiago was a vampire. His date was a vampire. As her grandmother always said, there can be happiness only when like marries like, a saying that had never been truer than now.

Regan tore her gaze from Santiago's and smiled at Mike while an impish little voice in the back of her head whispered that werewolves and vampires had a lot more in common than werewolves and mortals.

Chapter 21

Regan forced a smile as she bid Michael good night at the curb. They had enjoyed a leisurely dinner followed by coffee and dessert, and then spent the rest of the evening dancing. She had been all too aware of Santiago's presence, all too jealous of the woman he danced with. Once, Regan had thought he was going to ask her to dance, but he had walked past her as if she didn't exist.

He and the red-haired woman had left the restaurant a little after midnight. Off for a night of hunting, she thought, fighting off a wave of jealousy.

"I had a good time tonight, Reggie," Michael said, taking her into his arms.

"Me, too." It was partially true. She had been having a good time until Santiago showed up with the redhead.

"I'm off again tomorrow night. What do you say? Wanna catch an early dinner and a movie?"

She didn't, not really, but the thought of Santiago and the red-haired vampire made her smile and say, "Sure, why not?"

"Great, I'll pick you up at what, six-thirty, seven?"

"I'll check the Net for showtimes and give you a call."

"Sounds good. I've got court in the morning, so we'll have to make it an early night. Hey," he said, noticing the Speedster for the first time as she punched in the code to unlock the door. "When did you get that?"

"What?"

"The Speedster." He whistled softly. "Those things cost a small fortune."

"Oh, that, I . . . my car's in the shop and I . . . uh, borrowed this from a friend."

"Must be some friend."

"Yes. Well, good night, Mike."

He slipped his arm around her waist and kissed her good night. "See you tomorrow night."

With a nod, she slid behind the wheel, closed the door, and started the car. She waved to Michael as she pulled away from the curb.

Distracted, she punched her address into the Speedster's computer, then sat back and let the car do the driving. She wasn't taking the car back to Santiago this time; she didn't want to take a chance of barging in on him and the woman. If he wanted his car, he could darn well come and get it.

The Speedster pulled up to the curb and parked. The lights went out, the engine stopped, and the door opened.

Regan grabbed her handbag and got out of the car, only then remembering she hadn't left any lights on in her apartment. "Stop being such a coward," she muttered as she went up the stairs. "You're a vampire hunter and a werewolf. What is there to be afraid of?"

Even as she told herself there was nothing to

worry about, she pulled her gun out of her handbag. Better safe than sorry.

Turning down the corridor, she saw a tall, dark shape standing in front of her door.

"Nothing to worry about," she muttered as she aimed at the figure. "Right."

"Are you going to shoot me?"

"Santiago!" she exclaimed. "Damn you! You scared me out of a year's growth! What are you doing here? Why aren't you dancing with your redhead? Oh!" She clapped her hand over her mouth, horrified by what she had said and the unmistakable note of jealousy in her voice.

Shouldering her way past Santiago, she unlocked the door and hurried inside, her cheeks burning.

She bit down on her lower lip when she heard the door close behind her. She knew, without looking, that he had followed her into the room.

Her whole body tingled with awareness as she dropped her handbag on the coffee table and laid her gun beside it. He was here instead of with the redhead.

Heart pounding, she slowly turned to face him. "What are you doing here?" she asked.

"Do I need a reason?"

"So, you just came here because you had nothing better to do?" she prodded, thinking that if he said he had come for his car, she would smack him.

"I came because I wanted to see you." He took a step toward her. "I came because I saw you with another man and I wanted to rip his heart out." Another step. "I came because I missed you."

She let out a long, shuddering sigh. "Oh."

His arm curled around her waist. "I came because I hoped you missed me."

Her skin tingled where his hand rested on her hip. "Where's your dinner date?" she asked, pleased when her voice didn't tremble. "And what were the two of you doing in a restaurant, anyway? And how did she get past the barrier?"

"So many questions," he chided. His gaze moved over her face, as warm and tangible as a caress.

"Are you going to answer them?"

"An answer for a kiss."

Her heartbeat quickened.

He ran the tip of his finger over her lower lip. "Do we have a deal?"

Dry-mouthed, she could only nod.

Holding her gaze with his, he lowered his head and claimed her lips in a long, lingering kiss. When it was over, he said, "I took her home."

She nodded, and he kissed her again, his tongue exploring the depths of her mouth. "I was at the restaurant because you were there."

She wasn't sure she would survive another kiss like the last two, but she was willing to take a chance. He saved the best for last. If there had been an award for best kiss of the century, he would have won it, hands down.

When he took his mouth from hers, she felt as if he had taken a part of her soul as well.

"As for how Tatiana got past the barrier," he said, his voice low and husky with desire, "she does not reside in the park."

Regan stared up at him, all interest in the redhaired woman forgotten. Rising on her tiptoes, she pressed her lips to his, certain she would expire on the spot if he didn't kiss her one more time.

He pulled her up hard against him, so close that she couldn't tell where he ended and she began.

His mouth on hers did wonderfully magical, amazing things. She felt as if her feet had left the ground, as if she were flying through a rainbow world where colors had taste and substance and she was alive as never before. His hands cupped her buttocks, holding her fast. Feeling the heat of his desire fanned her own.

She moaned a soft protest when he took his mouth from hers, gasped with pleasure as his tongue traced the curve of her ear, then blazed a trail to the soft, tender skin along the side of her neck. The prick of his fangs came as a surprise, but not an unwelcome one.

A soft exclamation of sensual pleasure rose in Santiago's throat as he sipped the sweet nectar of her life force. The hunger rose up within him, demanding more, demanding that he take it all. She was sweet, so sweet; surely, if he drank his fill of the ambrosia in her veins, he would never be plagued by his hellish thirst again.

Lifting her into his arms, he carried her into the bedroom and stretched out beside her on the bed. He kissed her and caressed her until she was again pliant in his embrace and then he drank from her again, and again.

It wasn't until he realized her heartbeat was fluttering unevenly that the enormity of what he was doing penetrated the haze of pleasure that engulfed him. Rearing back, he stared down at her face. She was pale, so pale. What had he done?

"Regan? Regan!" Taking hold of her shoulders, he shook her. "Regan! Answer me."

Her eyelids fluttered open and she looked up at him, her gaze dreamy and unfocused.

Santiago swore. Bolting from the bedroom, he

went into the kitchen, quietly cursing himself for what he had done. He found a glass, filled it with grapefruit juice, and carried it back to the bedroom. Sliding his arm beneath her back, he lifted her to a sitting position. "Drink, Regan."

"Sleepy . . ."

"No, you must drink." He held the glass to her lips. "Drink, dammit!"

Startled by his gruff tone, she did as he asked.

When the glass was empty, he lowered her down to the bed, then returned to the kitchen. She needed sustenance, but what? He hadn't eaten food in hundreds of years and had no idea how to prepare most of the foodstuffs he found in the refrigerator or the cupboard. A sandwich, he thought. He had watched enough television commercials to know how to prepare a sandwich.

Moments later, he returned to the bedroom carrying a peanut butter and jelly sandwich and a glass of milk.

Sitting on the edge of the bed, he shook her gently. "Wake up, Regan. You must eat."

"Not hungry. Sleepy . . ."

Once again, he slid his arm beneath her. He coaxed her to eat and drink, all the while cursing himself for his selfishness. But for the blood of the werewolf in her veins, she would have died and it would have been all his fault. He had to be more careful in the future. She was far too tempting, and his resistance was far too weak where she was concerned.

When she finished eating, he gathered her into his arms and cradled her against his chest, frightened by how close he had come to losing her forever.

He held her all through the night, afraid to leave

her alone. In the early hours of the morning, he insisted she take more nourishment. Had she been an ordinary mortal, he would have given her his blood, but he wasn't sure how her body would react. He and Vasile had tasted each other's blood, but they had ingested only a small amount. He had no idea what effect his blood would have on Regan in her current state. It might make her stronger. It might be fatal. It was a risk he didn't dare take.

His skin tingled as dawn's first light brightened the sky, and still he held her, reluctant to let her go, afraid that if he left her, he would never see her again. He told himself he was being ridiculous. The color had returned to her cheeks. Her breathing and her heartbeat were normal. And still he held her, held her until it was too late for him to leave her house and seek his lair.

Swearing softy, he put her to bed, then went in search of a place to spend the day.

Regan woke reluctantly. She had been having such a beautiful dream, she hated to see it end. In it, Santiago had made love to her all night long—slow, sweet love that had satisfied her on every level and still left her hungering for more. She smiled, remembering. He had been a wonderful lover, creative, masterful, yet caring and tender. And because he was a vampire, he never grew weary, never had to rest. He had brought her to fulfillment again and again, made her weep with the beauty and the wonder of it. Now, she felt herself blushing as she remembered all the ways, and all the places, where they had made love. If only it hadn't been a dream . . .

She felt a little dizzy when she sat up. Once the

room stopped spinning, she glanced at her surroundings. She didn't remember going to bed last night; in fact, she didn't remember much of anything after coming home from her date with Michael. She frowned. Santiago had been here, waiting for her. He had followed her into the house. They had kissed and . . . She frowned. Her recollections grew hazy after that.

Rising, she went into the bathroom. She brushed her teeth, washed her hands, face, and neck . . . felt a jolt when her fingertips touched the skin beneath her ear. With a growing sense of trepidation, she turned her head to the side and looked in the mirror, blinked, and looked again. Good grief, were those bites on her neck?

Leaning forward, she examined the tiny puncture wounds more closely.

Vampire bites. She had seen enough to know what they looked like.

She went suddenly cold all over.

Santiago had bitten her last night.

And taken her blood.

She remembered now, though her recollection was none too clear. He had kissed her until she was lost in his touch and then he had taken her blood. She remembered his voice, thick with worry when he demanded that she eat, that she drink. He had held her all night long. She remembered waking several times, always in his arms, always hearing his voice, low and soothing, telling her to go back to sleep, assuring her that everything would be all right.

Returning to her room, Regan sat on the edge of the bed as a new thought occurred to her. The sun had been up the last time he had offered her something to eat. He couldn't have left the house when the sun was up. So, where was he now?

Recalling that he had slept under one of the motel beds when they were traveling, she stood and looked underneath her bed, but there was no sign of him. She checked the closet, even looked inside the cedar chest at the foot of her bed, though how he could fit his tall frame inside was beyond her.

But he wasn't there, either.

Putting on her slippers, she toured the house, looking in every conceivable place she could think of, but to no avail. Returning to the living room, she sat down on the sofa, her legs tucked beneath her. Where could he be? Remembering how he had cloaked his presence from her when they were in the cave, she knew he could be right in front of her and she wouldn't see him if he didn't want her to. A handy trick, she thought, and wondered if werewolves possessed that ability.

Too nervous to sit still, she went into the kitchen and punched in the code for a cup of coffee. When it was done, she carried it out onto the veranda and sat in the sun. The deck had been the main reason she rented the apartment. At night, she could see the lights of the city; during the day, she had a grand view of the mountains beyond.

She tried to relax but it was disconcerting, knowing there was a vampire in the house but not knowing where he was.

She thought about her date with Michael the previous night. He had sensed there was something different about her. How had he known? She looked the same on the outside. Did he have some sort of psychic power she wasn't aware of that allowed him to delve into her mind? Or had he sensed her internal unrest? Even when she wasn't consciously thinking about the next full moon or what had happened during the last one, the memory was always there, destroying her peace of mind, filling her with dread as she contemplated what was coming.

She was glad when the phone rang. Right now, any distraction would be welcome. "Hello?"

"Hey, Reggie."

"Michael. I was just thinking about you."

"Good things, I hope. Listen, I'm not going to be able to make it tonight. I had a phone call from my sister. Her husband was in an accident and she needs me to drive her to the hospital. I'll probably stay with her tonight."

"Sure, Mike, I understand." His sister, Jean, was pregnant and ready to deliver any minute. "Give her my love."

"Will do. I'll give you a call when I get a chance."

Regan said good-bye and hung up the phone, relieved that she wouldn't have to go out tonight and pretend everything was all right.

Picking up her cup, she sipped her coffee, aware of the taste and the aroma in a way she never had been before.

Werewolf. The word whispered through her mind. Sitting there, her face lifted to the sun, it seemed unreal, like a bad dream, but she knew it was all too true. She remembered it all so clearly, the intense pain as her body shifted, her heightened awareness of the world around her, the horrible hunger for flesh, any flesh, the giddy excitement of the hunt, and the exhilaration of the kill. Even in wolf form, she had been aware of Santiago's presence and found comfort in knowing she wasn't alone, just as she found a measure of comfort now, knowing he would be with her during the next full moon.

She shook her head. Why had this happened to her? And where was Vasile? She had to find him—and destroy him. It was the only way to break the curse.

She took a deep breath. She could do it. She had hunted vampires . . . but Vasile wouldn't be lying helpless in a coffin.

She wished Santiago could fight this battle for her. Unfortunately, it was something she had to do herself.

Either she would destroy Vasile or he would destroy her. Regan laughed humorlessly. Either way, she would be free of the werewolf's curse once and for all.

Chapter 22

Regan was curled up on the sofa that evening, reading a murder mystery, when Santiago suddenly appeared in the room.

"I hate it when you do that!" she exclaimed, one hand pressed to her heart. "Where have you been? I mean, where did you spend the day?"

"Under your bed."

His words sent a little shiver down her spine. He had been sleeping right below her. "Why didn't you want me to see you?"

"I was not hiding from you."

"Who then?" she asked, frowning. "No one else lives here."

He shrugged. "I have not survived this long by being careless."

She couldn't argue with that. She didn't want to argue with him at all. She just wanted to know exactly what had happened the night before.

"One minute we were making out," she remarked, "and then everything went blank." She lifted a hand to her neck, her fingertips probing the skin, but the marks were gone. "You drank from me, didn't you?" She heard the accusation in her voice. "That's why I felt so dizzy this morning."

He nodded, his expression unreadable. "I did not mean to take so much. I have no excuse except that . . ." He stopped, knowing that she would not want to hear what he had to say.

"Go on," she urged.

"Are you sure you want to hear it?"

"No, but tell me anyway."

He sat on the other end of the sofa. "I told you before, not all blood tastes the same. And yours is irresistible. I meant to take only a sip, but . . ." He shrugged. "It was like nothing I had ever tasted before. I knew if I took it all, I would never have to feed again."

"I don't believe you. Blood is blood."

"Perhaps. Or perhaps yours tastes so sweet because you mean so much to me."

"Joaquin . . ." She didn't want him to love her, didn't want to love him. But it was too late.

He smiled at her. It was a sad smile, as if he knew what she was thinking. And maybe he did.

She was trying to think of something to say when the doorbell rang. Muttering, "Who can that be?" she went to answer the door.

It was Michael.

"Hey, Reggie," he said cheerfully.

"Mike! I thought you were at the hospital with your sister."

"Yeah, well, as it turns out, Rob wasn't as badly hurt as they thought. He's going to be all right, although he's pretty banged up." He laughed softly. "Jean took one look at him and went into labor. She had the baby two hours ago. Prettiest little girl you've ever seen. The whole family's at the hospital, resting well." He smiled. "I know I'm a little late, but if you haven't eaten, we can still go out."

"What? Oh, well, about that, I wasn't expecting you, and . . ." Her voice trailed off when she realized Mike wasn't listening. He was looking over her shoulder. She didn't have to turn around to know what, or who, he was looking at.

"What the hell is he doing here?" Mike asked through clenched teeth.

"The same as you," Regan said, her temper flaring at the tone of his voice. "He came to, ah, visit."

"I see."

Regan felt her cheeks grow hot. She was afraid Mike saw things all too well.

"It didn't take you long to find another date, did it?" he said, his expression bleak.

"Mike . . ."

"I don't know what you see in him, Regan. Have you forgotten he's a vampire?" Mike asked, and then frowned. "How the hell did he get out of the park?"

Regan licked lips gone suddenly dry. "I . . ." She shrugged. "How should I know?"

"This is serious, Reggie," Mike said. "I'm going to have to report it to the department."

"I wish you wouldn't."

Mike shook his head. "I don't know you anymore." He glanced at Santiago, then looked at Regan again, his expression morose. "I just hope you know what you're doing, Reggie. Good night."

Helpless to explain, she watched him walk away. After closing the door, she turned to face Santiago. "Is he going to make trouble for you?"

Santiago snorted, as if the mere idea was ludicrous.

Drawing her into his arms, he kissed her cheek. "I must go."

"Why?"

"You grow more tempting each time I see you. I do not think it wise for me to be near you when I have not fed."

"Oh."

"I am only thinking of what is best for you."

She knew he was right but she couldn't help feeling as though he were abandoning her even as she told herself it was silly to feel that way. "I thought you could go a long time without . . . you know."

"Usually I can, but after last night, I find myself wanting to taste you again. And even if you were willing, I am afraid a taste would not be enough, so I think I should go."

Forcing a smile, she said, "If I don't see you before the next full moon . . ."

"I will see you before then," he said, rising. "I doubt I could stay away that long. Good night, Regan," he said quietly, and vanished from her sight.

She stared at the place where he had stood, feeling suddenly bereft. Since the night she had met him in the park, he had become a constant in her life, so much so that she could scarcely imagine her life without him.

At loose ends, she flipped on the Satellite Screen, surfing through the online guide. A thousand channels to choose from and she couldn't find a single thing she wanted to watch. Switching to one of the music channels, she turned the volume down low, then picked up the book she had been reading before Joaquin arrived. It had been written by one of her favorite authors, but tonight she couldn't concentrate, couldn't think of anything but Joaquin Santiago with his long black hair, deep sexy voice, and eyes that were both mysterious and mesmerizing.

Santiago, the vampire. The master of the city. He was the most fascinating, interesting creature she had ever known.

Chapter 23

Vasile stood in the moonlight, surrounded by all the members of the pack as he waited for his bride to join him. He wore a white shirt, open at the throat, and white slacks. His feet were bare.

There was a ripple in the night air as Zina appeared. She wore a long black dress and carried a bouquet of blood-red roses. Her feet, too, were bare.

She stopped at his side, her head high and proud. After this night, she would be the pack's alpha female.

Vasile turned in a slow circle, his gaze resting on the face of each one present. "I have called you here this night to witness my joining with Zina. From this night forward, she will be my mate. I will protect her and defend her with my life. Any one who dares to harm her, harms me, and will be dealt with accordingly. I now demand your allegiance and fealty to my mate. How say you all?"

Each member of the pack nodded in agreement.

Vasile took Zina's hand in his. "I now take you as

my mate, and pledge to you my loyalty and my protection. How say you?"

"I now take you as my mate," she repeated. "I pledge to you my loyalty and my devotion."

With a curt nod, Vasile said, "It is done." Blowing out a deep breath, he kissed his bride while the pack howled their approval.

Swinging Zina into his arms, Vasile carried her into the woods. She wasn't Marishka and would never be Marishka, but she would serve him well.

Chapter 24

Regan leaned back in her chair and rubbed her eyes. She had spent the entire morning surfing the Net in search of a job. To her dismay, opportunities for former vampire hunters were few and far between. The skills that she possessed were not in great demand in the business world. For a time, she had thought she might go back to her old job with the department, but the killings in the park had ceased. At any rate, the killer in the park hadn't been a vampire, but a werewolf. And Santiago had destroyed the vampire responsible for killing the Undead.

Two weeks had passed since she and Santiago had returned from the Black Hills. During that time, the city had been quiet. No murders had been reported. The mayor had opened the park to human traffic again, and life in the city had returned to normal.

She wondered if her life would ever be normal again. She was still trying to figure out how to find Vasile. She hadn't heard from Michael since their last disastrous meeting, but it was just as well. She had been thinking of ending their relationship, such as it was. He deserved a woman who would love him wholly and completely, and Regan couldn't do that. She hadn't heard from Santiago lately, either. In spite of his words to the contrary, she hadn't seen him since the night Michael came to call. She wondered if it was his guilt in taking her blood that was keeping him away, or if he had decided he had more of a future with the red-haired vampire.

Regan shook her head. She had spent far too much time and lost far too much sleep wondering about the female vampire and her relationship to Santiago. Was the woman a relative? A friend? A lover? What was she doing here in the city? Why wasn't she confined to the park? And why, Regan wondered irritably, hadn't she asked Santiago these questions when she had the chance?

With a sigh, Regan turned off her computer. She knew why she hadn't asked about the redhead. She had been too caught up in Santiago's kisses to think of anything else or to care about anything else. Where was he? Why hadn't he come to see her?

On more occasions that she liked to admit, she had started to go to him, only to turn around at the last minute and return home. As much as she wanted to see him again, what was the point? She wanted a home and a family and as normal a life as possible, though where she would find anyone who would marry her now was a mystery. No man in his right mind, including Michael, was going to want a werewolf for a wife or for the mother of his children. But she had to cling to the hope that she was wrong, that somewhere out there, there was a man she could love, one who would love her unconditionally in return. A little voice in the back of her mind told her that Santiago was that man, that even though he couldn't give her children, he would love her and cherish her all the days of her life. *And you could always adopt a child,* that same little voice whispered. She could hear her child now, introducing herself to the teacher on the first day of school.

"Hi. My name is Annica. My mom is an out-of-work vampire hunter and a werewolf and my dad is the master of the city."

With a wordless sound of despair, Regan went into the kitchen for a glass of water. Two weeks until the next full moon and she could already feel the tension growing within her.

Putting the glass in the sink, Regan picked up her handbag, checked to make sure her gun was inside, and left the house. For a time, she drove aimlessly through the city, her mind blessedly blank until she pulled up in front of You Bet Your Life Park.

Sitting there, she stared up at Santiago's apartment. Was he in there? Or was he at his lair in the Byways? And what was she doing here?

Exiting the car, she made her way to the office of the Vampire Arms, then shook her head. Idiot, she thought. There was no one on duty during daylight hours.

Leaving the office, she went into the lobby. An unnatural silence hung over the building. Taking a deep breath, she stepped into the elevator and said, "fifth floor."

"Fifth floor," the computer repeated.

The door closed with a swoosh and opened moments later in front of Santiago's apartment.

Squaring her shoulders, Regan knocked on the door. She waited a minute, then knocked again. No answer.

With a sigh, she left the building. It was probably just as well that he wasn't at home, she thought as she pulled away from the curb. In her current state of mind, there was no telling what she might have done, or what she might have let him do.

She turned on the radio and then drove to the mall where she spent the next three hours wandering aimlessly from store to store. She treated herself to a manicure and a pedicure and a full body massage, bought some new underwear and a pair of new sweats, and indulged her passion for chocolate by ordering a double-thick chocolate malt. She downloaded some new tunes for her Mbox, picked up some takeout Chinese food for dinner, and headed for home.

It was nearing sunset when she pulled up in front of her apartment. She gathered her purchases, her handbag, and her dinner and took the elevator up to her condo. Stepping out of the elevator, she wondered what Santiago was doing that night.

She found the answer waiting for her at her door.

Excitement fluttered in the pit of her stomach when she saw him standing there, tall, dark, and delicious. Looking at him, she lost her appetite for Chinese food. If only he was on the menu, instead!

"Hi," she said, unlocking the door. "What are you doing here?"

"You were at my place earlier, were you not?"

"Yes. Why didn't you answer the door?"

"I wasn't there."

"Then how'd you know I was there?"

He shrugged. "I caught your scent when I arrived."

"Oh, well, come on in," she said as she stepped inside and switched on the light.

He followed her inside and closed the door.

Regan tossed her shopping bags and her purse on a chair, then carried the takeout bag into the kitchen and put it in the refrigerator for later. When she turned around, Santiago was standing in the doorway, watching her.

"So," he said, "what did you want?"

You, she thought, *I want you*. Aloud, she stammered, "I . . . nothing really . . . I just . . . I mean . . ." She took a deep breath and started over. "I just wanted to see you."

He took a step toward her on silent feet, his gaze focused on her face. He moved like a panther, she thought, his body supple and dangerous and beautiful.

"Have you, by chance, been missing me?"

She nodded. Going to his place had been a really bad idea, she thought, her heartbeat speeding up. He was trouble, but he came wrapped in an irresistible package.

He took another step toward her.

Regan glanced over her shoulder but there was no place to run, no place to hide.

He canted his head to one side. "Do you want me to go?"

"Go?" Lordy, that was the last thing she wanted. It was just that he made her want things, feel things, that she wasn't prepared to handle, things that, once done, could not be undone. If she surrendered to him now, there would be no going back.

"Regan, what do you want from me?"

"Nothing," she said, not meeting his eyes. "Everything." She shivered when his arms went around her. "Joaquin . . ."

"Do not be afraid, my lovely one. I will not hurt you." He rubbed his cheek against hers. "Do you know how much I have missed you these past weeks?"

"Then why have you stayed away?"

"I wanted to give you time to sort out your feelings, and I needed time away from you." He smiled when she looked up at him. "You have no idea how you tempt me, love. I long to possess you, to make you mine for all time. To be near you and not touch you, not taste you, is like being invited to a banquet and being forbidden to eat. Do you understand?"

"I guess so." She rested her head against his shoulder. "I want you, too; you must know that. But I'm so confused . . . and so afraid."

"Of me?" he asked, silently cursing himself for his lack of control the last time they were together.

"No. Mostly I'm afraid of the changes in me. Sometimes I don't recognize myself. I . . ." She looked up at him. "I've never liked rare meat, but lately that's all I eat. I know it's the curse, but it frightens me. It's not a horrible thing, but it's not like me. Even Mike . . ." Her voice trailed off.

"Go on."

"When I went out with Mike, he said I looked different. Do I?"

"You look the same to me." Taking her by the hand, he led her into the living room and settled her beside him on the sofa. "Perhaps he sensed your inner struggle, though most mortals are unaware of such things."

With a sigh, she rested her head against his shoulder. "Nothing in my life seems the same as it was. I feel like I'm sitting on a time bomb, just waiting for it to blow up. I hate it!"

"It will get easier with time," he said reassuringly. "Try not to worry so much. It will change nothing and only make things worse."

"I know."

"Regan."

She tilted her head back so she could see his face and felt a shiver of awareness sizzle through her when their eyes met. He was going to kiss her and she was going to let him.

She closed her eyes as he lowered his head. He was right. What good had worrying ever done? She was a werewolf. In less than two weeks, the moon would be full. She would go to Santiago's lair and he would take care of her. She would find Vasile. Maybe not this month or the next, but she would find him and destroy him and get her life back. But that was in the future and Santiago was here now, his mouth warm on hers, his tongue sweetly dueling with hers, his hands gentle as they caressed her.

Somehow, they were lying side by side on the sofa, arms and legs entangled, hands slowly exploring, learning, arousing.

She loved touching him. She reveled in the latent strength in his arms, broad shoulders, and hard, flat belly. She loved the feel of his hair against her cheek, the weight of his leg lying over hers.

Wanting to be closer, she pressed herself against him, her hands slipping under his shirt to stroke his back. His skin was cool and firm beneath her curious fingertips.

"Regan." Her name was a groan on his lips. An unspoken plea.

How could she refuse him when she wanted him as badly as he wanted her?

She was about to suggest they continue their lovemaking in the bedroom when there was a knock at the door.

"Leave it," Santiago said, his voice a low growl.

Whoever it was knocked again, harder this time.

There was no sense pretending she wasn't home. The lights were on. Her car was parked out front.

"I'll just be a minute." She kissed Santiago quick and hard. "Don't go away." Gaining her feet, she adjusted her clothing, then went to open the door. It was the last person she expected to see. "Mike!"

"Hi, Reggie." He handed her an enormous bouquet of wildflowers. "I'm sorry for the way I acted the other night."

"It's all right."

"No, it's not. I didn't have any right to . . . dammit!" Mike said, glancing past her. "Doesn't he ever go home?"

"Mike . . ."

He shook his head, his face mottled with barely suffused rage. "It's obvious you've made your choice. I won't bother you again."

"Mike, listen . . ."

"Good-bye, Regan."

Murmuring, "good-bye," she closed the door.

"Are you sorry to see him go?" Santiago asked.

"Yes," she said, going into the kitchen for a vase. "We were friends." She filled the container and placed the flowers inside. It had been a long time since anyone had given her flowers.

Turning, she found that Santiago had followed her. "Do you wish to have him here in my place? If so, call him back and I will take my leave."

"No, of course not. But we were friends," she said again. "Do you even know what it's like to have friends anymore?"

"Are we not friends?" he asked, closing the distance between them.

"I don't know. Are we?"

With a muttered oath, he swept her into his arms.

"We are friends and more than friends, and were it not for that fool's intrusion, we would have been lovers by now."

"Would we?" she asked impishly.

"You know it as well as I." He brushed a kiss across her cheek. "There is still time." He studied her face, one brow raised inquisitively. "I see you have changed your mind. Shall I change it back again?"

"I don't know. Joaquin, I'm so confused about everything. My life has turned upside down since . . ."

"Since you met me?"

She smiled up at him. "You're part of it, of course. My associations with vampires have never been social, you know."

He grunted softly. "No 'hello, how are you?' before you lop off their heads?"

She grimaced. "It isn't just you. It's everything. I'm out of a job, I'm almost out of credits, I was bitten by a werewolf, and I'm . . ."

"Go on."

"I'm afraid I've fallen in love with you."

"And that makes you unhappy?"

"No, but . . ." She shook her head. "It's a complication, you must admit."

"I should not have come here tonight," he said, "but I could not stay away."

"I'm glad you're here. My life seems incredibly dull when you're not around."

His palms slid up and down her sides, his thumbs lightly skimming over her breasts. "I could change that."

"I'm sure you could but I'm just not ready."

"I can wait."

"I'm sorry."

"You need not be sorry, Regan. I will wait until you are ready, no matter how long it takes," he said with a wry grin. "I have nothing but time." He drew her close, his arms tightening around her as his lips brushed the crown of her head. "I must go now, but I will see you at the Byways when the moon is full."

"All right."

He kissed her then, a lingering kiss that spoke of his love for her and his yearning, and then he was gone.

With a sigh, she sank down on the sofa, wondering if she should have asked him to stay.

Chapter 25

Vasile was waiting at the door when Nadia's father arrived.

"The moon will rise shortly," Stefan announced.

Vasile nodded. He would have preferred to avenge Nadia's death himself, but he couldn't deny Stefan the right to avenge his daughter's death.

Vasile understood the need for vengeance all too well. His yearning to destroy Santiago burned as bright and hot within him as it had the day he destroyed Marishka. A day he would never forget. A day that had changed his life forever.

He had loved her from the moment he first saw her dancing in front of a Gypsy wagon. In the fire's light, she had been enchanting, her body moving fluidly to the strains of a Gypsy violin.

He had loved her, and had thought she loved him. While he had been blindly pursuing her, she had been meeting Santiago on the sly.

Santiago. He spat into the dirt. He would not rest until he had destroyed the bastard.

But first he and Stefan would pay a visit to the villager who had killed Nadia.

With a feral cry, Vasile shifted and ran into the night. He did not look back to see if Stefan followed.

It took only minutes to reach the house of the man responsible for Nadia's death. Light shone from the windows. Smoke curled from the chimney.

Vasile could see a woman inside, preparing the evening meal. For all the conveniences of the modern world, few had reached this small village, whether by choice or fate. A corral held a flock of sheep. Two large dogs slept near the gate. One of them woke as Stefan approached and immediately began to bark a warning.

Moments later, the door of the cottage opened and a man emerged, a lamp in his hand. "Who's there?" he called, peering into the darkness. "Is anyone there?"

When the dog continued barking, the man walked toward the sheep pen.

The other dog was awake now. Vasile quickly dispatched them both while Stefan stalked the villager.

The man never knew what hit him.

Chapter 26

Regan woke knowing that the moon would be full that night. It was something she had dreaded every night. Filled with a sense of apprehension and with her nerves on edge, she skipped breakfast and had a thick chocolate malt for lunch. She cleaned house with a vengeance, straightened the kitchen cupboards, did her laundry, and washed her car.

She went out for an early dinner and ordered a steak, rare, and ate it with gusto, even as she was inwardly repulsed.

Shortly before dusk, she changed into a pair of old sweats and sandals and drove to Santiago's lair in the Byways.

He was at the door waiting for her when she arrived.

He stood back, allowing her entrance, then closed the door and keyed in the lock code.

"So," she said. "What do we do now?"

"Whatever you wish. I can lock you in my lair, or we can drive out to the country and you can run under the moon. The choice is yours."

The thought of being locked in the vampire's lair, with his coffin, gave her the creeps. "Do we have time to get out of the city before the moon rises?"

He nodded. "Is that what you wish to do?"

"I think so." As she said the words, she was surprised to find she was looking forward to running through the night. In spite of her revulsion at being a werewolf, there was an undeniable thrill to being a wolf, a sense of freedom that she had never known before.

Santiago took her in his arms, one hand stroking her back, her hair.

"What are you doing?" she asked. "Shouldn't we be leaving?"

He pressed a finger to her lips. "I will carry you there."

Before she could question him further, they were out of the city.

Regan turned in a slow circle. They were in a heavily wooded area. Tall trees surrounded her on every side. For all she knew, they could have been hundreds of miles from the nearest town.

"Where are we?"

"A wild animal sanctuary outside of Clanton." Clanton was a large metropolis about eighty miles from the city.

"I've heard of this place. People aren't allowed in here."

Santiago glanced at the sky. "In a moment, there will not be any people here."

Even as he spoke the words, Regan felt the familiar but unwelcome burning sensation that signaled the onset of the change. She looked at Santiago, who sensed what was happening and obligingly turned his back to her. Hands shaking, she threw off her top and stepped out of her sandals and sweatpants. She hadn't bothered with a bra or panties.

She howled with pain as the werewolf took control of her body, transforming her nails into claws and her skin into fur. Her bones stretched and shifted until the change was complete. She howled again, this time with triumph, as she bounded into the darkness, her nose testing the wind for prey.

Quickly shifting into wolf form, Santiago ran after her. He had long ago accepted his existence as a vampire. He reveled in his preternatural powers and strength and his expanded senses, but there was something about being a wolf that surpassed even that. There was a wildness, a sense of freedom and exultation that was unmatched in any other form.

He soon overtook Regan and fell in alongside her.

And the fun began.

They flushed a red fox, a couple of deer, a bull moose, a pair of coyotes, and a jackrabbit.

Regan went after the rabbit.

Santiago watched her with a wolfish grin as she gave chase, laughed inwardly when the rabbit eluded her snapping jaws by diving into a hole. Lifting her head, she howled her frustration to the moon and the stars.

He saw her stiffen as an answering cry was borne to her on the wind. Moments later, three wolves materialized out of the shadows. Fangs bared, hackles raised, they walked stiff-legged toward her.

Santiago went to stand beside Regan, his own hackles raised, a snarl rising in his throat. It was obvious from their stance that the wolves meant to fight.

Santiago swore inwardly. Why hadn't he realized there would be wild wolves here and that they would be protective of their territory? He never should have brought Regan here, but it was too late now.

She pressed herself against him as the wolves closed in. Santiago spoke to her mind, telling her not to be afraid, and not to run, but to stand her ground, and then he moved forward to confront the alpha male.

Growling, they circled each other. Santiago felt his blood run hot at the prospect of a fight. He let the alpha male attack first and then, with savage fury, he lashed out. Even so, he held back, not wanting to kill the other wolf. He bit down hard on the wolf's left flank, his mouth filling with the warm coppery taste of blood. Animal blood was never as satisfying as human blood, but now, in the heat of battle, it tasted like the sweetest elixir.

It wasn't until he heard Regan's cry that he realized the other two wolves had attacked her. Enraged, he quickly disabled the alpha male, then went to Regan's defense, but there was no need. She fought like one possessed, biting and snapping until the two females tucked their tails between their legs and ran off. Limping badly, the male followed.

Tail wagging, Regan pranced toward Santiago. She circled him, then rolled onto her back, whining softly.

Santiago licked the blood from her face, stifling the urge to mate as he did so. Even in wolf form, blood and desire were closely linked, but he restrained himself, certain that Regan would be outraged.

With a yip, he backed off, his tail wagging.

Regan rolled to her feet and trotted off into the forest.

After a moment, Santiago followed.

The rest of the night passed quickly. They chased each other through the woods, dined on a deer that Regan brought down, slept beside a shallow stream.

Santiago woke when he felt dawn's approach, his body automatically shifting to its natural form. Regan had done likewise while she slept. He spent a moment simply looking at her, admiring the sheer beauty of her body, the rise and fall of her breasts, the softness of her skin, the wealth of her hair, the shapely length of her legs, her narrow waist, and the curve of her hips. His fingertips brushed her cheek, caressed her throat, slid over her shoulder.

Muttering an oath, he jerked his hand away. He had no right to touch her, should be ashamed of himself for the lustful thoughts tumbling through his mind.

Aware that the sun would soon be rising, he gathered Regan into his arms and raced back to his lair in the Byways. He arrived just as the sun rose over the horizon, felt its deadly heat on his back as he ducked into the building and slammed the door.

Once inside, he went into the bedroom. He settled Regan in his bed and pulled the blankets over her. It was a shame to cover such beauty, he thought, thinking that he would love to crawl in beside her and gather her into his arms, to hold her and make slow, sweet love to her until his body demanded that he succumb to the Dark Sleep.

A soft sigh escaped her lips. Was she dreaming of

him? Unable to resist, he slid into her mind and smiled at what he saw . . .

They were walking through a forest much like the one they had just left. She wore a sleeveless white sundress that fluttered in the breeze. Her hair fell loose around her shoulders, shimmering in the sun like a veil of gold silk. She looked up at him, her eyes aglow with love and desire.

A waterfall appeared ahead and she ran toward it, beckoning him to join her. At the pool, she shed her clothing and slipped into the water. Shedding his own garments, he dove in after her. For a time, they cavorted under the waterfall like carefree children. She let out a shriek when a fish brushed against her foot. Moving closer to the shore, she splashed him and then swam away, laughing. He immediately gave chase. She squealed with mock terror when he caught her, her body writhing against his as she struggled to free herself. Her skin was slick and smooth, her breasts warm and firm against his chest, firing his desire and he took her there, in the shallows near the edge of the pool, slaking his lust for her sweet flesh even as he bent his head and surrendered to the desire for her life's blood . . .

Regan woke with a cry of denial on her lips, her eyes widening when she saw Santiago standing beside the bed. "Did you . . . ?"

He shook his head. "It was only a dream." He studied the expression on her face. "Or perhaps a nightmare."

"Whose dream?" she asked. "Yours or mine?"

He lifted one shoulder and let it fall. "It started as yours."

"How can you do that?" she demanded angrily.

"How can you be in my dreams? How can you twist them to suit you?" She started to sit up; then, realizing she was naked beneath the sheet, she pulled the blankets up higher, her eyes shooting angry sparks at him.

"It is just another of my powers."

"What else can you do? What else have you done to me?"

"I can hypnotize you. I can bend your will to mine. I can erase whatever memories you have of me from your mind and your heart."

Her eyes widened. "Have you ever done any of those things to me?"

"No."

She looked skeptical.

"Trust me, Regan. I would not lie to you."

"I don't have much choice, do I?"

"I will never betray you, or defile you, or lie to you," he said, though he knew there would likely be times in the days ahead when, for one reason or another, he would refrain from telling her the whole truth.

"I believe you."

Sitting on the edge of the bed, he took one of her hands in his. "How do you feel?" He loved being near her, touching her, feeling the warmth of her skin.

"I feel all right. Why? Is something wrong? Did something happen last night?"

"No."

Holding the blanket to her chest, she sat up. "I had fun last night," she remarked, her voice barely audible. "How can that be? I don't want to be a werewolf. I don't want to get used to it."

"Would that be so bad?"

She snorted softly. "Would you want to marry a werewolf?"

His gaze moved over her face, lingering on her lips and the line of her throat. "I would not mind."

She shook her head. "My grandmother said true happiness can only be found when like marries like. Birds don't marry fish, dogs don't marry cats."

"We are alike," he said fervently. "Both cursed, or blessed, depending on your point of view."

"Joaquin . . ."

He cupped her cheek in his palm, his thumb stroking back and forth. "Forgive me. I know you want a home and a family, a normal life."

She nodded, tears stinging her eyes.

"I will do my best to see that you have everything you want." Leaning forward, he brushed a kiss across her lips. "And now I must go and take my rest."

She nodded again, her throat tight with unshed tears. Somehow, she would find Vasile and put an end to the curse that plagued her. She only wished that Santiago could do the same.

Chapter 27

"You're leaving?" Zina exclaimed. "Where are you going?"

"To the States," Vasile snapped. "I'm leaving in the morning."

"You've been here less than a month."

"So?"

"I had expected you to stay longer."

He shrugged impatiently. "I have unfinished business to attend to."

Zina's eyes flashed angrily. "That woman?"

Vasile nodded. "I told you I intended to make her my mate; have you forgotten?"

"No." She lifted her head proudly. "I have not forgotten. But you have a duty to me, now. I want you to stay until I'm pregnant."

Vasile stared at her, his eyes narrowed. He started to admonish her for her audacity, but on what grounds? He had married her to conceive a child and the task was not yet done. Perhaps it was his fault. Lying with a woman for whom he had no real affection had proved more difficult than he had expected.

Annoyed with himself and angry with her, he grabbed her by the arm and dragged her into the bedroom, determined that she would be gravid before the next full moon.

Chapter 28

Michael Flynn stared into the half-empty glass of whiskey in his hand. He had spent the last hour trying to understand what Regan saw in that blood-sucking bastard Santiago—and trying to figure out how the former master of the city had slipped through the barrier that surrounded the park. He had reported the fact to his superiors, who had assured him they would look into the matter.

Michael had spent the last few nights staking out the vampire's condo, hoping to catch Santiago leaving the park; unfortunately, there had been no sign of Santiago, causing Michael to wonder if the vampire had left town. Of course, leaving the city without notifying the authorities was also against the law.

He wondered suddenly if the fact that the murders had stopped abruptly had anything to do with the vampire's disappearance, and then wondered why the devil he hadn't considered the possibility before. Was Santiago the killer? He swore softly. Wouldn't that peel the hide off the hog?

Draining his glass, Michael ordered another drink.

He had been in love with Regan since the day he met her. They had both been working at the time, and there had been nothing the least bit romantic about the circumstances, but later that night, while they were filling out reports, he had asked her out for coffee and they had spent a pleasant hour unwinding and getting acquainted. They had dated on and off since that time; in the last year, neither of them had dated anyone else. Michael had been thinking about asking Regan to marry him at the upcoming department Christmas party. But that had been before Joaquin Santiago arrived on the scene.

Once again, Flynn asked himself what she saw in the vampire. He couldn't believe she was serious about the creep. Fascinated, maybe. After all, vampires were rumored to have some sort of supernatural charm that mortals found hard to resist.

Michael glanced at his surroundings. What the hell was he doing in a dive like this? Muttering an oath, he tossed off his drink. He should just go on home, he thought morosely. There was nothing for him here—and nothing for him there.

He was about to order another drink when a woman sat down beside him. Her perfume surrounded him, cutting through the cloud of smoke and perspiration that hung in the air. Her hair was the vivid red of a sunset, her eyes were the deepest, brightest shade of blue he had ever seen. And her mouth . . . it could only belong to an angel—or a temptress.

Feeling his gaze, she looked over at him and smiled, displaying even white teeth.

Michael swallowed hard. He had never been shy around women; in college, he'd had a reputation for being a ladies' man. But this woman, clad in a skintight black dress and black stiletto heels, made him feel like a callow youth.

She smiled at him again. "Would you like to dance?"

The thought of holding her in his arms had him suddenly believing in Santa Claus. Rising, he offered her his hand.

The dance floor was small and crowded, but Michael wasn't aware of anything or anyone but the woman whose body was pressed intimately against his own. He could feel every feminine curve. No doubt she was equally aware of his body's response to her nearness.

"Do you come here often?" he asked, thinking that if she said yes, he was going to be spending a lot of time here himself.

"No, this is my first time." Her gaze devoured him. "Perhaps it was fate that brought me here tonight. Do you believe in fate?"

"I never did before." He studied her face, thinking she looked vaguely familiar.

She laughed, a deep sexy laugh that brushed over his skin like velvet over sandpaper. "Have you a name?"

"Michael."

"Hello, Michael," she purred. "I'm Tatiana."

Chapter 29

Santiago wandered the dark streets of the city. A week had passed since the night of the full moon. He had not seen Regan since then. Though he longed for her company, it seemed wiser to stay away. She had made it clear that in spite of her affection for him, he was not what she wanted. Which was too bad, he mused, because she was exactly what he wanted. Human or werewolf, it didn't matter. He loved her as he had never thought to love again, yearned for her with every fiber of his being, ached to take her in his arms and possess her fully and completely.

He muttered an oath as he turned a corner. He could take her by force. He could bend her will to his, make her want him and no other, make her forget she had ever wanted anything or anyone else, but what kind of love would that be? He wanted her love, freely given, he wanted her to need him with every breath in her body, every beat of her heart. All or nothing, he thought, and knew he would have to settle for nothing. He would be there for her when the moon was full for as long as she needed him. He would help her find and destroy Vasile. And then he would never see her again.

Santiago paused in front of the nightclub at the end of the street. The place was a dive, one of many in this part of the city. He had come here on occasion, sometimes just to pass a quiet night, sometimes to hunt for prey.

For a moment, he listened to the slow, heavy beat of the music spilling out into the night and then he went inside.

He stood inside the doorway for a moment, his gaze quickly perusing the room and its occupants, and then he grinned, amused by the sight of Michael Flynn dancing with Tatiana. It was obvious, even from a distance, that the cop was thoroughly smitten. But then, who could blame him? Tatiana was perhaps the most blatantly beautiful and sensual female Santiago had ever known. In days long past, they had relied on each other for companionship. They had hunted together and taken their rest together and occasionally, on a long and lonely night, they had found solace in each other's arms, but then Santiago had met Marishka, and Tatiana had decided to go off and see the world.

Moving to the end of the bar, Santiago ordered a glass of red wine. Looking into the mirror behind the bar, he continued to watch the vampire work her magic on the detective. Not surprisingly, every other man in the room was also watching her.

When the music stopped, Tatiana took Michael by the arm and led him toward the entrance.

Muttering an oath, Santiago followed them outside. Though he had no love for Flynn, he knew Regan was fond of the man.

Santiago kept his distance until Tatiana drew Flynn into the shadows behind a tall hedge.

"What are you doing?" Santiago heard Flynn ask.

"You'll like it," Tatiana purred. "Trust me."

"That's enough," Santiago said, rounding the hedge.

"Joaquin!" Tatiana exclaimed with mock enthusiasm. "What a nice surprise!"

Santiago grunted softly. Hunger radiated off of her in waves, like summer heat shimmering off blacktop. He didn't miss the faint glow in her eyes, or the way she held on to Flynn, her arms imprisoning him in the guise of affection. Santiago knew it would be affection only so long as Flynn didn't try to escape.

Michael Flynn glared at him over the top of Tatiana's head. "What the hell are you doing here?"

"Saving your neck," Santiago retorted. "And I mean that literally."

Flynn glanced at Tatiana, then back at Santiago. "What are you talking about?"

"She is a vampire."

Flynn stared at him. "A vampire?"

Santiago nodded.

Flynn looked at Tatiana as if he had never seen her before. "Is he telling the truth?"

She shrugged. "Does it matter?"

"Damn right!" Flynn said. He tried to get away from her, but there had never been a mortal who could equal the strength of a vampire. Fear surfaced in Flynn's eyes. "Get away from me!"

"Tatiana, let him go."

Her gaze locked with his, her eyes blood red with hunger.

"Let him go," Santiago repeated.

With a harsh laugh, she released her hold on Flynn. Moving toward Santiago, she raked her nails across his cheek, drawing blood. "All right, I'm going." Standing on her tiptoes, she licked the blood from his cheek. "But you owe me one," she said, and with a wave of her hand, she vanished from sight.

Flynn stared after her and then, ever so slowly, turned toward Santiago. "I'm grateful," he said brusquely, "but I'd still like to know what you're doing outside the park."

"Saving your ass," Santiago replied, his voice equally harsh.

"And why isn't she confined," Flynn went on as if Santiago hadn't spoken. "And I intend to find out the answers to both questions."

"I would advise you to mind your own business," Santiago said, "or I might not be there next time."

And then, he, too, disappeared from sight.

Muttering an oath, Flynn drove to Regan's, determined to get some answers once and for all.

Regan was sitting at her computer, scrolling through the help-wanted section, when the doorbell rang.

Hoping it was Santiago, she hurried to answer the door, but it was Michael. After their last parting, she had never expected to see him at her doorstep again.

"Mike!" she exclaimed. "What a surprise. Do you want to come in?"

"Thanks." He followed her into the living room and sat on the sofa, one arm draped across the back.

Regan sat on the other end of the sofa. "So, what brings you here?"

"I want you to tell me everything you know about Joaquin Santiago."

"What makes you think I know anything?"

"Come on, Reggie, don't play games with me. How does he get out of the park? Why doesn't the barrier affect him?"

"I don't know, Mike, honest. I asked him once, but he never told me. Are you all right?"

He rubbed his hand over his neck. "Sure, for a guy that was almost dinner."

She frowned at him. "What are you talking about?"

"I was at the Blue Zodiac tonight. A woman asked me to dance, then she asked me to walk her home." He cleared his throat. "Turned out she was a vampire."

"Good heavens, Mike, are you all right?"

"Yeah. Your buddy Santiago showed up and saved my butt. I need to find out why she's not registered in the park, and how he's crossing the barrier. People need to know they're not as safe as they think. If there's a glitch in the barrier, then the superintendent in charge of security needs to know, as well."

"The barrier works on most of the vampires, Mike. I think it doesn't work on Santiago because he's so old."

He nodded. "Makes sense, I guess, but it doesn't matter if it's one bloodsucker getting out or a hundred. I'm sworn to protect the people in the city and as long as even one of them can get out, we're not safe."

"Mike, don't you think you're overreacting?"

"Hell, no! If Santiago hadn't showed up tonight,

I might have been the next victim. You're a hunter, Regan. We need to find the female and get her housed in the park before she turns the city into her own private buffet."

"Have you cleared this with the department?"

"No, but I will." He drummed his fingertips on the back of the sofa.

Regan nodded. Maybe Santiago could help her find the vampire in question. "Do you know where she lives? Her name?"

"She said her name was Tatiana."

Good grief, Regan thought. That was the name of Santiago's friend. "Does she have red hair and blue eyes?"

"Yeah, do you know her?" Even as he asked the question, Mike suddenly remembered where he had seen the vampire before. She had been at Charlie's one night, dancing with Santiago. "You making friends with the Undead now?"

"No. All I know is that she's Santiago's friend."

"I guess that means hunting her is out of the question, doesn't it?" Flynn asked, his voice laced with contempt.

She lifted her chin defiantly. "I'm afraid so."

Mike swore softly. "Regan, how serious are you about this bloodsucker? You're not . . . you wouldn't . . ."

"There's nothing going on between us, Mike. He's a vampire, remember?"

"See that you remember that."

"Not to worry," she said, forcing a smile. "I haven't seen him in weeks."

"Regan, you know how I feel about you. Nothing's changed that." He took a deep breath. "Is there any chance for us?"

She laid her hand over his. "I'm sorry, Mike. I just don't love you the way you deserve."

Mike nodded, then gained his feet and headed for the door. "Be careful, Regan," he said, "I'm afraid humanity isn't as safe from the monsters as we thought we were."

Regan stared after him, wondering what he would say if he knew she was now one of the monsters.

Chapter 30

Zina stood at the window of Vasile's house, smiling as she stared out into the night. He had left for the States only moments ago.

No longer would she have to endure his physical and verbal abuse. She had wanted only one thing from Vasile and now she had it. She placed her hand over her womb, her heart swelling with love for the child she carried. Never again would she submit to Vasile's cruelty. If he ever laid a hand on her again, she would kill him. Though she had come to accept being a werewolf, she had never forgiven him for biting her. She had been a teenager when he attacked her. Before Vasile, she had dreamed of becoming a model or an actress, but Vasile had changed all that. He had bitten her and brought her here. She had been too afraid and too ashamed of what she had become to leave. But now . . .

"I could be free," she murmured, and wondered why she hadn't thought of it years ago. All she had to do was kill him and the curse would be broken. Her child would be born free of the curse. Killing Vasile . . . the thought gave her pause. It was against pack law for one werewolf to kill another, but she had a child to think of now. With Vasile dead, she could take her baby away from this place and live a normal life.

The more she thought about it, the more she warmed to the idea. She would be better off without him. The pack would be better off without him. Vasile ruled out of fear. In the past, the pack had been content to follow her in his absence. They would not miss him if he was gone a week, a month, or forever.

A familiar tingle told her that the moon was rising. Shedding her shoes and her clothing, Zina stepped out into the gathering darkness. Soon, the rest of the pack joined her. As soon as they all shifted, they gathered around her, rubbing their bodies against hers. They knew at once that she was with child.

With joyful yips and barks, the members of the pack bounded into the night, their humanity and all its cares left behind. There would soon be a new member of the pack. It was cause for rejoicing.

Feeling fulfilled for the first time in her life, Zina threw back her head and howled her happiness at the moon.

Chapter 31

Leaning back in her chair, Regan stretched her arms and legs. Of all the jobs she had considered, teaching hadn't been one of them, but here she was, teaching a six-week class at the Academy on how to recognize and destroy vampires. She had been surprised when the chief of police called to offer her the job, surprised and pleased. At last, she was working again, feeling productive again, and earning credits again. The number of her students would vary from class to class, depending on the number of Academy recruits, but her pay remained the same whether she had ten students or a hundred.

It was a dream job. According to her schedule, she would teach for six weeks, have four weeks off, then start a new class. Best of all, the classes were held during the day, sparing her the necessity of having to worry about coming up with reasons to stay home when the moon was full.

Sitting up again, she opened the file in front of her. It held the results of the test she had given her class earlier that day. Her students wouldn't be graded on this test. It was merely to determine the scope of their paranormal knowledge and discover where their strengths and weaknesses were. If they already knew basic vampire lore, so much the better.

She picked up the first test.

<u>Circle all answers that apply:</u>

Vampires
a. have hairy palms
b. can turn into mist
c. are repelled by crosses and garlic
d. cast no reflection in a mirror
e. can control the weather
f. have bad breath
g. can change shape
h. can shield their presence
i. will be burned by holy water and/or silver
j. can be destroyed by burning or beheading
k. can't cross running water . . .

Regan found herself mentally answering the questions as they applied to Santiago while she graded the paper. Santiago didn't have hairy palms. Quite the contrary, his hands were smooth and gentle when they caressed her. He had told her he could turn into mist. She didn't know if he was repelled by crosses, but she had it from his own lips that a vampire's aversion to garlic was just a myth. He could see himself in a mirror, but she didn't know if he could control the weather. He most definitely didn't have bad breath. She had seen him change into a wolf, and quite a handsome wolf, at that . . . odd, that Vasile looked ugly and misshapen in wolf form while Santiago simply looked like a wolf. She knew he could shield his presence when he wished. She didn't know what the effects of holy water or silver would be on him, but she assumed both would burn him, just as beheading or fire would destroy him. She was pretty sure the running water thing was a myth. After all, he had crossed oceans . . .

Santiago, Santiago, no matter where she was, he was constantly in her thoughts. Though she disliked being a werewolf, it assured her of seeing him two nights of every month.

It wasn't enough. What if she never found Vasile? Not that she was looking, but only because she had no idea where to look. She didn't know if he had left the city or left the country. Santiago was certain that the werewolf would return soon, but werewolves, like vampires, didn't view the passage of time the same way mortals did. Soon could be a month from now, or a year, or a century.

To live so long, she thought, and realized for the first time that she, too, could expect to live a very, very long time. What if Vasile eluded her for five years? Ten? Fifty? Did she want to remain alone all that time? As long as she was a werewolf, she couldn't enjoy a normal relationship with a human male. When viewed through the lens of a hundred years or more, did it really make sense to refuse Santiago? She might tire of him in a century or so. He might grow weary of her. But until then, why was she denying herself the joy she found in his company? He was the only one who truly understood her. And he loved her, loved her enough to respect her wishes, to run at her side when the moon was full. And she loved him. They could have a good life together . . .

Even as the thought crossed her mind, a little voice asked if she would feel the same if she managed to rid herself of the curse. Would she still be happy to share her life with a vampire? And what of children? Santiago couldn't father a child, but there were other ways. Adoption. Sperm donors . . . She shook her head. She could see herself now, sitting on the bed with her child, trying to explain why daddy couldn't take him to the zoo or go to the park and play catch on a summer day, and why mommy turned furry when the moon was full.

She shook the thought aside. Kids were flexible. Having a dad who couldn't go outside in the daytime wasn't much different than having a dad who worked nights and slept days. But a mother who turned into a wolf? How would she explain that?

With a shake of her head, she stuffed the tests into her briefcase and left the building. Vampires, werewolves, children, marriage—none of it mattered. What mattered was that she loved Joaquin Santiago and she wasn't going to let another day go by without asking him to forgive her for being such an idiot. She loved him and she needed him and she intended to have him, all of him, now, tonight.

Whistling softly, she jumped into the car and headed for his place, glad that it was Friday night. If she was lucky, they could make love all weekend long.

Santiago stared at the woman standing in the doorway. Was she really there, or had his insatiable need for her conjured her image?

"Regan?"

"Hi," she said softly. "Can I come in?"

She wasn't a figment of his tortured imagination after all. "Of course."

He stepped back, allowing her entrance to his lair in the Byways, then closed and locked the door. He stood there a moment, inhaling the fragrance of her hair and skin, the alluring scent of her blood, appreciating the beauty of her face and form. He didn't know why she was there, but it didn't matter. The fact that she was there was like an unexpected gift and he intended to savor it for as long as possible.

He gestured toward the sofa. "Please, sit."

She remained standing, her fingers fidgeting with the hem of her sweater. "Am I interrupting anything?"

"No. Is something wrong?"

"No. Yes." Taking a deep breath, she crossed her arms over her chest. "I . . ."

He tilted his head to one side. "Go on."

"I love you."

He lifted one brow. "I know."

"Do you still love me?"

He frowned at her. "Of course."

"Remember when you said you wouldn't mind marrying a werewolf?"

A faint smile touched the corners of his mouth. "Yes."

"Would you mind marrying me?"

"Are you proposing?"

"Yes. Should I get down on one knee?"

He laughed softly as he drew her into his embrace. "No, my love. I will marry you whenever you wish." He dropped kisses across her cheek, her nose, her lips. "What has changed your mind?"

"I guess I just came to my senses. I love you and I need you and tonight I asked myself why we were apart. I'm happy only when I'm with you."

"What of children?"

"I don't know. Maybe we could adopt or . . . I don't know. I just know I don't want to live another day, or night, without you."

"Regan, do you remember the promise I made you?"

"You promised to see that I have everything I want."

"Yes. Are you sure this is what you want? That I am what you want?"

"Very sure."

"What of the future? What if you destroy Vasile and break the curse? I cannot promise that I will let you go if you change your mind."

"I won't change my mind. I've given it a lot of thought," she said, laughing softly. "I don't think I've thought of anything else in the last few weeks."

He looked at her a moment, as if weighing her sincerity, and then he kissed her, long and hard, and she knew there was no going back. This was where she belonged. Werewolf or mortal, for now and always, this was where she wanted to be.

When he would have broken the kiss, she wrapped her arms around his neck and held him close, her tongue sliding over his lower lip, her body pressing against his in silent invitation.

"Regan." He murmured her name, his voice ragged. "Are you sure?"

"Yes, aren't you?"

"I do not want you to be sorry later."

"I won't be," she said, and taking him by the hand, she led him into the bedroom. "I want you," she whispered, her voice husky. "More than ever."

She didn't have to tell him again. Drawing her into his arms, he kissed her, his hands making short work of her clothing until she stood naked before him.

Naked and blushing furiously.

He found it most becoming.

Biting down on her lower lip, she drew his shirt over his head, unfastened his belt, and removed his trousers.

Her blush deepened at the visible sign of his desire.

She sighed when he drew her into his arms and carried her to bed.

"You are beautiful," he murmured.

"So are you."

"Indeed." He kissed her then, a long deep kiss that made her toes curl with anticipation while her imagination conjured images of their entwined bodies writhing on black satin sheets.

Lifting her into his arms, Santiago drew back the covers on the bed and lowered her to the mattress, then stretched out beside her.

Regan shivered with trepidation when she felt the cool reality of those satin sheets against her bare back.

"Still sure?" he asked, sensing her hesitation.

"Yes, it's just that . . . well, you see, I've . . ."

"Go on."

"I've never done this before," she confessed in a rush.

"Never?" He shook his head in disbelief. "How can that be?"

"Well, I . . . I just . . ." She looked away, her face heating with embarrassment. "I promised my grandmother I'd wait until I was married or twenty-one, whichever came first."

"Are you telling me you are not twenty-one?"

"No, but, well, when I went into vampire hunting, dates got kind of scarce."

"What of Flynn? You never . . . ?"

"We've only been dating seriously for a few months. Besides, I never loved him that way."

Santiago rolled onto his back, one arm across his eyes.

Wishing she could just disappear, Regan pulled the covers up to her chin. "I thought you'd be pleased."

He rolled onto his side to face her. "I am," he said, "more than you can imagine."

"Then why did you stop?"

Leaning forward, he kissed the tip of her nose. "I have thought of this moment since the first night I saw you, but I did not expect you to be untouched. To my surprise, I find that I do not want to take my bride's virginity before we are wed."

"So you're turning me down?"

"Only for an hour or so." Taking her by the hand, he pulled her into a sitting position. "Get dressed," he said with a grin, "and let us get married."

Regan shook her head as reality set in. "No one will marry us." It was against the law for vampires and humans to marry. The law defined marriage as a union between a man and a woman. That didn't include the Undead.

"Let me worry about the details," Santiago said.

"I need a dress," Regan said. "Shoes. And what about my parents . . ." She frowned. Inviting her parents might not be such a good idea. Her mother would want to know every tiny detail of how Regan and Santiago met, and every tiny detail of his life before that. "Well, I definitely need a dress."

"Tomorrow evening then?" Santiago asked. "I will pick you up at seven."

She didn't want to wait, but she had never been married before and if she couldn't have a big ceremony with her family in attendance, she at least wanted to wear a beautiful white wedding gown. After all, she deserved it!

Laughing, Regan threw herself into Santiago's arms.

"What is so funny?" he asked, his brows drawing together in a frown.

"Nothing," she said, "I'm just so happy." Happier than she had ever been before, and that alone told her that she had made the right decision.

Santiago groaned softly. "I cannot guarantee you will be a virgin tomorrow night if you do not get up and get dressed."

"Find me tempting, do you?" she asked with a saucy grin.

"More than you can imagine."

She ran her finger down his chest. "I find you very tempting, too, you know."

"Regan." His voice was low and husky. "I am warning you."

"Oh, all right." Wrapping the sheet around her, she got off the bed. "I've waited this long. I guess I can wait one more night, but it won't be easy."

He grunted softly. His whole body, his every sense, was attuned to Regan. He smelled her desire, her excitement, her trepidation.

"Turn around," she said.

He lifted one brow. "A little late for modesty, is it not?"

"Never mind," she said primly. "Just turn around."

With a shake of his head, he put his back to her.

He didn't have to see her to know what she was doing. He heard the rustle of the sheet, the whisper of soft cotton as she drew on her underwear, the heavier sound of her clothing sliding over her skin.

"Aren't you going to get dressed?" she asked over her shoulder.

"Of course." With a complete and utter lack of modesty, he rose and reached for his briefs. "You may watch, if you wish."

Heat flooded her neck and washed into her cheeks, but she didn't turn around. Clad in nothing but a pair of snug black silk briefs, Joaquin Santiago, vampire, was the most exotic, gorgeous creature she had ever seen.

And tomorrow night, all that mouthwatering masculinity would be all hers.

Chapter 32

As might be expected, Regan slept late the following morning. Rising, she took a long hot shower and then, dressed in a pair of black slacks and a short-sleeved pink sweater and matching sandals, she ate a quick breakfast of toast, orange juice, and coffee, and headed for the nearest mall where she spent the rest of the morning and the early part of the afternoon trying on wedding dresses, veils, and shoes, and buying sexy lingerie and a black nightie that was so sheer, it was nearly invisible. And always, in the back of her mind, a happy little voice reminded her that she would be Santiago's wife before the night was over.

Mrs. Joaquin Santiago. Nothing in her life had ever sounded so good or felt so right. Never before had she been so sure that she was doing the right thing, and that everything would work out for the best. Deciding she might as well grab something to eat before she went home, she stopped at her favorite Italian restaurant for a late lunch.

She had just been seated when Mike came in.

He saw her, hesitated, and then made his way to her table.

"Hey, Reggie," he said, his eyes lighting with pleasure at seeing her.

"Hi, Mike."

He glanced around. "Are you here alone?"

She nodded. "Yes, you?"

"Yeah. Mind if I join you?"

"No, of course not. Are you working?"

"Yeah, but things are mighty slow. The most excitement I've had this afternoon was a false alarm over on Fifth and Tigrina."

The waitress arrived then to take their order. Regan ordered a turkey sandwich, then searched her mind for a safe topic of conversation while Mike spoke with the waitress. She knew she should tell Mike she was getting married, but somehow she didn't think that would lend itself to congenial small talk.

She smiled at Mike when the waitress moved away from the table. "So . . ."

Mike cleared his throat. "I'm leaving the city. Tomorrow's my last day."

Regan stared at him. "What? Why? You didn't quit?"

"No, I asked to be transferred to another division."

"But why? Is it because they promoted Holloway in front of you?"

"No."

She felt a rush of guilt because she knew with sudden certainty that he was leaving because of her. "Mike . . ."

He held up a hand, staying her words. "Don't say anything, Reggie. I'm not blaming you. Anyway," he said with forced enthusiasm, "I'm glad I ran into you. If there's ever anything I can do . . . if you ever need anything . . ." He pulled a business card out of his pocket and handed it to her. "This is where I'll be."

Taking the card, she tucked it into her pocket. "Thanks, Mike."

They made desultory conversation during lunch, careful to keep things light between them.

When the meal was over, he walked her to her car. "Keep in touch, Reggie."

"You, too." Opening the door, she slid behind the wheel and punched in the ignition code. Nothing happened. She hit it again, thinking she might have entered it wrong. Nothing.

She slammed her hand against the steering wheel. She didn't have time for this. She was getting married in less than four hours.

"Looks like it needs charging," Mike suggested.

"I guess so. Can you give me a ride home?"

"Sure, come on."

"Wait, I've got some packages in the trunk." Thankfully, her wedding dress had been packed in a box, then placed in a large sack. She was careful to keep the name of the store hidden against her leg as she carried the package across the street to where Mike stood beside his car.

When he opened the back door, she laid the sack logo side down and piled her other packages on top of it.

"I guess I don't have to ask what you did today." Mike said, holding the door open for her.

She forced a laugh. "I went on quite a shopping spree."

"Any special occasion?"

"No," she said quickly. "Why do you ask?"

He shrugged. "I've known you quite a while and I've never known you to like shopping."

"Well, sometimes shopping's a necessary evil, like going to the dentist."

He pulled up in front of her condo a few minutes later. Being Mike, he offered to help carry her bags inside, and because she couldn't think of any logical reason to object, she let him carry everything but her dress. In the living room, she dropped her handbag on the sofa, then hurried into the bedroom. She hung the dress in the closet and then closed the door.

Pausing in front of the dresser, she picked up her brush and ran it through her hair.

"Mike, do you want some coffee before you go?"

Instead of an answer, she heard a heavy thud.

"Mike?" she called, walking toward the bedroom door, "You're in big trouble if you broke my new . . ."

Her voice trailed off when she reached the living room and saw Mike lying facedown on the floor. Concern for his welfare was swallowed up in stark fear for her own life when a tall figure stepped into view.

"You!" Her gaze flew to her handbag, lying out of reach on the sofa.

"Hello, Regan," Vasile said with a wicked grin. "I've come to take you home."

Santiago rose with the setting sun. He showered and dressed, then went out to feed before driving to Regan's apartment.

Regan was going to be his bride. It was a miracle, he thought, and he had long ago stopped believing in miracles.

He glanced up at the sky. He had long ago stopped believing in just about everything but his own abilities. Perhaps he had been wrong to stop believing.

"I will make her happy," he murmured, "every day of her life."

Happy. A small word. Mortals used it for so many things. Graduating from college would make them happy. A pizza would make them happy. A new car would make them happy. More money, a bigger house, a trip around the world, a nose job, a tummy tuck; all would bring them happiness yet never did.

But he would make Regan happy. He would grant her anything within his power to give no matter how large or how small.

Happy, Santiago thought. For the first time in hundreds of years, he, himself, was happy.

He was smiling when he pulled up in front of Regan's condo. Whistling softly, he got out of the car and ran up the stairs, eager to see his bride.

His steps slowed as he neared her apartment, his nostrils filling with a familiar, unwelcome scent.

Muttering an oath, he knocked on the door, swore again as it swung open and the smell of blood and impending death surrounded him.

"Regan!"

But it wasn't Regan's body lying in a pool of blood on the floor.

Kneeling, Santiago rolled the body over. It was the cop, Michael Flynn. His body had been badly savaged.

Flynn groaned, his eyelids fluttering open. "Regan . . ."

"Where is she?" Santiago demanded.

Flynn shook his head weakly. "A man . . ."

"Vasile? Was it Vasile?"

"Don't . . . know." Flynn's eyes closed. "Find . . . her."

"Do you know where he was taking her?" Santiago shook Flynn. "Where, dammit, where did they go?"

Flynn's eyes opened again and with his last breath, he whispered, "Home . . ."

Santiago closed Michael Flynn's eyes. He stared at the dead man a moment, then swore a vile oath. Vasile had taken Regan. Judging from Flynn's wounds and the way the blood had congealed, Santiago figured Vasile had a good head start—three hours, maybe four.

Rising, Santiago left the house. Outside, he closed his eyes and opened his senses. Sifting through the multitude of smells that assailed him, he sought for Regan's unique scent.

It was faint, hours old. It led him away from the city to the airport. Going into the terminal, he checked all the flights that had left in the last four hours. None were headed to Romania.

Going to one of the windows, Santiago smiled at the woman behind the counter. "Hi, Sarah," he said, reading her name off the badge she wore on her breast pocket. "I need to know if a private flight left here in the last five hours."

"I'm sorry, sir, but I'm not allowed to give out that kind of information."

Santiago swore under his breath. He didn't have time for this. Capturing her gaze with his, he said, "I need to know, Sarah, and I need to know now."

"Yes, of course, sir, I'll find that for you right now." She typed a few words into her computer. "A private jet took off four and a half hours ago bound for Romania."

Santiago muttered an oath. "Do you know if there was a woman on board?"

"No, sir."

"Is there anyone here who would know?"

"The ground crew might have seen something, sir."

"Thank you, Sarah." Releasing her mind from his control, Santiago left the terminal and went outside to speak to the ground crew.

It took only moments to discover that a man and a woman had boarded a private plane on runway number eight.

"The woman," Santiago said, "what did she look like?"

"I'm sorry, sir, we never saw her. She was ill."

"The man," Santiago said, fear for Regan's life growing with every passing moment, "was he tall, with long blond hair? Spoke with a faint accent?"

"Yes, sir."

Santiago released the man with a wave of his hand and strode away, his fear and his anger growing as he returned to the terminal. He found a public phone and dialed information. Ten minutes later he had chartered a private plane to fly him to Romania. The flight was scheduled to leave tomorrow at dusk.

He only hoped he would reach his destination before it was too late.

Chapter 33

Regan woke with a headache, a horrible taste in her mouth, and a sense of disorientation.

Where was she?

Glancing around, she saw that she was in a small bedroom. The walls were a forgettable shade of beige; the curtains at the single window were brown. A glance to the left showed a closed door; a large dresser took up most of the wall to her right. She lay on a canopied bed. Feeling as if she had been asleep for a week, she tried to sit up, only to discover that her arms were drawn above her head and her hands were tied to the bedposts.

Fear was a cold hard knot in the pit of her stomach.

She took a deep breath. She told herself not to panic and repeated it over and over again in her mind. *Don't panic, Regan, don't panic, don't panic . . .*

Too late, she thought as she tugged frantically against the ropes. She had gone beyond panic! Nothing good ever came of being tied up in a strange place.

Where was she?

Vasile . . . oh, Lord, she remembered now. Vasile

had been in her apartment. And Michael . . . where was Michael?

She closed her eyes, praying that this was all just a bad dream, that she would wake up and everything would be all right. It had to be a nightmare . . . nothing this awful could be real.

When she woke again, a middle-aged woman with short, dark hair was staring down at her. The expression in the woman's eyes sent a chill down Regan's spine. Never, in all her life, had anyone looked at her with such hatred.

It took every ounce of willpower Regan possessed to meet the woman's baleful stare, but she knew somehow that looking away or showing any sign of fear would be the worst thing she could do.

The woman glared at her for another few moments, then turned and left the room without saying a word.

As soon as she was alone again, Regan began to struggle against the ropes that bound her to the bed. She didn't know where she was, but she was certain Vasile was nearby, and that she wouldn't like whatever it was he had in store for her.

After ten minutes of intense concentration, she felt the rope on her right wrist loosen just a little. Hope soared through her and she tugged harder, ignoring the pain of the rope cutting into her skin and the blood dripping down her arm.

One last hard pull and her wrist slipped free. Sitting up, she quickly untied her other hand and got off the bed. After tiptoeing to the window, she drew back the curtain and peered outside.

A number of small square houses were arranged around a central courtyard. There was a fountain in the center. Two young girls sat in the shade of a huge tree. One was reading a book, the other was playing with a doll. Tall trees rose behind the houses across the way, their branches interwoven, their trunks so close together that nothing was visible beyond them.

Tiptoeing to the bedroom door, Regan opened it a crack and looked out. She didn't see anyone or hear anything. Opening the door wider, she made her way down the short hallway to the living room. It, too, was empty.

Squaring her shoulders, she opened the front door and stepped outside. The two girls looked up. Regan smiled at them. After a moment, they smiled back and then returned to what they were doing before. Regan walked casually to the corner of the house, as if she had every right to be there, and then walked without hurry toward a heavily wooded area located behind the house.

Once Regan was out of sight of the girls, she began to run. She didn't know where she was running to, but any place had to be better than where she was.

She ran until she was out of breath and her legs felt like rubber. With one hand pressed against her aching side, she dropped to the ground and closed her eyes. She had to find help, but where? And where was she?

Lifting her head, Regan glanced around. Trees. Nothing but trees and a tall mountain in the distance—a mountain with a castle on top. She frowned, thinking that the castle looked vaguely familiar. Something to do with Dracula . . . it couldn't be his castle, she thought. That one lay in ruins, but it was said that Dracula had stayed at another castle. Was this the one? It was quite lovely, with rusty colored turrets and lots of windows.

Rising, she began to walk rapidly, going deeper into the forest. In an effort to avoid thinking about Vasile or the fact that he might be after her, she tried to recall everything she had read about Dracula. While learning to be a vampire hunter, she had studied the famous count's life, since there were some who believed he had been the first vampire. Though he had been a cruel, unforgiving man, he was hailed as a hero for defending Walachia against the invasion of the Turks centuries ago. It was said that on one occasion, when foreign emissaries refused to remove their turbans in his presence, Dracula nailed their turbans to their heads. Of course, he was famous, or infamous, for impaling hundreds of his enemies for various crimes, a punishment that resulted in days of excruciating agony for the victims.

Regan walked for what must have been hours, until she couldn't take another step, and then she walked some more, woodenly placing one foot in front of the other, her fear of being caught by Vasile stronger than her growing thirst.

Vasile shook Zina's shoulders. "Where is she?" he demanded. "What have you done with her?"

"I didn't do anything." She spat the words at him. "She was there the last time I looked."

"How long ago was that?"

"I don't know. Two hours ago, maybe three."

He shook her again. "How long?"

"A little after noon."

Four hours ago! With an oath, Vasile flung the

woman away from him. She staggered backward, striking her head against the wall. The smell of blood filled the air.

Without waiting to see if Zina was alive or dead, Vasile stormed out of the house, his body shifting as he went. Outside, he sniffed the ground, his nostrils quickly picking up the woman's scent.

He would have her before nightfall.

He was coming.

Fear lent wings to Regan's feet but she was too tired, too thirsty, and too hungry to sustain it for long. She had been a fool to think she could outrun a werewolf. With his increased senses, he would find her no matter where she went, and out here, in this seemingly endless forest, there was nowhere to hide.

She was scrambling up a slight incline when her legs refused to support her any longer. With a sigh of resignation, she dropped to the ground, overcome with a sense of doom and a sudden fear that she had been running in circles for the last few minutes.

Closing her eyes, she prayed for strength and courage, and then, holding onto a tree, she gained her feet and staggered onward. She had no doubt that Vasile would find her, but she wasn't going to surrender without a fight!

She was crossing a stream when the wind shifted and she caught Vasile's scent. Glancing over her shoulder, she saw a fair-haired wolf loping effortlessly toward her. With a wild cry, she darted across the stream and scrambled up the other side, her weariness forgotten as she ran for her life.

She screamed when his weight slammed into her back, cried out in pain as his momentum carried her to the ground. She landed face-first. Lights exploded behind her eyes. Grunting softly, she struggled to wriggle out from under him, but it was no use. Tears of pain and frustration filled her eyes as she realized there was no escape.

She lay there, unmoving, trying to get her breath back.

And then she felt his body shift.

She made one last effort to escape, shrieked when his hand closed around her ankle, dragging her backward across the rough terrain.

Effortlessly, he flipped her over, then straddled her hips, his hands pinning her arms above her head.

"Did you really think you could escape me?" he asked.

She stared up at him, refusing to answer, refusing to give him the satisfaction of begging for mercy. She knew it would only amuse him.

"Go on," she said, "kill me and get it over with."

"Kill you?" He laughed in her face. It was a dark, ugly sound. "I'm not going to kill you. Don't you know it's against pack law to kill a member of the pack? And you, my dear, are a member of my pack now. I made you, and I'm sworn to protect you. And protect you I will."

"What are you going to do with me?"

He cupped her chin in his palm and gave it a painful squeeze. "Do with you? You're going to take Marishka's place at my side." He laughed that ugly laugh again. "I'm going to make you my queen."

Regan stared at him. His queen? She would

rather be dead. Screaming, "No, no!" she began to struggle against him again.

"Yes," he said, his voice and his gaze as hard as iron. "Tomorrow night, when the moon rises, you will become my bride."

Chapter 34

Santiago hated flying. He wasn't sure why—perhaps because he wasn't in control of the aircraft, or perhaps because a plane crash usually involved flaming wreckage, and fire was one of the few things he feared and respected.

But he would have walked through the fires of hell itself to find Regan. He drummed his fingers on the armrest, willing the plane to go faster, hating the hours and the miles that separated him from his bride. She had been at Vasile's mercy since yesterday. The very thought filled him with an ever-increasing sense of dread. What sort of revenge would the werewolf exact from her? Would he kill her quickly, or torment her? There were so many ways to inflict pain on both body and soul, and Vasile knew them all.

Regan. He could no longer envision a world, or the rest of his existence, without her in it. He had become accustomed to having her around. He loved her laugh, lived for her smile, hungered for the sound of her voice, the touch of her hand, the sweet taste of her lips. Regan. She would be his bride now but for Vasile's unending hatred and his perpetual need for vengeance . . .

Santiago swore under his breath. What right did he have to condemn Vasile when he, himself, had once been guilty of the same relentless need for revenge? But his eternal longing for revenge had been snuffed out in his love for Regan.

He clung to the faint hope that she was still alive, certain that he would know if she wasn't.

"Hang on, Regan," he murmured. "I will find you."

Wracked with fear for her safety, he began to pace the plane's narrow aisle, his hunger growing with his agitation.

Would this flight never end!

There was less than an hour to sunrise when the plane landed. Santiago opened the emergency door and leaped out of the plane before it had stopped on the runway.

He found shelter in the cool earth beneath a stand of timber moments before the sun's light brightened the horizon.

Chapter 35

Regan paced the small, dark confines of the room where Vasile had imprisoned her.

His bride. She was going to be his bride at the moon's rising. The very thought made her sick to her stomach.

Yet even as she swallowed the nausea rising in her throat, some cruel imp inside her mind kept repeating, "There can only be happiness when like marries like." As if she could ever be happy with a monster like Vasile. She had seen his handiwork. She knew what cruelty he was capable of.

She was going to be Vasile's wife, and if that wasn't bad enough, she wouldn't even be his first wife. The woman she had seen in the bedroom earlier had been waiting for Vasile when he returned with Regan in tow. The woman, whose name was Zina, was not at all happy with Regan's presence, or with the fact that Vasile intended to marry her that night. Zina had poured out her anger and jealousy in the most vitriolic and spiteful tirade Regan had ever heard.

Vasile had listened for a short time and then

he'd struck the woman across the face, bloodying her nose and mouth. Zina had made no attempt to wipe the blood away. She had glared at Vasile, her eyes narrowed with hatred, and then, shoulders back, she had turned and walked away.

Regan blew out a sigh. Her prison had no windows and she had no idea how long she had been locked up, or if it was day or night.

She blinked back the tears she had been holding and then, sinking down on the floor, she gave in to the misery that engulfed her.

But for Vasile, she would be Joaquin's bride now. Instead, she was going to become Vasile's wife. Strange, that Joaquin no longer seemed like a monster, while Vasile had become the master of evil. But then, Joaquin had a tender side that she doubted Vasile had ever possessed.

She would never see Joaquin again, never hear his voice, feel his arms around her, or taste his kisses. That thought made her tears fall harder and faster. Why was life so unfair? She had finally found a man to love, and it turned out that he was a vampire. And now, when she was ready to give herself to him heart and soul, Fate had stepped in again, snatched her away on the eve of her wedding, and brought her here. Oh, it just wasn't fair!

Rising, she went to the door and turned the knob. It was locked, of course. She had known that. Nevertheless, she twisted the knob back and forth, over and over again, and when that failed, she slammed her shoulder against the door, tears of frustration washing down her cheeks when it refused to give. There was no way out. No way out . . . no way out. She was doomed to be Vasile's bride. Fear congealed in her belly as a new, horrible thought occurred to her. Oh, lord, would he come to her as a man or a werewolf on their wedding night?

She froze when she heard the snick of the lock being turned. The door opened with a frightful creak, and Vasile stood in the doorway, haloed by the sun's fading light.

When she tried to dart past him, he grabbed her by the arm and pulled her body up against his. When she struggled, he wrenched her arm behind her back and gave it a painful twist.

"Stop fighting me," he said with a growl. "You will be mine tonight." Eyes glittering, he cupped the back of her head with his free hand and kissed her. His kiss was hard and cruel, a brutal branding, a threat of what was to come. She gagged when he forced his tongue into her mouth, and then she bit down. Bile rose in the back of her throat when she tasted his blood.

Muttering an oath, he jerked his mouth from hers, then dragged her across the compound to his house. He shoved her inside, slammed the door behind him, and pushed her up against a wall, his body imprisoning hers.

"You will not fight me," he said, his face only inches from her own. "You will accept me as your mate without argument. If you shame me in front of my pack, you will regret it many times before this night is over. Do you understand me?" When she didn't answer, he shook her so hard her teeth rattled. "Do you understand?"

She glared at him, but wisely nodded.

Vasile glanced out the window. "The pack is gathering." He shoved her toward the bedroom. "Go clean yourself up, and change your clothes. You will find a dress in the bedroom. And don't bother

trying to escape. One of my men is standing outside the window."

With a curt nod, Regan went into the other
room and closed the door. She stood there a
minute, then went into the bathroom. She didn't
bother to lock the door. If she refused to come out,
Vasile would just break it down.

After a moment, she went to the sink and looked
at her face in the mirror.

What could not be changed must be endured.

That which does not break us can only make us
stronger.

"This is no time for platitudes," she muttered.
"I need an escape plan." She laughed humorlessly.
There was no way to escape. She was surrounded
by werewolves.

She washed her hands and face, brushed the dirt
and leaves off her clothing as best she could, finger
combed her hair, and all the while, she thought of
the beautiful wedding dress hanging in her closet.
She would never wear it now.

After returning to the bedroom, she changed
into the dress lying on the bed. She didn't bother
looking in the mirror. What difference did it make
how she looked?

She blinked back her tears, wishing that she and
Joaquin had made love, that she had given her virginity to the man she loved instead of having it
taken, by force, by a monster. All that waiting and
all those cold showers for nothing, she thought.
She had intended her virginity to be a gift for her
husband. Instead, it would be taken violently as an
act of vengeance.

She wondered where Santiago was, if Michael

was all right, and if she would ever see her home or her family again.

She blinked back her tears when she heard Vasile's voice outside the bedroom door.

"It's time," he said.

Determined to hang on to her dignity as best she took, Regan took a deep, calming breath, opened the door, and with her head held high, went out to meet her fate.

She wondered if Vasile could hear the nervous pounding of her heart as he led her outside. She felt a sudden sense of embarrassment that she was about to be married in a hand-me-down dress, and then wondered why she cared. She didn't want to be here. She didn't want to marry Vasile. She didn't know any of the people who had gathered to watch her being forced into a marriage she didn't want.

Vasile came to a stop and the pack surrounded the two of them in a loose circle.

Regan's heart pounded slow and heavy in her breast. This was it. There was no escape.

Zina stood on Vasile's other side. She could feel the woman's hatred rolling over her like thick black smoke.

Vasile lifted his hand and the crowd fell silent. "This woman is mine," he said in a loud voice. "I have made her a member of the pack, and I now declare that she is my mate and that you will treat her as such from this night forward." He turned his gaze on Regan. "From this night forward, you will be my mate. I promise you my protection and my allegiance."

Regan stared at him. Up until this moment, she

had secretly hoped for some last-minute miracle. She knew now that her hopes had been in vain.

"Repeat after me," Vasile said. "From this night forward, you will be my mate."

"From this night forward, you will be my mate."

"I swear to you my loyalty and my devotion."

She spoke the words slowly, feeling as if they were being torn from her throat.

"It is done," Vasile said, and taking her by the hand, he led her back to his house and into the bedroom.

With a leer, he closed the door, then pushed her down on the bed.

"You are mine now," he said.

Regan slared at him defiantly. "Do what you will, say what you will, I will never be yours."

"Willing or not, you will be mine this night." And so saying, he ripped the dress off her body, then stripped away her underwear, his eyes hot as they moved over her. With his gaze riveted on her face, he stood beside the bed and removed his shirt, revealing a chest covered with a mat of thick blond hair.

Regan glared at him. She couldn't do this. She couldn't just lie there and let him rape her without putting up a fight.

She waited until he sat down to remove his shoes and then she bolted off the bed and headed for the door.

Her hand was on the knob when he grabbed a fistful of her hair and gave it a sharp yank. She cried out in pain as she stumbled backward. Snarling at her, he shoved her down on the bed and fell on top of her, his mouth covering hers, his body pinning hers to the mattress.

She writhed beneath him, her nails raking his

cheek. He struck her across the face. She bit his shoulder and his cheek.

It was a violent, bitter struggle. Regan was certain he was going to kill her when, suddenly, his body went limp.

Peering over his shoulder, Regan saw the woman, Zina, standing beside the bed, a club in her hand.

"He's mine," Zina said.

"You can have him, and welcome," Regan muttered. "Just get him off of me."

Zina shook her head. "I don't want him. I just want to kill him."

"No!" Regan wriggled underneath Vasile's limp form. "No." She couldn't let anyone else kill Vasile. It was something she had to do herself.

Zina stared at her, obviously confused. "Would you rather have him alive?"

"No, I want him dead! But I want to do it myself."

Zina nodded, her eyes filled with understanding. "I'm sorry, but I have to do this." She placed her hand over her stomach. "Not for me," she said, withdrawing a gun from the pocket of her skirt, "but for my baby."

Before Regan could protest, before Zina could fire the gun, Vasile rolled off Regan. With a roar of outrage and betrayal, he shifted. When Regan tried to get out of his way, his jaws closed over her neck. Flinging his head to the side, he threw her off the bed as if she weighed no more than a small child. Blood sprayed from her throat, splattering over the blankets, the ceiling, and the wall.

Regan landed on her back, hard, and lay there, too stunned to move. She could feel the blood flowing over her shoulder and down her arm. So much blood . . . She knew instinctively that it was a killing wound, but somehow it didn't seem to matter.

Growling low in his throat, the wolf turned on Zina.

White-faced with fear, the woman scrambled backward, firing blindly as she went. The first shot missed, as did the second, and then the wolf was on her.

With a roar, Vasile swatted the weapon from Zina's hand. He was about to rip out her throat when a black wolf burst through the window in a spray of broken glass.

Vasile turned to meet his new attacker, a wolfish grin on his face as he recognized the intruder.

Hackles bristling, fangs bared, the two wolves circled each other, oblivious to everything but putting an end to the centuries-old feud between them.

Regan stared at the gun that was lying only inches from her hand. She needed a gun, but she couldn't remember why. She looked at the blood running down her arm. It seemed a shame for all that blood to go to waste. Too bad Santiago wasn't here . . . She looked at the weapon again. She owned a gun . . . she wanted to kill Vasile. It was important for her to kill him, but again, she couldn't remember why.

She glanced at the wolves. They were still fighting ferociously. Both were splattered with blood. The fair-haired one was limping; blood oozed from a deep cut on its foreleg. The black one was also bleeding from several places.

The wolves parted for a moment. Breathing heavily, tongues lolling, they growled at each other.

Regan looked at the fair-haired wolf. He had bitten her. And now she was dying from the wound he had inflicted on her. With all the energy at her command, she reached for the gun. It was heavy, so heavy. She dragged it closer, her finger curling around the trigger. Using both hands, she summoned the last of her energy and lifted the weapon. It was too late for her, she thought dully, but she intended to make sure that Vasile sired no more werewolves.

As if divining her thoughts, he turned to look at her, his eyes filled with savage hatred.

She didn't flinch. Meeting his gaze, she squeezed the trigger and shot him right between the eyes.

He stood there a moment and then he dropped to the floor. There was a charge in the air, like electricity before a storm. The fair-haired wolf shimmered and then it was gone and Vasile lay in its place, a neat round hole between his sightless eyes.

It was over.

The gun fell from Regan's hand. With the last of her energy, she looked at the black wolf. Tears filled her eyes. He had come to save her, she thought, but it was too late. Too late.

"I . . . love . . . you," she whispered, and then, with a sigh of resignation, she closed her eyes and waited for death.

With a harsh cry of denial, Santiago shifted to his own form. Kneeling beside Regan, he drew her into his lap. Her face was drained of color. Blood continued to ooze from the terrible gaping wound in her throat. He started at it in horror. So much blood.

Hardly aware of the other woman, who had

gained her feet and was now backing into a corner, Santiago gathered Regan into his arms and carried her to the bed. After placing her on it, he ripped the top sheet into strips. He folded one into a thick pad and placed it over the ugly wound in her neck, then he used one of the other strips to hold it in place. He muttered an oath when blood quickly soaked through the makeshift bandage.

She needed a doctor, he thought desperately, and they were miles from civilization, miles from a hospital.

Cursing softly, he swaddled her in a blanket and then, gathering her into his arms, he went outside. A crowd had gathered around the front of the house but he paid them no heed. With all the preternatural speed at his command, he carried her to the nearest village. It cost him precious time to find a doctor. The man took one look at Regan and got to work.

After laying her on a metal table covered with a white sheet, the doctor unwrapped the bandage from her throat. He looked up at Santiago through narrowed eyes. "Did you do this?"

"No."

"Do you know her blood type?"

"A negative."

"What type are you?"

Santiago hesitated a moment, then said, "O."

"Sit down and roll up your sleeve."

Santiago shook his head. "I cannot . . ."

"Do you want her to live?" the doctor demanded brusquely. "Then do as I say. We have no time to waste."

Muttering an oath, Santiago sat on the chair beside the bed. How would his blood affect Regan?

Would it kill her? Taken via a transfusion, it wouldn't turn her into a vampire, but what would it do? And what would the doctor say if he knew whose blood he was about to take?

Santiago clenched his fist as the doctor prepared to take his blood. Watching, he couldn't help but laugh inwardly at the thought of a vampire donating blood to a mortal woman. Surely it was a first!

"Is she going to be all right?" Santiago asked, though how anyone could survive such a terrible wound was beyond his comprehension.

"Only time will tell."

The doctor slapped a bandage on his arm. "I will need to stitch her. You can wait outside."

"No."

"Yes. Go."

With a curt nod, Santiago left the room. As much as he longed to stay, he needed to feed, needed to replace the blood he had lost.

Leaving the doctor's office, he ghosted down the dark streets in search of prey.

She was lost in a dark fog. No matter where she went, no matter how she searched, she couldn't find what she was looking for, couldn't find the light. Her body felt weak, adrift. Lost.

Was this death? Had her spirit left her body? Did one have to search for heaven?

Or, oh horrible thought, had killing Vasile condemned her to hell? She refused to accept that. Vasile had been a monster. Surely killing him was a good thing!

Why couldn't she find the way out?

Why couldn't she find him?

She tried to call his name but the words wouldn't come and then she remembered that he was a monster, too, and that she shouldn't want him, shouldn't love him. She wished that they had made love. Right or wrong, it was her one regret.

"Joaquin." His name formed in her mind. Had she said it aloud? She wanted Joaquin, wanted him to hold her hand and promise her that everything would be all right. They would find the shaman and he would cure her . . . but then she remembered that the shaman was dead.

"Pahin Sapa? Are you there? Is anybody there?"

She tried to open her eyes, but her eyelids were heavy, so heavy. When she tried to move, she felt a sharp, burning pain in her neck where Vasile had bitten her.

But he was dead now, and so was she. So many things she would never be able to do. She would never see her family again, never have a family of her own, never see Santiago . . . Joaquin, Joaquin! She loved him, but the world was growing darker . . .

Santiago stood at Regan's bedside. Her complexion was deathly pale, her breathing shallow, her heartbeat faint and thready. He looked up at the doctor, unwilling to believe what his eyes were seeing.

"Is she going to live?"

The doctor shook his head. "I'm sorry," he murmured, and his eyes were kind.

"Is there nothing you can do?"

"She's too weak. She's lost too much blood. The wound in her neck . . . how did she get it?"

"An accident."

"It looks like the bite of a large animal. The authorities . . ."

"How much longer does she have?"

"A few hours. Perhaps until morning." The doctor laid a sympathetic hand on Santiago's arm. "Can I bring you anything? Coffee? Whiskey?"

"No, nothing."

"I have patients to visit," the doctor said. "Stay as long as you wish. Call me when . . ." He patted Santiago on the shoulder. "I'm sorry."

After the doctor left the room, Santiago took Regan's hand in his. It was cold, too cold. He was losing her.

Dammit, he couldn't let her go! "Regan! Listen to me! You will not die, do you hear me? I cannot live without you."

He had not wept in hundreds of years, had thought he had lost the power to do so long ago, but he felt the sting of tears in his eyes as he gazed down at her. She lay so still, as if she was already gone.

Using the power of his mind, he commanded her to wake up.

She moaned softly and then her eyelids fluttered open.

He squeezed her hand. "Regan!"

She stared up at him, her gaze unfocused. There was no recognition in her eyes.

"Regan, listen to me."

"You're here," she said, her voice little more than a whisper. "You're the one I've been searching for."

He frowned. "What?"

"I looked for you . . . in the light . . . but you weren't . . . there."

He lifted her hand to his lips and kissed her palm. "I am here with you now."

"I . . . love . . . you."

"And I love you."

"I wish . . . I could . . . stay."

"Regan, listen to me. I cannot let you go."

A faint smile flitted over her lips and was gone. "You can't . . . stop me."

"Yes, I can. Let me bring you across."

She blinked at him and then shook her head.

"Dammit, I will not let you go! Do you hear me? I need you in my life."

"I can't . . . be a vampire . . . I hunt . . . vampires."

"And you have found one who will never let you go."

"I'm . . . sorry . . ." Her eyelids fluttered down; her hand went limp in his.

He gazed down at her, trying to imagine his existence without her in it, but it was impossible. Without her, he had no reason to go on. She had become his life, the light in his darkness, his purpose for rising in the evening. Without her, what was there to look forward to? He had no need for the world; the world had no need of him.

"Very well," he said, stroking her cheek. "Rest in peace, my love. I will join you in the morning."

Her eyelids flew open as her fingers tightened around his. "No! No . . . you must . . . not. Promise . . . me."

He shook his head. "I have no reason to go on if you are not here. If I cannot have you with me in this life, then I will join you in the next. Surely a merciful heaven will not keep us apart."

She looked up at him, her eyes clear. "You don't mean that."

"I do. I have existed alone long enough. I will not do it any longer."

"This is . . . blackmail," she said accusingly.

"There is an old saying: 'All is fair in love and war.' And I love you, Regan Delaney, as I have loved no other. In life or in death, you will be mine."

"Let it be life, then," she murmured, closing her eyes. "A long, long life."

Chapter 36

At her words, Santiago lifted her from the bed, blankets and all, and carried her out the back door of the doctor's office.

With preternatural speed, he made his way out of the village toward a heavily wooded area, searching until he found a small cave that was cut into the side of a hill and hidden behind a tangled mass of shrubbery and foliage.

Inside the cave, he spread the blankets on the ground and then, sitting down, he gathered Regain into his arms. There was little time to waste. Her heartbeat was already so faint that even with his preternatural ability, he could scarcely hear it. Smoothing her hair away from her neck, he kissed the sweet curve of her throat and then, taking a deep breath and praying it wasn't too late, he bent over her, his fangs piercing the tender skin below her ear.

Ah, the warmth and sweetness of her life's blood. It filled him with a sense of euphoria such as he had never known. He drank it all and then, tearing a gash in his wrist, he held the bleeding wound to her lips.

"Drink, my love," he coaxed, stroking her throat to make her swallow. "Drink and live."

Regan woke slowly. Sitting up, she stretched her arms over her head. She felt wonderful. And then she frowned. Why did she feel wonderful? Why was she naked? And where was she?

Glancing around, she realized she was lying on a blanket in a cave. A cave? What was she doing in a cave? Had they returned to the Black Hills? Where was Santiago? She touched her hand to her neck where Vasile had bitten her. There was no bandage and no ragged wound, only soft, smooth skin.

"All right," she muttered, "let's sort this out. I'm alone in a cave and . . ." She bolted to her feet. Had Santiago left her for dead? Had he buried her in a cave?

She wrapped the thin blanket around her, toga-style, and then moved quickly toward the entrance, only then wondering how she could see so clearly in the dark.

She frowned again, her gaze darting right and left. She could see everything with crystal clarity, and she felt different somehow.

"You're just being silly," she said, moving closer to the entrance. "It's probably because you're not a werewolf anymore and you're just feeling normal again."

But she didn't feel normal.

As she stepped out of the cave, she realized she was hungry, not for food, but for something to drink. That wasn't normal, either.

She had recently been close to death. Perhaps that was the answer to everything.

She paused outside the cave, more confused than ever. Her senses were enhanced, the way they had been when she was a werewolf, yet she wasn't in wolf form and she knew that that part of her was gone, destroyed with Vasile. Why, then, were her senses so sharp? She could hear the tiny black beetle crawling on a leaf to her left, see clearly though the sky was dark and overcast, smell the grass and the dirt and the trees. She knew there was a small stream a few yards away and a honeycomb in the branches overhead, and that a small fox was cowering in a hole not far from where she stood.

She took a deep breath and Santiago's scent was borne to her on the evening breeze, and then she saw him striding toward her. He smiled when he saw her, though his eyes were guarded.

"How do you feel?" he asked.

"Never better," she replied, thinking he was more handsome than ever. "What's wrong with me?"

"What do you mean?"

"Why do I feel so good? I should be dead."

He took a deep breath. "Undead," he said quietly.

The word hung between them in the air as bits and pieces of what had happened the night before rose in her memory. The wolves fighting. The weight of the gun in her hand. Santiago's voice telling her that he loved her, telling her that if she died, he would join her in the morning.

"You did it," she said, a note of wonder in her voice. "You made me a . . ."

He nodded. "Vampire."

"I don't feel dead." She ran her hands over her arms, across her breasts, over her face. "I feel as if I could fly." She tilted her head to the side. "You told me that it was painful when you were brought across. Why didn't I feel anything?"

"It happened while you were unconscious."

"I'm a vampire." She looked at him, her eyes wide. "Does this mean I have to live in the park?"

Grinning, he drew her into his arms. "No, my love. We can live wherever you wish."

"Are you still going to marry me?"

"Just as soon as I can."

She stared up at him. "Can we get married tonight?"

"I do not think so. At home, I know a priest who will marry us, but here . . ." He shrugged. "I am a stranger here."

Reaching up, she trailed her forefinger across his brow, down his cheek, and over his lower lip. "Can we have our honeymoon now and get married tomorrow night?"

He took her finger into his mouth and suckled it a moment before asking, "Is that what you want?"

She nodded, surprised to feel a blush heat her cheeks. "I almost died last night and all I could think about was how sorry I was that we hadn't made love. I don't want to wait any longer."

He understood her need even better than she did. She had been through a number of terrible ordeals in the last few months. She had been turned into a werewolf and been near death, and now she was a newly made vampire, unsure of her future, wondering if she had made the right decision. Few things were as life-affirming as the act of love.

He brushed a kiss across her cheek. "A blanket in a cave was not what I had in mind for our wedding night."

"Don't you know it isn't the place that matters," she said, "it's who you're with?"

"Nevertheless," he said, swinging her up into his arms, "I do not intend to spend our first night together in a cave."

"No?" She glanced around. "I don't see a hotel."

"There is one in the village," he said, striding swiftly through the night.

The inn was old and small and quaint, with a pointed roof and a bright red door. The grizzled clerk gave Regan and Santiago an odd look when they walked into the lobby hand in hand. Regan couldn't blame him. Even though Santiago had scrounged up a dress from somewhere, she still looked as though she had been ridden hard and put away wet.

The clerk, who, as it turned out, was also the owner, insisted on being paid in advance. Regan couldn't blame him for that, either.

She glanced around the lobby while Santiago signed the register. An ancient tapestry depicting a king riding to hounds hung from one wall. A small, round, mahogany table and four elegant chairs occupied one corner. The chairs looked so old and fragile, Regan doubted if all of them put together would hold her weight.

There was no elevator. Santiago took her hand and they walked up the curved stairway to the second floor.

Their room was located at the end of a narrow hallway that was lined with old portraits. Regan wondered if the inn was a family business and the portraits were of the former owners.

A murmured, "Oh, my," escaped Regan's lips when Santiago swung her into his arms, opened the carved oak door, and carried her across the threshold. The tiny parlor was done in blue and white with peach accents and was perhaps the loveliest room she had ever seen. The sofa was curved, with a high back. A matching chair sat at a right angle to the sofa. Dainty white doilies, as delicate and lacy as spider webs, covered the arms of the furniture. The framed pictures on the walls were scenes of days gone by—a horse-drawn carriage driven by a man in blue and gold livery, a man and a woman in Victorian clothing strolling alongside a placid lake. Old-fashioned lamps with fringed shades provided the room's light. Patterned rugs covered the floor. A fire was laid in the marble hearth, needing only the touch of a match.

"Not bad," Santiago said, glancing around.

"Not bad?" Regan punched him on the shoulder. "It's beautiful."

He kissed the top of her head, murmuring, "You are."

Turning her in his arms, he slowly lowered her feet to the floor. Her body made a slow, sensuous descent down the length of his and by the time her feet touched the floor, she was as aroused as he was.

But this was her wedding night, and she wasn't going to bed smelling of fear and perspiration and dirt. "I need a shower."

"An excellent idea," Santiago said agreeably.

When Regan started to undress, he gently batted her hands away. "Let me," he said, his voice rough with desire.

Regan stood there, blushing, as Santiago slowly bared her body to his gaze. She felt a rush of feminine power as his eyes grew hotter.

Santiago toed off his boots and was about to slip

off his shirt when she said, "My turn," and with hands that trembled with eager excitement, she removed his shirt, trousers, and briefs.

He was, in a word, gorgeous, from his inky black hair to the soles of his feet. And he was hers, for this night and every night for as long as she lived. It was a heady thought.

Swinging Regan into his arms, Santiago headed for the bathroom.

"I can walk, you know," Regan said dryly.

"Of course you can," he replied easily. "But why should you?"

She laughed softly. "Are you going to carry me everywhere?"

"Perhaps." He kissed her cheek, the tip of her nose, the curve of her jaw. "You do not wish to deny me the pleasure, do you?"

Regan smiled a sultry smile. "I wouldn't think of denying you anything that would bring you pleasure."

Chuckling softly, Santiago opened the shower door. Muttering, "how quaint," he turned on the old-fashioned shower and adjusted the temperature. When the water was just right, he stepped under the spray. Then, as he had before, he slowly lowered Regan to her feet.

She shivered with pleasure as her body slid over his. Never in all her life had she experienced anything quite as erotic as the feel of Santiago's water-slick skin against her own.

Moments later, when he picked up a bar of lavender soap, lathered his hands, and began to wash her breasts, she knew she had been mistaken. Nothing could be more sensual, more arousing, than the touch of his soapy hands sweeping over her flesh.

"Joaquin . . ."

"Yes, my love?"

"I'm going to melt at your feet if you don't stop that."

"Then melt, my love," he said, his voice growing husky as his hands, his wickedly clever hands, slid over her belly, slowly moving lower, lower, until, groaning with pleasure, she arched against him.

Unable to wait a moment longer, Santiago took her there, in the shower, with the water sluicing over their bodies and their mouths fused together.

He swallowed her cry when he breached her maidenhead, his hands gentle as they stroked her face, her back, her hair.

Regan writhed against him, certain she was going to explode into a million pieces as Santiago moved deep inside her, his voice urging her to go with him, to let go and let it happen.

With her arms wrapped tight around his waist, she buried her face in his neck and felt a sudden sharp pain in her gums. Needing to relieve the pressure, she bit his neck. Caught up in a world of sensation, it took her a moment to realize that she was feeling what he felt, that his groan was not one of pain, but ecstasy. His blood was like sweet nectar on her tongue.

Moments later, the wave of pleasure she had been riding crested, sending ripples of pleasure through every part of her being. It was unlike anything she had ever known, and more wonderful than anything she had ever imagined.

Spent and sated, she rested her head against Santiago's shoulder. "That was incredible," she murmured. "Can we do it again?"

* * *

It was near dawn when Regan crawled under the covers. They had indeed done it again. And again. And again. On the sofa. On the floor in front of the fire. In the bed. After the last time, they had taken another shower.

Now, lying in bed while Santiago secured their room, she felt her body grow heavy. It was a frightening feeling, as if she were being weighed down. Was this a natural part of being a vampire?

She tried to sit up as Santiago entered the room, but she lacked the strength.

"Joaquin!"

Hearing the note of panic in her voice, he hurried to her side and sat on the edge of the bed. "I am here."

"I feel so strange. I can't even sit up. It's like I've been drugged or something."

He smoothed his hand across her brow. "Relax, my love, do not fight it. It is the Dark Sleep."

"I don't like it."

"The sensation of being weighed down will pass, in time."

"So, it's normal?"

He nodded.

"You won't leave me, will you?"

"No."

She frowned. "Why aren't I hungry all the time, the way new vampires are supposed to be?"

"Because I am a very old vampire. My blood is stronger than most because I have only made one other vampire during my existence. My strength is now yours." He grinned at her. "And you drank from me earlier, remember?"

How could she forget? In the throes of passion,

she had bitten his neck and tasted his blood—and liked it so much she had done it again, and again.

"Vampires do not usually feed on each other," Santiago remarked.

"Why not?"

He shrugged. "I really do not know. I think the reason you are able to drink mine is because the doctor gave you my blood via transfusion."

"You gave me your blood?" Even though the darkness was dragging her down, she laughed. "A vampire *giving* blood," she said, yawning. "That has to be one for the books . . ."

Her voice trailed off as the Dark Sleep caught her in its grasp.

Santiago's heart swelled with love as he gazed down at his bride. She was so lovely, so sweet. And now she was his, and would always be his.

He sat at her side, stroking her hair and caressing her cheek with his fingers, or simply watching her, until his own body demanded rest.

With a sense of contentment, he slid into bed beside her. For the first time in centuries, he wasn't alone as he took his rest.

It was, he thought, a welcome change that had been a long time coming.

Chapter 37

Regan looked out the window of the plane. She had been wondering how they were going to get home. One thing she hadn't expected was to have a private jet waiting for them at the airport.

"You must have an awful lot of credits saved up," she remarked, glancing over at Santiago.

"I have a few."

"A few?" She glanced at the plane, with its plush seats and opulent interior. Pilots that flew private planes were expensive; pilots that would fly you across the world and wait until you were ready to return were even more so.

"It is easy to accumulate wealth when you have centuries at your command to do so and your material needs are few."

She made a soft sound of assent. She hadn't thought of it like that. Then a new thought crossed her mind.

"Joaquin! What am I going to tell my family?" She shook her head, trying to imagine how she would explain to her parents and her brothers that she now belonged to an endangered species and wouldn't be able to have brunch with them on Easter Sunday or open presents on Christmas morning. Sure, they were liberal in their thinking, but they'd never had a vampire in the family before.

"Do they love you?"

"What a silly question. Of course they do."

"Then they will accept you as you are."

"I don't know. My father's a senator. He's been working on a law to repeal the Endangered Vampire Act. Somehow I don't think he'll be too thrilled to learn about my new, ah, role in life."

Santiago grunted softly. "In that case, I doubt they will approve of your choice of a husband, either, but I would think that, given a choice between having a daughter who is a vampire and a daughter who is dead, your father would prefer the former."

"I guess so. It should certainly make for some interesting conversation when the family gets together."

"You are all the family I need."

"I love you, too." She glanced out the window, thinking of all the things she hadn't even considered when she agreed to let Santiago bring her across. Her parents' reaction hadn't occurred to her. Of course, she hadn't been thinking all that clearly at the time. And Mike . . . how would she ever tell Mike?

"What is wrong now?" Santiago asked, seeing her woebegone expression.

"It's Michael. How will I ever tell him?" She shook her head. "I'll never be able to tell him about any of this," she remarked, "or about us. He'd never understand. He's so . . . Joaquin?" She frowned as his face went blank. "What is it? Is something wrong with Mike?" She shook his arm. "What is it? Tell me."

"He is dead."

"Dead?" She stared at him. "When? How?"

"He was dying when I found him."

Regan felt a rush of guilt. "It was Vasile, wasn't it? That night, at my house . . ."

Santiago nodded. "It was Flynn who told me where to find you."

Tears welled in her eyes. All this time, she had never wondered what had happened to Mike. She had just blithely assumed that he was all right and that he would be in the city when she returned. Resting her head on Santiago's chest, she let her tears fall. "It's all my fault. If it wasn't for me, Mike would be alive now."

"It is not your fault," Santiago said. "You must not think like that."

How could she help it? She hadn't been in love with Michael Flynn, but she had loved him as a friend—a good friend. She felt a sudden delight in the knowledge that she had killed Vasile. She only wished she could do it again, for Mike.

Regan stood beside Joaquin, her hand clasped in his as they waited for the priest to arrive. They had returned to Santiago's lair in the Byways just before dawn the day before. Regan had succumbed to the Dark Sleep almost as soon as they reached Santiago's lair. Now she stood beside him, her gaze slowly moving around the room. It was a beautiful old church, with burnished wooden pews and intricate stained glass windows. A sweet-faced Madonna stood in one corner, her hand raised in benediction. Flickering candles set in scrolled wall sconces cast a warm glow.

The soft sound of a door opening drew Regan's attention. Glancing to her left, she saw an aged priest walking toward the altar. Short, slender, and gray haired, he leaned heavily on a wooden cane.

A smile spread over the priest's face as he approached the altar.

"Ah, Santiago, my old friend, forgive my tardiness," he said, his brown eyes twinkling.

"Time is something I have in abundance, Father Paul," Santiago replied.

"Would that I could say the same." The priest took Santiago's hand in his. "Some nights the spirit is willing but this old body just wants to go to bed."

"We appreciate your taking time to do this, Father," Santiago said, his voice tinged with genuine reverence and respect.

"Well, now, I can't have the two of you living in sin, can I?" the priest said chuckling. "Who is this lovely young woman?"

"Father, this is my bride, Regan Delaney. Regan, this is Father Paul."

Smiling his good-natured smile, the priest took Regan's hand in both of his. "Delighted to meet you, my dear," he said, his eyes twinkling. "I didn't think my friend here would ever find love again." Eyes narrowed, he tilted his head to the side, his gaze locked on hers. "You are as he is." It wasn't a question, but a statement of fact. "Were you brought across of your own free will?"

"Yes, Father."

"Very well, then, join hands, won't you, and we'll begin."

Regan looked at Joaquin, her heart swelling with love for the man who would soon be her husband. His voice was soft and low and intense as he spoke his vows. Regan couldn't help smiling when he promised to love her as long as he lived. The good Lord willing, they would have centuries together.

"I now pronounce you man and wife," the priest said, his voice and expression solemn. And then he smiled broadly. "You may kiss the bride."

"Gladly," Santiago murmured. Drawing Regan into his arms, he kissed her tenderly, gently, and then he kissed her again. There was nothing tender or gentle in this kiss. It was a brand, sealing her as his for all time.

"Go in peace, my children," the priest said.

"Thank you, Father," Santiago said.

Regan kissed the old man on the cheek. "Yes, thank you."

Taking her by the hand, Joaquin led her out of the church.

"How do you happen to be friends with a priest?" Regan asked when they were outside. "I mean, it seems odd, doesn't it?"

"Perhaps. I have known the good Father for over forty years."

"However did you meet?" she asked. "He's not a vampire, is he?"

"No. I saved his life one night. It happened in Spain. He was a young priest at the time, on his way back to the church after visiting a parishioner who lived in the slums outside the city. It was raining heavily when two young hoodlums jumped him . . ."

"They attacked a priest?"

"They didn't know he was a priest. He was wearing a heavy raincoat at the time."

"Go on."

"One of the young men was about to stab him in

the back when I came along." Santiago shrugged. "I chased the boys away, then escorted the good Father home."

"Did he know what you are?"

"Not at first."

"And he didn't care, when he found out?"

"He was a bit of a rebel in his youth. I rather think he enjoyed having a vampire acquaintance. When I saved his life, he promised me a favor in return. Tonight he fulfilled that promise."

"You waited quite a long time to collect that favor, didn't you?"

"I wanted to save it for a special occasion. He is the only one I know who would marry us without a license."

"He's a long way from Spain."

"His order sent him here five years ago. And now, my lovely bride," he said, his gaze warming as he looked at her, "we have the whole night ahead of us. Is there anything you would like to do before we go home?"

"There is one thing I need to do," she said. "It won't take long."

The cemetery was located on a green hill east of the city. Regan paused at the entrance, knowing that she couldn't go on with her life until she told Michael good-bye.

"Go," Santiago said, "I will wait for you here."

With a nod, Regan opened the large iron gate and made her way along the narrow stone path until she found Mike's final resting place. She read the short epitaph on the headstone:

> *Michael Seamus Flynn*
> *Beloved son of Timothy and Gladys*
> *May the good Lord keep you safe in His care*
> *Until we meet again*

She stood there a moment, remembering the first time she had met Mike and how kind he had been to her, a brand new vampire hunter who had lost her lunch at her first crime scene. He had always been protective of her. She remembered a time when she had been sick with the flu. It had been Mike who had looked after her. He had driven her to the doctor, made sure she had food in the house, and even changed the sheets on her bed. He had been so sweet and so kind and yet, try as she might, she hadn't been able to love him as he deserved. And now he was gone.

Funny how life turned out, she thought as she placed a single white rose on his grave. They had met because she was a vampire hunter and now she was a vampire.

Kneeling, she placed her hand on the grave. "I'm sorry, Mike, so sorry." No matter what anyone said, she would always feel responsible for his death. Tears stung her eyes. "I'm sorry I couldn't love you, but I promise I'll never forget you." She wiped the tears from her eyes. "Never."

She felt a subtle shift in the air as Santiago came up beside her.

"Regan? Are you all right?"

"Yes."

Taking her hand, he lifted her to her feet. "Is there anything I can do?"

She shook her head. "Remember when you asked me if I'd rather be a vampire or a werewolf?"

He nodded, his expression impassive as he waited for her to go on.

"Well," she said, looking up at him, "I've been mortal, werewolf, and vamp . . ."

She watched a muscle clench in his jaw, but he didn't say anything; he simply stood there, waiting, as if he wasn't sure he wanted to hear what else she had to say.

"This way is the best way." Standing on her tiptoes, she cupped his face in her hands and kissed him deeply. "Come on," she said, taking him by the hand, "let's go home."

Amanda Ashley's next book from Zebra,
NIGHT'S TOUCH,
will be available in bookstores in July 2007.
A stunning sequel to NIGHT'S KISS,
this is a most surprising
and exciting novel!

ONE KISS CAN SEAL YOUR FATE . . .

Cara DeLongpre wandered into the mysterious
Nocturne club looking for a fleeting diversion from
her sheltered life. Instead she found a dark, seductive
stranger whose touch entices her beyond the safety
she's always known and into a heady carnal bliss . . .

A year ago, Vincent Cordova believed that vampires
existed only in bad movies and bogeyman stories. That
was before a chance encounter left him with unimag-
inable powers, a hellish thirst, and an aching loneliness
he's sure will never end . . . until the night he meets
Cara DeLongpre. Cara's beauty and bewitching inno-
cence call to his mind, his heart . . . his blood. For Vincent senses the Dark Gift shared by Cara's parents, and
the lurking threat from an ancient and powerful foe.
And he knows that the only thing more dangerous
than the enemy waiting to seek its vengeance is the
secret carried by those Cara trusts the most . . .

Chapter 1

Cara Aideen Delongpre sipped her drink, too preoccupied with her own thoughts to pay any attention to the crowd and the noise that surrounded her. She had grown up knowing her mother and father weren't like other parents. Once she had started going to school, she had discovered a whole new world. Other kids went on vacation with their parents when school was out. They went out to dinner and to the zoo and to Disneyland and Sea World. They had birthday parties at Chuck E. Cheese's. Other kids had brothers and sisters, aunts and uncles, and cousins and grandparents. When Cara asked why she didn't have brothers or sisters or aunts and uncles, her father had explained that her mother couldn't have children, and that he and her mother didn't have any siblings, and that her grandparents had all passed away.

It was a perfectly logical explanation, but it didn't make her feel any less lonely. It would have been nice to have a sister she could share confidences with.

What wasn't logical was the fact that, in over twenty

years, her parents hadn't changed at all. She told herself she was being foolish, that she was overreacting, imagining things. But there was no arguing with the proof of her own eyes. They both looked exactly the way they had when Cara was a little girl. Her mother never gained or lost an ounce. Her face was as smooth and clear as it had always been. The same was true of her father. Roshan DeLongpre looked like a man in his mid-thirties, and he had looked that way for as long as Cara could remember. He had taken her to the movies one night last week and they had run into a couple of Cara's acquaintances. Before she could introduce her father, her friend, Cindy, had taken her aside and asked how long she had been dating that "good looking older man."

Cara stared into her drink, wishing she had the nerve to ask her parents why Di Giorgio aged and they didn't, why their lifestyle was so different from everyone else's. She knew about their aversion to the sun and their liquid diet, but why did that keep them from other normal activities? Why did they encourage her to make friends, but discourage her from bringing them home? And why did they keep the door to their bedroom locked during the day? What were they doing in there?

She looked up as a man sat down beside her. He smiled, then pointed with his chin at her drink. "Can I buy you another?"

"No, thank you."

He lifted a hand. "Hey, no problem. You just looked a little down. I thought you might like some company."

He had a nice voice, blond hair, and dark brown eyes. What harm could it do to share a drink with him?

"Are you sure you won't change your mind?" he coaxed, as if sensing her indecision.

"Well, I would like another."

"What are you drinking?" he asked, signaling for the bartender.

"A virgin pineapple daiquiri."

He ordered her drink and a scotch and water for himself, then held out his hand. "I'm Anton."

"Cara." She hesitated a moment before taking his hand. Though she had been on her share of dates, she tended to be shy around strangers. She wasn't sure why. Maybe because she had never forgotten her father's warning that he had "ruthless enemies." Still, she told herself there was nothing to worry about. Frank was here.

Anton's grip was firm, his skin warm. "Do you come here often?"

"No, this is my first time. I was just passing by and I heard the music and . . ." She shrugged. "I thought it might cheer me up."

"If you tell me what's got you feeling so blue, I might be able to help."

"I don't think so, but thanks for offering."

Cara glanced out at the dance floor as the lights dimmed. The music, which had been upbeat, changed to something slow and sensual with a dark, sexual undertone. It called to something earthy deep within her.

"Would you like to dance?" Anton asked.

Again, she hesitated a moment before agreeing.

Anton took her by the hand and led her out onto the floor. "So," he said, taking her in his arms. "Tell me about yourself."

"What do you want to know?"

"Let's see. What do you like to do for fun? Do you work, or are you an heiress? Who's your favorite

singer? And, most important of all, are you a choco-
holic like every other woman I've ever met?"

She laughed. "Guilty on the chocolate," she said,
and then frowned as she realized she had never
seen her mother eat or drink anything chocolate.
Even the most rigid dieters cheated every now and
then.

"Did I say something wrong?" he asked.

"No. I work at the library, and I don't really have
a favorite singer." She didn't tell him that she was,
in fact, an heiress. After all, he was a stranger and
she wasn't a fool. Not that she had anything to
worry about, not with Frank Di Giorgio sitting at
the far end of the bar watching her like a hawk.

"You're a librarian?" Anton exclaimed.

"Is something wrong with that?"

"No, no, but . . . well, you're a knock-out. I sort of
thought you might be a model or an actress."

Cara smiled, flattered in spite of herself. "Disappointed?"

"Not at all."

When the music ended, he escorted her back to
their seats. Their drinks were waiting for them. Cara
sipped hers, thinking how glad she was she had
stopped in here tonight. Di Girorgio had tried to
dissuade her, but she had insisted. Once inside, she
almost hadn't stayed, it was such a strange place. For
one thing, she was the only one in the place who
wasn't wearing black. Voodoo masks and ancient
Indian burial masks decorated the walls. Tall black
candles flickered in wrought iron sconces, casting
eerie shadows over the faces of the patrons; a good
number of them wore long black cloaks or capes
with hoods.

"So," Anton said, "what do you think of The Nocturne?"

"I'm not sure. Why is everyone wearing black?"

"This is a Goth hangout."

"Oh! Silly me, I should have guessed."

He grinned at her. "I take it you're not into the Goth scene."

"Not really," she replied, and then frowned, thinking that her father would be right at home in a place like this. He had an affinity for dark clothing, and he had a long black cloak. But it was more than that. From time to time, she had sensed a darkness in her father that she couldn't explain and didn't understand.

Cara finished her drink, then looked at her watch, surprised to find it was so late. "I should be going," she said reluctantly. "My folks will be worried."

"Don't tell me you still live at home with mom and dad!"

Cara shrugged. "I like it there." And she did, although sometimes, especially when the days were long and the nights were short, it was like living alone.

"One more dance?" he coaxed.

"I don't think so. I really need to go," she said, and then wondered why she had to be home before midnight. She wasn't a child anymore. Why did she still have a curfew? Lately, she'd had so many questions about the way she lived. Why did she still live at home? Why did she still need a bodyguard? She was twenty-two years old and no one had ever tried to kidnap her or molest her or so much as given her a dirty look. Of course, Di Giorgio was probably responsible for that. A man would have to be crazy to try anything with The Hulk lurking in the background. Still, maybe it was time to sit her folks down and ask the questions that had been plaguing her more and more in the last few months.

"Thank you for the drink and the dance," she said, rising.

"Any chance you'll be here tomorrow night about this time?" he asked.

She tilted her head to the side, considering it, and then smiled. "I'd say the odds were good."

"Great. I'll see you then."

Leaning back against the bar, Anton Bouchard watched his enemy's daughter leave the bar, followed by a big bear of a man who looked as if he could easily take on every other man in the place without breaking a sweat.

Anton grunted softly, thinking how pleased his mother would be when he told her he had put the first part of her plan into operation.

If you loved this Amanda Ashley book,
then you won't want to miss any of
her other fabulous vampire stories
from Zebra Books!
Following is a sneak peak . . .

DESIRE AFTER DARK

Cursed to an eternity of darkness,
Antonio Battista has wandered the earth,
satisfying his hunger with countless women,
letting none find a place in his heart.
But Victoria Cavendish is different.

"You wish something?" he asked.

She shook her head. "No. Good night."

She started past him only to be stayed by the light touch of his hand on her shoulder. She could have walked on by. He wasn't holding her, but she stopped, her heart rate accelerating when she looked up and met his gaze.

Time slowed, could have ceased to exist for all she knew or cared. She was aware of nothing but the man standing beside her. His dark blue gaze melded with hers, igniting a flame that started deep within her and spread with all the rapidity of a wild-fire fanned by a high wind.

Heart pounding, she looked at him, and waited.

He didn't make her wait too long.

He murmured to her softly in a language she didn't understand, then swept her into his arms and kissed her, a long searing kiss that burned away the memory of every other man she had ever known, until she knew only him, saw only him. Wanted only him.

He deepened the kiss, his tongue teasing her lips,

sending flames along every nerve, igniting a need so primal, so volatile, she thought she might explode. She pressed her body to his, hating the layers of cloth that separated his flesh from hers. She had never reacted to a man's kisses like this before, never felt such an overwhelming need to touch and be touched. A distant part of her mind questioned her ill-conceived desire for a man she hardly knew, but she paid no heed. Nothing mattered now but his arms holding her close, his mouth on hers.

Battista groaned low in his throat. He had to stop this now, while he could, before his lust for blood overcame his desire for her sweet flesh. The two were closely interwoven, the one fueling the other. He knew he should let her go before it was too late, before his hunger overcame his good sense, before he succumbed to the need burning through him. He could scarcely remember the last time he had embraced a woman he not regarded as prey. But this woman was more than mere sustenance. Her body fit his perfectly, her voice sang to his soul, her gaze warmed the cold dark places in his heart, shone like the sun in the depths of his hell-bound spirit.

He felt his fangs lengthen, his body tense as the hunger surged through him, a relentless thirst that would not long be denied.

Battista tore his mouth from hers. Turning his head away, he took several slow, deep breaths until he had regained control of the beast that dwelled within him.

"Antonio?" Vicki asked breathlessly. "Is something wrong?"

He took another deep breath before he replied,

"No, my sweet." Summoning every ounce of willpower he possessed, he put her away from him. "It has been a long night. You should get some sleep."

She looked up at him, her eyes filled with confusion. He expected her to sleep, now?

He forced a smile. "Go to bed, my sweet one."

Vicki stared at him a moment; then, with a nod, she left the room. That was the second time he had kissed her and then backed away. Was there something wrong with the way she kissed? But no, he had been as caught up in the moment as she. She couldn't have been mistaken about that.

She closed the bedroom door behind her, then stood there, trying to sort out her feelings. She knew very little about Mr. Antonio Battista. She had no idea where he came from, who he was, if he had a family or friends, or what he did for a living. But one thing she did know: no other man had ever affected her the way he did, intrigued her the way he did, made her want him the way he did.

Tomorrow morning, she thought. Tomorrow morning she would find out more about the mysterious Mr. Battista.

NIGHT'S KISS

The Dark Gift has brought Roshan DeLongpre
a lifetime of bitter loneliness—
until, by chance, he comes
across a picture of Brenna Flanagan.

After awhile, Brenna lost interest in the images she was watching. Instead, she found herself sliding glances at Roshan. He had a strong profile, rugged and masculine.

She wondered if he liked being a vampire. He had told her he had no vampire friends. It seemed unlikely that he would have mortal friends. Did he then spend all his time alone?

She knew little of what that was like, could not imagine living without friends or family for hundreds of years. Such a lonely existence. She wondered why anyone would want to live like that.

"Brenna?" His voice scattered her thoughts and she realized she had been staring at him. "Is something wrong?"

"Everything," she replied. "I do not belong in this time or this place." She stroked the cat's head. "I do not think I will ever belong."

"Sure you will. It might take a little while for you to get used to it, but you're young. You'll learn."

A single tear slid down her cheek and dripped onto the cat's head.

"Ah, Brenna." Reaching for her, he drew her into his arms. At first, she held herself away from him but then, with a sigh, she collapsed against his chest. With a low hiss, Morgana slipped out from between them and curled up in front of the hearth.

Brenna's tears dampened his shirt. Her scent filled his nostrils, not the scent of her blood, but the scent of her skin, and her sorrow. He stroked her hair, ran his hand down her spine, felt her shiver in response to his touch.

Placing one finger under her chin, he tilted her head back, his gaze meeting hers.

Though a maiden innocent in the ways of men, her eyes revealed that she recognized the heat in his.

She shook her head as he leaned toward her. "No."

"No?"

"Kissing," she said with a grimace. "I like it not."

"Indeed?" He cupped her head in his hands. "Perhaps I can change your mind," he murmured, and claimed her lips with his own.

Eyes wide open, Brenna braced her hands against his shoulders, prepared to push him away, but at the first touch of his mouth on hers, all thought of pushing him away fled her mind. His lips were cool yet heat flooded her being, arousing a fluttering in her stomach she had never felt before, making her press herself against him.

Closing her eyes, she wrapped her arms around his waist, wanting to hold him closer, tighter. She melted against him, hoping the kiss would never end, a distant part of her mind trying to determine why John Linder's kiss had not filled her with liquid fire the way Roshan's did. But it was only a vague thought, quickly gone, as Roshan deepened the kiss, his tongue sweeping over her lower lip. She gasped at the thrill of pleasure that engulfed her, moaned softly as he repeated the gesture.

She was breathless when he took his lips from her. Lost in a world of sensation, her head still reeling, she stared up at him.

"More," she whispered.

"I thought you didn't like kissing."

"I was never kissed like this." Feeling suddenly bold, she slid her hand around his nape. "Kiss me again."

A WHISPER OF ETERNITY

When artist Tracy Warner purchases
the rambling seaside house
built above Dominic St. John's hidden lair,
he recognizes in her spirit the woman he has
loved countless times over the centuries.

She wasn't surprised when Dominic appeared in the doorway. He wore a long black cloak over a black shirt and black trousers. His feet were encased in soft black leather boots. Though she had refused to admit it, she had known, on some deep level of awareness, that this was his house.

He inclined his head in her direction. "Good evening. I trust you found everything you needed."

"Yes." Her fingers clenched around the brush. It was hard to speak past the lump of fear in her throat. "Thank you." Though why she should thank him was beyond her. He had brought her here without her consent, after all.

He took a step into the room.

She took a step back.

He lifted one brow. "Are you afraid of me now?

"How did I get here? Why am I here?"

"I brought you here because I wanted you here."

"Why didn't I wake up?"

"Because I did not wish you to."

The fear in her throat moved downward and congealed in her stomach. She started to ask another question, but before she could form the words, he was standing in front of her, only inches away. She gasped, startled. She hadn't seen him move.

"I will not hurt you, my best beloved one."

"Where are we?"

"This is my house."

"But where are we?"

"Ah. We are in a distant corner of Maine."

"So, I'm your prisoner now."

"You are my guest."

"A guest who can't leave. Sounds like prison to me."

"We need time to get to know each other again. I will not be shut out of your life this time. I will not share you with another. This time, you will believe. This time, you will be mine."

"So you're going to keep me locked up inside this house?" She stared down at her hands, noticing, for the first time, that she was holding the brush so tightly, her knuckles were white. "And what if I believe and I still don't want you? Still don't want to be what you say you are?"

"Then I will let you go."

AFTER SUNDOWN

Edward Ramsey has spent his life hunting vampires.
Now he is one of them.
Yet Edward's human conscience—and his heart—
compel him to save beautiful Kelly Anderson.

After dinner, they drove to the beach and walked barefoot along the shore. It was a calm, clear night. The moon painted ever-changing silver shadows on the water.

After a while, they stopped to watch the waves. Ramsey's gaze moved over Kelly. She looked beautiful standing there with the ocean behind her. Moonlight shimmered like molten silver in her hair; her skin looked soft and oh, so touchable. He wished, not for the first time, that he possessed a little of Chiavari's easy charm with women.

"Kelly?" He took a deep breath, the need to kiss her stronger than his need for blood. He knew he should turn away, afraid that one kiss would not be enough. Afraid that a taste of her lips would ignite his hellish thirst. But she was looking up at him, her brown eyes shining in the moonlight, her lips slightly parted, moist, inviting. He cleared his throat. The kisses they had shared at the movies had been much in his mind, but he had lacked the courage to kiss her again, afraid of being rebuffed. "I was thinking about the other night, at the movies. . . ."

"Were you? So was I."

"What were you thinking?" he asked.

"I was thinking maybe we should kiss again—you know, to see if it was as wonderful as I remember."

"Kelly . . ." He swept her into his arms, a part of him still expecting her to push him away or slap his face or laugh out loud, but she did none of those things. Instead, she leaned into him, her head tilting up, her eyelids fluttering down.

And he kissed her, there in the moonlight. Kissed her, and it wasn't enough. He wanted to inhale her, to drink her essence, to absorb her very soul into his own. She was sweet, so sweet. Heat sizzled between them, hotter than the sun he would never see again. Why had he waited so long?

"Oh, Edward . . ."

She looked up a him, breathless. She was soft and warm and willing. He covered her face with kisses, whispered praises to her beauty as he adored her with his hands and his lips. He closed his eyes, and desire rose up within him, hot and swift, and with it the overpowering urge to feed. He fought against it. He had fed well before coming here, yet the Hunger rose up within him, gnawing at his vitals, urging him to take what he wanted.

"This is crazy," she murmured breathlessly. "We hardly know each other."

"Crazy," he agreed. Her scent surrounded him. The rapid beat of her heart called to the beast within him. He deepened the kiss, at war with himself, felt his fangs lengthen in response to his growing hunger.